GET
EVEN

JADE CHURCH

Get Even by Jade Church First published in Great Britain by Jade Church in 2022

Exterior artwork by Brittany Keller

Paperback ISBN 978-1-916522-24-4

Ebook ISBN 978-1-7398968-2-9

Hardback ISBN 978-1-7391457-0-5

Conditions of Sale

CONTENT WARNING

Get Even contains themes and content that some readers may find triggering, this includes: *cheating (past, ex), references to anxiety and depression, misogyny, racism, homophobia, references to addiction and abuse, slut-shaming, alcohol and drug use, death of a grandparent (Off-page, brief mention), revenge porn, sexual harassment and cyber bullying.*

ALSO BY JADE CHURCH

Temper the Flame

This Never Happened

In Too Deep

Three Kisses More

The Lingering Dark (Kingdom of Stars #1)

Coming soon:

Fall Hard

Tempt My Heart (Living in Cincy #2)

The Clarity of Light (Kingdom of Stars #2)

Keep in touch!

Don't want to miss new release details, behind the scenes sneak peeks, cover reveals, sales, and more? Then sign up to my newsletter to get swoony romance updates straight to your inbox!

https://linktr.ee/authorjadechurch

PLAYLIST

OPTIONAL LISTENING FOR MAXIMUM VIBES

1. Enemy - Imagine Dragons, J.I.D.
2. Wait a Minute! - WILLOW
3. When You're Out - Billen Ted, Mae Muller
4. Girl - The Internet, KAYTRANADA
5. idfc - blackbear
6. dramatic - Cat & Calmell
7. R U Mine? - Arctic Monkeys
8. Done for Me - Charlie Puth, Kehlani
9. Better Now - Post Malone
10. I See Red - Everybody Loves an Outlaw
11. Dirty Thoughts - Chloe Adams
12. bellyache - Billie Eilish
13. So High - Doja Cat x High Enough - K. Flay
14. I Feel Like I'm Drowning - Two Feet
15. Say So - Doja Cat
16. Crave You - Flight Facilities, Giselle
17. Love Me Land - Zara Larsson
18. River - Bishop Briggs, King Kavalier
19. In My Mind - Lyn Lapid

20. Heaven - FINNEAS
21. As the World Caves In - Sarah Cothran, Wuki
22. The Jeweller's Hands - Arctic Monkeys
23. No.1 Party Anthem - Arctic Monkeys
24. Slow - Rumer

ABOUT THE AUTHOR

Jade Church is an avid reader and writer of spicy romance. She loves sweet and swoony love interests who aren't scared to smack your ass and bold female leads. Jade currently lives in the U.K. and spends the majority of her time reading and writing books, as well as binge re-watching *The Vampire Diaries*.

For everyone content to let the bed burn

GET
EVEN

SUN CITY #1

JADE CHURCH

CHAPTER ONE

ENEMY - IMAGINE DRAGONS, J.I.D.

THERE WERE A FEW THINGS YOU SHOULD PROBABLY know. The first was that boys at college were horny. The second was that the girls were horny too. Lastly, I was a firm believer of *Don't get mad, get even*—but I also didn't like to do things in halves. That's how I ended up sandwiched between my ex-boyfriend's brother and best friend.

Brad was moaning in my ear, his breath uncomfortably hot as he pounded away underneath me, wringing small sparks of pleasure from my body. Cody echoed him like this was some kind of pack mating exercise as he moved over me, grunting as he pushed into me shallowly and then harder. The sex wasn't bad. In fact, it was highly satisfying because I knew that Aaron was going to just *die* when he found out about this. Well, maybe next time he promised he loved someone he wouldn't go ahead and fuck their best friend. *Asshole.*

Despite the moral satisfaction, my body was not hugely interested in these guys—mostly because they were idiots and I did generally like to find some sort of intellectual connection in the people I slept with. But... they were pretty, so I focused on

1

the way Cody's golden body flexed in the mirror opposite the bed and the warmth of Brad's hands as they squeezed my breasts. I ran my hands down Brad's abs and gave him a smug smile, there were a lot of them—more than Aaron had for sure. He groaned, tweaking my nipple in one large hand as I sat up and pushed back into Cody's warmth and hardness. His breath stuttered at the change in position and I let out a moan to encourage him on and he began quickly moving again, faster this time. I took the hand Brad still had on my boob and tugged him up so I was sitting in his lap with Cody kneeling behind me, then I directed his hand downwards and pressed his fingers to my clit, giving a loud cry of appreciation. Suddenly they're both scrambling, trying to fuck me harder or faster and I rocked between them with a gasp—*finally*. Whoever said you couldn't have your cake and eat it too was wrong and revenge tasted sweet.

Cody pressed hot little kisses to my neck and heat flooded through me as I reached back and tugged at his blonde curls. I was getting close to the edge as I felt them hit a spot Aaron had never managed to find and suddenly I was shaking through my release, tightening around them until they panted in unison. Brad gripped my waist as they worked themselves to a climax too and Cody slumped against my back as he finished, hair tickling my skin until Brad eased me off them. I was a sweaty mess and I shivered as the cold air rushed over my skin, feeling oddly lonely without them pressed against me. The boys collapsed to the bed on either side of me after ditching their condoms and I smiled at them, kissing one and then the other —now for the *piece de resistance.*

"Say 'fuck me'." I giggled, brushing my dark hair away from my face and holding up my phone to take a very naked photo of the three of us looking thoroughly fucked with our sweaty, flushed skin and smug smiles. Then I found Aaron's contact and hit send, my finger hesitating for only a second over the button.

"Well, this has been fun boys—I'd say call me but, well, don't." My smile was sweet and they looked bewildered as I stood and searched the floor for my clothes—not that they covered much anyway. I'd come prepared to seduce two guys, thinking they might be a little hesitant about betraying Aaron, but really... it had taken surprisingly little effort. My phone vibrated in my hand and my stomach tightened in anticipation of his response. It had been a scant twenty-four hours since I'd got home early and found my boyfriend in my best friend's bedroom—unbeknownst to them. At first I'd gone straight to my room, sat numbly on my bed and waited for my pulse to stop pounding in my ears quite so loudly. Then I'd stood up and walked to the door, ready to burst in there, cause a scene and humiliate them both. But there was something that would hurt them more—*public spectacle.* Plus I wanted Aaron to know exactly how much he meant to his brother. *His* best friend. I'd spoken barely two words to them, just shown up in my skimpy outfit and gave Brad *fuck me* eyes and suggested he bring Cody along for the ride. That was it. They'd sold him out that quickly.

"You're leaving?" Cody asked, pushing out his full bottom lip into a pout that really was cute but dropped it when I nodded my head. I pulled on the lacy black panties I'd been wearing and Brad sat up, concern starting to muddy those big brown eyes.

"Hey, you're not going to mention this to Aaron, are you?"

I smiled. "Oh no, I don't intend on speaking to him again, but you know how he is with secrets."

Brad looked unsure about whether to be worried about his brother and Cody bit his lip. I walked a little closer and brushed a kiss across his mouth. "Wasn't it worth it though?" I asked

3

and Cody melted, a sleepy grin pulling across his face as he decided it was, in fact, worth betraying his best friend for. I supposed I should be flattered.

A knock sounded at the door and the boys both froze like naughty kids with their hands caught in the proverbial cookie jar. I hadn't foreseen a direct confrontation with Aaron at the scene of the crime, considering he'd still been in Taylor's bedroom when I'd left over an hour ago, but this definitely could be fun.

But when I opened the door it wasn't Aaron staring back at me, it was Ryan, their other housemate. His eyes dropped to my still-bare chest and I leaned against the door frame lazily as his gaze found my see-through underwear.

"Do you always open the door in just your panties, Jamie?" he asked with a small smirk and I looked down at myself as if only just remembering my clothes—or lack thereof.

I giggled like he'd just said the funniest thing I'd ever heard. "Oh, no, I don't make a habit of it. I guess my head still isn't back in the real world yet after spending the last hour with these two." I nodded behind me to where Cody and Brad still lay naked on the bed and Ryan's mouth tightened in disapproval.

"I guess I know why Aaron's on the warpath now," he said, waving his cell phone in our direction, and the boys looked at each other in horror.

"How the fuck did he find out so fast? My dick's barely dry," Brad said and I bit back a grimace at the imagery.

"Something about a picture? I don't know, but if you don't want an awkward scene then you should probably go," he directed the last at me and I batted my long lashes at him innocently while the boys stared at me in something like shock as they realized what I'd done.

"Oh, of course. I'd hate to be an inconvenience to poor, baby Aaron."

Ryan looked like he almost wanted to smile until his gaze dropped to my chest again and he cleared his throat. "You might want to get dressed quickly then."

"Right, yes, it won't take me long. I wasn't wearing much when I got here."

A look of pain crossed his face that only increased as I bent over and stepped into the short black dress crumpled on the floor by the bed and found my shoes. I blew the boys a kiss and they dazedly smiled before frowning, like they weren't quite sure what had just happened and whether they were allowed to have enjoyed it.

"See you later, Ry," I said and he stepped out of the way. He was a complicated one—actually seemed to have a brain rattling around inside his pretty head and a genuine sense of humor. Fuck knows why he chose Aaron, Brad and Cody for housemates. I felt Ryan's gaze on me all the way down the hallway until I walked down the stairs and out of sight.

Sometimes, revenge was a dish best served hot. Sure, I could have walked into Taylor's bedroom, found her and Aaron tangled together and had that image burned into my brain— but I'd chosen a messier path because I wanted them to *hurt*. Aaron would hate my public fuck-you and Taylor was about to get what was coming to her too. She'd clung to me since Freshman year and I could admit that I had clung right back, I'd never had real friends before and I'd thought I'd found that with Taylor and Aaron. But the truth was, Taylor needed me more than I needed her. I'd always been independent, never really had much choice in the matter, but she had always had someone willing to bail her out, to wipe her tears or throw money at her problems. Usually her mom.

At the end of the day, Taylor was a rich white girl and her mom had taught her the most important rule: *never cause a scene.* If she knew half the shit her precious baby girl got up to...

I smirked but shook my head as I closed the front door behind me. I didn't want to involve her mom. I wanted Taylor to know what it felt like to be alone, to have the person she trusted kick her in the teeth. Figuratively, of course. I wasn't going to beat her ass, even if she deserved it, because that would make *her* the victim. I was done giving her chances or excuses. Sometimes you had to cut off a limb before the poison could spread any further and that's exactly what Aaron and Taylor felt like, poison in my veins, burning me from the inside out until all I felt was white-hot rage. Their mistake, really. The cheating would have pissed me off, but the *lying* was something I couldn't tolerate. Ever. It hit my trigger button like nothing else, probably thanks to my own, sweet mother, and practically ensured that I wouldn't have been able to stop at payback. I didn't need revenge, I needed to *win*. I smiled as my phone vibrated three more times in my hand, Aaron no doubt losing his mind over the photo and the added insult of being ignored. I didn't give a single fuck. There would be time for tears later. For now, I had to go and confront my best friend.

CHAPTER TWO

WAIT A MINUTE! - WILLOW

AARON AND I HAD BEEN TOGETHER FOR JUST OVER A year now, up until he'd made the executive decision to sleep with my best friend and roommate, Taylor. One of the big perks of the relationship was the house he shared with Brad, Cody and Ryan, it was just a ten-minute walk from campus and was so new that the boys had managed to keep it relatively clean. Though we still tended to spend more time at my place for privacy, that was how he'd met Taylor. I snorted as I followed the winding sidewalk towards the park. It had been staring me in the face, really. The long looks, the sudden silence between them when I'd walked in the room, casual touches that now represented so much more... I was an idiot. That was the hardest part. I was furious with them, but I was also so angry at myself for not seeing it sooner.

The dry heat of the Arizona air brushed against my skin pleasantly and I sighed. This wasn't a walk of shame, more like a march of victory, but from the sneers and dry amusement on a few faces it was clear nobody else got the sentiment. Then again, it was two o'clock in the afternoon on a Thursday—but revenge doesn't wait for convenience and if I'd had to sit in my room for another second, imagining what was going on across the hall, I would have murdered him. By now, he'd definitely got the message that I knew what had happened between him and Taylor and that we were over.

I smirked and finally glanced down at my phone as I walked. Three missed calls and a barrage of texts lit up the screen and I ignored them as I opened up the message app and scrolled past Aaron's bullshit to find the photo I'd sent him of the three of us simply captioned, *Touché*. I laugh reacted to his message calling me a sadistic bitch, declined another of his calls and grinned up at the sky. It was a deep blue and I inhaled the pre-summer air longingly. It was April, I was single, and this was the year *things* were going to happen. I could feel it.

Sun City in the summer was truly something else, the trees came alive and bushes, planters and shrubbery burst with color. Though, it was going to be a little less fun now that I had nobody to spend it with. I tended to run a little more on the loner side of things and now that I'd firmly kicked my boyfriend from my life (and soon my ex-bestie for good measure) my social calendar was looking a bit tragic.

My good mood faded slightly as I thought about what might be waiting for me back at my apartment. With any luck, Taylor would be out and I could deal with her later—or maybe Aaron had already warned her that I knew. I clamped down on a slightly hysterical giggle, as if Aaron gave a crap about anyone other than himself. I took a deep breath as I walked on, deciding not to think about Aaron again, I had a history paper to work on later and nothing cleared the mind and realigned the chi like a revenge threesome.

My apartment was on the other side of town, closer to the bars than it was to campus, but I didn't mind. I'd bought it for cheap when I'd moved down here in my freshman year. I'd waited before I'd come to college, working full-time at a club for a year back in Phoenix and saving every single tip I could and then scrounging it all together alongside a small inheritance that I'd been left with when my Grandmother had died. It had been enough to get me my own place and rent out the second bedroom. Aaron had helped me fix it up when we'd met, repainting the walls, sanding down floors... I sighed. I was going to have to redecorate and find a new roommate.

Taylor and I had met in our freshman year, she had been staying in the on-campus housing and I'd been friends with one of her friends. I squinted into the sun, wishing I had my sunglasses as I tried to remember the girl's name—Sara? Ivy? I shook my head and breathed a sigh of relief as I found my way beneath the canopy of trees that sheltered the long walk-way up to the main crossing that led back into town. Taylor and I had bonded over our love of karaoke on a night out and when it came time for her to re-apply for housing or find somewhere else, I'd offered to rent out the second room in my apartment to her. The rest, as they say, was history. Until she'd fucked my boyfriend.

I clamped down hard on my emotions, not wanting to shed a single tear over those two fuckwits. Tonight I was going to get rip-roaringly drunk and then tomorrow I was going to have to advertise for a new roommate.

Cocoa & Rum appeared in my eyesight and suddenly I was gasping for a bucket-sized iced coffee, never mind the fact that I was now only ten minutes away from home and could make one myself. Homemade iced coffee was never as good as the real thing and iced coffee, especially from *Cocoa & Rum*, was one addiction I did not mind feeding.

It was probably my favorite coffee house in town and as the familiar scent of coffee beans washed over me, I felt my shoulders relax. I'd actually had several messy nights here too, in the evening the place opened up into a cocktail bar with a small dance floor and the signature cocktails were to die for— and potent as hell.

The barista from behind the counter seemed new, her green-brown eyes were pretty and her smile was wide and for a second I let a hint of interest grip me. I *was* single now. If I wanted to ask out a cute girl, there was nothing stopping me... except, I couldn't risk fraternizing with the place that made the best coffee in town. That was a recipe for disaster. I placed my order and lingered at the opposite end of the counter, admiring the way the sunlight poured in through the large glass-front windows. It was only spring and already the heat was ramping up, everything starting to smell like warmth and sunlight again, maybe I'd even be able to build up my tan this summer. My olive skin was temperamental, I either became a glowy golden brown or I burnt. There was no in-between.

I accepted my coffee gratefully when the barista called my name and immediately started gulping it down as I walked slowly towards my apartment. I winced as brain freeze started to settle in and looked longingly out towards the lush green park sprawling on the walk-way behind the town. *No.* I clenched my jaw, realizing that I was putting off the inevitable. I'd had my caffeinated fortification and now it was time to face the music.

My apartment had always felt like a sanctuary and when I'd invited in Taylor, my former best friend, it had felt like a home. My Mom and I weren't close and my dad had never been in the picture, it was only really my grandmother that I'd had any real familial connection with. Then she'd died, I'd moved to Phoenix and eventually I'd ended up at Radclyffe-U.

I'd been on my way home from a class trip when I'd discovered Aaron and Taylor were boning. It was tragic how predictable it was really—came home sooner than expected and went straight to my room, intending to freshen up and surprise

Aaron. Taylor had sounded... busy, in her room and I'd smirked, wondering who she'd managed to pin down now. Obviously my amusement had quickly faded away when I'd re-opened my bedroom door in time to see Aaron closing Taylor's behind him as he walked into her bedroom.

Standing outside my apartment door now, I felt the twinges of deja-vu hitting me. For this more than anything else, I hated Taylor. This was my home. *Mine.* All that security, that peace that had come with finally having something to call my own, something good I could point to and say *I did that,* had been tainted by her and Aaron's rampant fucking hormones.

I huffed out an angry breath and twisted the door handle viciously as I walked in. I was *not* going to feel like this, damn it. They were the ones who had fucked me over. Aaron was... well, I knew he wasn't going to be the forever kind of boyfriend. But Taylor? She was supposed to be my friend and that made it ten times worse.

My hallway was painted a cheerful cherry red but even the sight of the familiar walls couldn't ease the anxiety building in my chest as I stomped through and to the kitchen. I passed through the living room without a glance and it wasn't until Taylor called out that I even realized she was still here. I let out a long breath.

What the fuck? Surely she had to have heard from someone that I knew what had happened? So why was she still here? Did she think we were just going to talk it out, hug and move on? I was more likely to poop rainbows and fly around the kitchen than I was to hug it out with this fake-ass bitch.

I pasted on a smile as I scooped the drink I'd just made off of the side and strolled casually into the living room and took in Taylor, sprawled on our couch. *No.* That was *my* couch and this was *my* home. Though, Aaron had been *my* boyfriend, so clearly Taylor didn't care a lick about boundaries.

"Hey," she called again, flicking a glance away from the TV and smiling. "Where have you been? I thought we were getting breakfast once you got back this morning."

"Yeah, sorry I had to take care of something."

"Oh?" Taylor's blonde eyebrows rose so high they almost blended in with her equally blonde hairline. "Anything interesting?"

I waved a hand airily and sipped my juice. "Just stuff between me and Aaron." That finally caught her attention and her eyes held mine, taking in my lacy black outfit with something close to jealousy passing across her face. "It's funny really..."

"What?" Did she know how curt her voice had become? Had their relationship really been staring me in the face for this long without me even realizing it?

"Well, Aaron's okay in bed—as I'm sure you know," Taylor's face whitened, her blue eyes looking bright against her deeper pallor, "but I really just didn't expect his brother to be *that* much better. Though, I suppose with Cody helping out too it evened the playing field a little."

"Jamie, I—"

"If you're about to lie to me, don't. Don't disrespect me or yourself more than you already have." My voice was cold and I felt like ice, like I was gazing at this scene from a distance and I wondered whether I would remember the minute details about this moment in the future—the tampon ad playing on the TV, the trees swaying beyond the blinds shading the window, Taylor's face, slowly clouding from horror to anger.

"I'm the disrespectful one?" Taylor stood, her blonde hair fluttering about after her like she was the heroine in a movie.

"Sorry, are you saying you *didn't* fuck my boyfriend? In my apartment?"

Taylor laughed, a sneer taking over her face as she looked me up and down. "It's not my fault that he was bored of you—I mean, who could blame him with the way you dress? Have you ever heard of that saying *giving the milk away for free?*"

Was she calling me a slut?

I didn't bother to respond to that. I liked sex. I'd previously mostly-enjoyed sex with my boyfriend. Monogamously. My current outfit was a game in seduction and not what I'd normally wear out for a walk through campus and town, so I had no idea what she was talking about and honestly? I didn't care anymore. I wanted her gone.

"Pack up your shit and get out."

Her blue eyes widened, mouth angling to catch flies as she stared. "What?"

"You thought you could bang my boyfriend, call me a slut instead of apologizing—not that it would have helped—and still live here?" Taylor's mouth opened and closed like a fish and her eyes filled with tears, the standard way she got out of anything she found distasteful, and I folded my arms across my chest, waiting to see if she had anything else to spit out.

"Okay," I said when her silence stretched on. "Nice knowing you—well, not really, actually."

"You're kicking me out?" The whine in her voice grated along my nerves and I felt my control snapping even as I wanted to crow in triumph. This was the thing that would hit Taylor where it hurt—her privilege. Girl had never been told *no*.

"What did you think was going to happen?" Taylor looked away and I let out a short laugh. "Right, you thought I'd never find out. Just so you know, you two are both way too fucking stupid to pull that off long-term. Go and pack up your shit before I do something I might regret."

She ran past me on her way out of the living room, heading to the room that was opposite mine, and I heard her crying down the phone to someone—Aaron maybe? If she thought he was going to put her up she had another thing coming. Aaron was a dick and Taylor had been single for a *long* time, maybe I'd been stupid leaving and expecting them not to hook up.

No. I wasn't responsible for their shitty actions. I finally uncrossed my arms and took a few deep breaths, trying to fight the rising tide of anger that was warring with the newfound loneliness. I'd just lost the closest thing to family I'd had since my grandmother died. *You'll make new friends.* Sure, but it wouldn't be easy. People tended to find me a little... direct. Which was fine! But it wasn't an approach that everyone liked. I couldn't change who I was and I guess it turned out that Taylor didn't really like me very much anyway if she thought I was a slut and had gone after my boyfriend.

I sank down onto my couch, running my hand over the soft gray material and sighing. The thrill from earlier had faded and now I was left in a messy situation with even messier feelings.

"Jamie?"

I looked up, startled, to find Taylor standing in the doorway, her hair scraped up into a messy bun and her mouth scrunched up in the way that only happened when she was upset.

"What?"

"I'm sorry."

I glanced away, staring at the sun beyond the window. It was less painful than looking at the girl who was supposed to be my friend, who I'd known for two years and counting and who had screwed everything up for a quick fuck with a guy who didn't even love her. *Unless he did?* I didn't reply, just nodded slightly.

"Aaron doesn't want to see me, he won't let me stay with him and I was wondering—"

Second choice yet again, huh? "Oh, so you only apologized once you were sure my ex-boyfriend wouldn't take you in?

14

Nice. Go and crash with those sorority girls you ass-lick twenty-four-seven—I don't care, but I want you gone. Sooner rather than later if I'm going to have any chance of getting the stink of desperation out of the furniture."

I finally looked up and found the space where she'd stood empty. Good. Who needed liars and cheaters in their life anyway? I grabbed the remote from the coffee table and flicked the TV off, it was playing a Vampire Diaries re-run and right now I didn't want to have to look at Damon Salvatore's perfect face—it would only make me feel worse about my own messed up romantic life. Though, of course, if Damon Salvatore walked into a bar and asked for a vein I'd *gladly* let him tap that.

A different set of familiar blue eyes floated through my head unexpectedly and I shook my thoughts free of Ryan's killer lashes and toe-curling smirk. It wasn't the first time I'd had to do so, but he was off-limits. Fellow co-captain of the football team and Aaron's 'nemesis' (Aaron's words, boys were fucking dumb, like *seriously*, nemesis?)—unfortunately, Ry was also an absolute smoke show. I'd avoided him as much as possible when I had been dating Aaron, which had been hard considering they lived together. I didn't really understand why, considering they seemed to hate each other's guts. Men. Can't live with them... well. I guessed I'd manage.

I sank back against the couch, listening to Taylor crying down the phone to someone else in the other room as she rustled bags and clattered about. My hands shook and my eyes fluttered closed. How had my life become this cluster fuck of such epic proportions? I bit my lip as the emotion I'd been holding back finally threatened to overwhelm me and a tear trickled down my cheek, followed by another. I'd give myself a few minutes to cry and that was it. They didn't deserve my tears and these were for myself anyway, for whatever came next. For the uncertainty that the future now held without Aaron and

Taylor in it. Taylor's door creaked open and I dashed the tears from my face quickly, setting my jaw and not even flinching when the front door opened and then closed. I stood and walked through the hall to Taylor's room. Clothes were strewn across the floor, make-up littered her desk as if she'd upended her bag and a suitcase sat on the bed waiting to be filled. All that was left of a two-year friendship.

The front door opened and I turned away as Taylor walked in.

"Jamie, please—" Taylor tried again and I walked into my bedroom, closing the door firmly behind me and resting my back against it as the sounds of Taylor packing resumed.

They say the best way to get over someone was to get under someone else—I could tick that off the proverbial list. Now, it was onto phase two of *Erase Aaron Matthews From My Brain/Heart:* getting ferociously drunk. I could only hope he would take the memory of my best friend with him.

CHAPTER THREE

WHEN YOU'RE OUT - BILLEN TED, MAE MULLER

THE BOX WAS LOUD ON A FRIDAY NIGHT, THAT WAS why Thursdays were my favorite day to come. There were several reasons why *The Box* was one of my favorite places in Sun City: firstly, the booze was cheap. Secondly, it looked pretty, with a flower wall along one side and pink lighting that deepened to red as the evening wore on. Lastly, their karaoke and live music nights. I loved to sing, so Wednesday nights I was usually here, setting up my guitar and ready to belt out whatever cover I'd been working on that week. I was a regular and Kat, the bartender working tonight, eyed me worriedly as I threw back my third tequila shot since I'd walked in ten minutes ago. We didn't know each other that well beyond the odd drunken ramble at the bar and the one night that we'd done karaoke together, but I liked her. Kat was honest if nothing else and she had let me rant to her about Aaron when I'd invited him to watch me sing at open mic night and he'd blown me off. I gave her a tight smile and patted her hand. "It's been a long day, babe. Keep 'em coming."

She squeezed my hand and refilled the shot glasses, waving

away my card as I reached out to pay. "This one's on me, okay? Let me know if you need anything, Jay."

My smile wobbled and I quickly grabbed another shot, downing it and then smiling widely. "You're the sweetest, thank you Kat." *See? You have more friends than Taylor and Aaron.* I groaned. I'd gone almost an hour without thinking about either of them while I enjoyed the sunset and walked to *The Box*. How drunk did I need to be before I wouldn't be able to remember their names?

Kat gave me one of her trademark sweet smiles, green eyes crinkling at the corners and cheeks dimpling, before she moved off to serve someone else.

I liked to people watch, sometimes it was nice to be surrounded by people and yet be completely alone in your thoughts—it sounded emo as fuck, but there was something peaceful about it. Usually, anyway. Tonight my thoughts were a swirling mess of *What did I do wrong? Am I really so unbearable?* And oddly and most stupidly of all, *Ryan saw me naked.*

I ran a hand through my short hair in agitation, a mixture of irritation and confusion dogging me. Who gave a singular fuck what Ryan Sommers thought?

"Come on, baby, I'd love to have your number. You look lonely."

The smarmy voice cut through my inner monologue and I rolled my eyes, glancing to my right to find the owner of that voice sitting two stools down. He was a skinny, greasy looking guy with a long face and dark hair with too much gel. He'd been attempting to sweet talk the pretty girl sitting next to me for the last ten minutes and her replies had become more and more clipped each time the guy ignored her clear signals to back the hell off. Maybe it was the tequila, maybe it was the frustration that continued to make my blood hum at the thought of Ryan, but I turned and leaned forward, draping my arm around the shoulders of the girl next to me.

She tensed momentarily before looking at me out of the corner of her eye and relaxing, apparently deciding I wasn't here with the creep harassing her. The guy frowned at me like he'd only just noticed I was there on the other side of her and *holy hell* I could see why. She'd been facing the other way the entire time I'd been sitting here, watching the door, so this was my first good look at her and I felt a brief stab of pity. She must get assholes fawning over her all the time. With her honey-hued skin, deep brown eyes and glossy hair ,she would be considered gorgeous—throw in the full lips, long legs that were currently crossed demurely in her tight jeans and curves for days and she was a knock-out.

"Have you finished playing yet, doll?" I cooed in her ear, loudly enough for the sleaze to hear me.

"Excuse me?" he spluttered, eyes bulging like a frog and a bit of spittle hit the bar.

"You're excused," I said, smiling brightly, pouting my red lips for full effect as he stared at me in shocked silence.

"Who the hell do you think you are?"

"Hers," I answered, linking my other arm around the brunette's neck and staring intently into her eyes as I leaned in, pausing as I hovered over her mouth and letting her close the distance if she chose. I could feel her stuttered breaths ghosting over my lips lightly before her mouth pressed to mine in a kiss that I deepened after a few seconds, letting my tongue briefly stroke across hers before pulling back. "Satisfied?" I said breathlessly without looking away and saw the sleazeball leave out of the corner of my eye.

"Very," the girl murmured and I laughed, pulling away. "I'm Olivia, but since you just had your tongue in my mouth, you can call me Liv."

"Nice to meet you," I said, settling back onto my own stool and ordering a cocktail from the other bartender, whose name I didn't know. "My name's Benjamin, but you can call me Jamie."

"That's... unusual?"

I gave her a wry smile and thanked the bartender a moment later as he placed the Sex on the Beach down in front of me. "My Mom thought she was having a boy and decided to keep the name regardless."

Liv let out a laugh that drew a few appreciative glances her way as her long brown hair swayed with the movement. "Wow. Well, thank you for... kissing me, I guess?"

I smirked. "Happy to be of service. Are you meeting someone?" I half-hoped she'd say no—and not just because the kiss had been good. I could use the company and it would be... nice to meet some new people. Not a thought I often had, but I was putting it down to the alcohol and the shitty forty-eight hours I'd just lived.

"Oh." She glanced down at her hands folded in her lap, her lashes were long and full and I realized that though I would happily take her back to my place, I could use a friend more than a fuck buddy right now. "Yeah, but I don't think they're going to show." She had a light accent that might have been Southern and her apparent worry made the twang thicken. I smiled and gestured for Kat to bring over another cocktail.

"Well, that's their loss and my gain I guess!" I dropped her a wink as Kat set her drink down. "Tell me, do you like karaoke?"

Three more cocktails, two shots ,and a timeless rendition of Careless Whisper later, I'd told Liv and Kat (who had joined us at nine once her shift had ended) what had gone down with Aaron and Taylor.

Kat shook her head. "I never liked him. He's too..." Liv and I leaned closer to Kat as she took a long sip of her mojito, "cookie-cutter. Like, you know when you see guys in ads that are supposed to be super clean cut and all-American?"

I nodded as I bit down on the lime and almost choked laughing at the face Olivia made after taking her tequila shot. "Yeah I get that. He's the other sort of all-American though— Mr. Nice Guy. Except, he does coke in the evenings and thinks grinding to music is dancing."

Liv looked horrified as Kat burst out laughing. "Is that... common?"

"What?" I raised an eyebrow. Liv seemed... innocent. I mean, not prudish or anything, just like she maybe wasn't that experienced. Her mouth had hung open for a solid five minutes after I'd told her about my revenge sex that afternoon.

"The drugs," Liv whispered. Except, we were all pretty drunk so she wasn't really that quiet. Even Kat was keeping pace, the five tequila slammers had definitely helped her catch-up to our level.

"Liv, I'm going to ask you something and I don't want you to be offended or anything because the answer doesn't really matter that much."

"Okay," she said, biting down on her lower lip.

"Are you a freshman?"

Liv gasped and Kat howled, though that might have been because a squeeze of lime juice shot in her eye. "I am *not* a Freshman."

I raised my hands in supplication and fluffed my fringe off my face with my hand. God was it just me or was it boiling hot in here? "I said not to get offended! It's just that this all seems very new to you."

"That's because it is." She shrugged lightly. "I'm in my second year. I just transferred to Radclyffe from St Agatha's."

Kat and I blinked at her in shocked silence before I managed to make my tongue work again. "You transferred out of one of the most strict religious schools in the US to a college named after a lesbian?"

"Well, sort of. I was actually kicked out." Oh my god. Who *was* this new friend I'd made?

"Spill," Kat said, eyes glittering dangerously as she sensed good gossip and I shot her a warning look.

"Why were you kicked out?" I made my voice gentle. It wasn't a tone I used often.

"Um, I got caught having sex."

I was pretty sure I gasped aloud. "You have to be chaste at St Agatha's?"

"Not really, I mean they prefer no sex before marriage. Like, *heavily* prefer it. But it was who I was caught sleeping with that was the issue."

"You're killing me here," Kat whined and I frantically shushed her.

"Was it a teacher?"

"I mean, that certainly didn't help." I wasn't sure my eyes could get any wider. Had I really said I thought she wasn't very experienced? "But it was more the fact that she was a girl that was the nail in my coffin. My parents screamed down our halls of residence and the Matron decided it would be best if I transferred out to another school of my choice with a full scholarship, since my parents were now refusing to pay my tuition."

Holy shit. She'd caused a lesbian scandal at one of the most religiously zealous colleges around, Olivia might just be my new hero. I grabbed for her hand and clasped it in mine. "They tried to give you hush money?"

"Essentially." Liv let out a long breath before looking up at us as though she hadn't just divulged something that was clearly pretty raw and that made something inside of me ache. I wasn't good with people or emotions, I was even worse at combining the two without the aid of alcohol or maybe some good weed. The fact that she trusted us enough to open up like that... karaoke and tequila truly were the key to starting any good friendship. "So yeah, this is all kind of new to me. Drugs, frats, karaoke and booze—like I'm not completely inexperienced but it just wasn't this... wild for me before."

Kat grinned but her eyes were as gentle as my voice had been earlier. "Well, you stick with us. This one here is particularly good at finding trouble."

I laughed as she nudged me and I squeezed Liv's hand before letting go. "I'm sorry you had to go through that, but hey, it brought you here to us—so I can't be *too* sorry." I winked and she laughed just as I'd hoped. "So where are you staying?"

"Right now I'm in temporary on-campus housing. I was supposed to be meeting someone here today about renting a room but they didn't show."

"This is perfect!" I crowed and Kat shot me a look to say I was being insensitive. I waved her off. "Well, not that they didn't show. I mean that I just kicked out my best friend for sleeping with my boyfriend, remember?"

"How could we forget? The post-revenge-hookup pic was hot." Kat laughed and I rolled my eyes.

"So, I'm saying I have a spare room I'm renting out."

"Oh my gosh, really? That would be amazing!" Liv beamed at me, her straight white teeth making me a little dizzy.

"Erm, yeah," I said, slightly dazed as the full force of that smile hit me. "We can work out the details tomorrow but you can crash at mine tonight, same for you Kat if you like."

"No, that's okay, but thanks. I should actually get home. I

have an early lecture tomorrow, but we should do this again sometime." Kat smiled and it eased something in my chest that had been hurting since I'd heard Taylor's door close and watched Aaron disappearing inside, clad in just boxers.

"I'd love that," I said and smiled when she grabbed my phone and input her number before doing the same for Liv and waving goodbye. "Guess we should be buying that dickwad from earlier a drink, right? Who knew sticking my tongue in your mouth would be so fortuitous—but I'm leaving here slightly less angry and with two new friends." I wasn't usually a huge sharer and in that moment I remembered why I didn't drink tequila anymore, but I had a good feeling about Liv, she seemed genuine and nice and maybe a little naive. Like she needed someone just as much as I did.

Liv laughed. "I'd say we're both due for a little luck, right?"

CHAPTER FOUR

GIRL - THE INTERNET, KAYTRANADA

MY HEAD FELT LIKE A COTTON BALL HAD BEEN stuffed inside, doused in tequila and set alight. I groaned as I rolled over in bed, scrubbing a hand over my eyes and fighting a wave of nausea as the warmth from my covers stifled me and my eyeballs throbbed. There was only one thing that would cure this.

Liv found me in the living room twenty minutes later sparking a joint, my short hair sticking up at wild angles. She sniffed delicately and I sighed. "Sorry, last night was sort of a blur. I half-forgot you would be here. I can go outside if you like?"

"Oh no, it's okay. I'm just not really used to the... smell, is all."

I dragged in a slow toke and let the smoke curl out past my lips as I held it out to her in offering, shrugging when she shook her head. "My entire face hurts and I have class in like two hours. Trust me, it's the best hangover cure out there."

A knock rang out far too loudly and I groaned, inhaling again as I made my way through the hall, my bones feeling unfairly heavy. I was only twenty-one! I should still be able to handle my tequila, yet, here I was. I pulled open the door and stumbled a little, wincing as the light from the hall flooded in, and then groaned when I saw who was waiting.

"What do you want?" I snapped and my ex-boyfriend gave me a sweet smile, as if that was going to make me forget what he'd done. "Taylor's not here."

"I don't give a shit about Taylor," he said in his smooth, even, voice and I rolled my eyes. Like that made it better. "I'm here for you. We need to talk about this, Jay."

"We really, really don't. You know what they say, right? A picture is worth a thousand words."

Aaron's perfectly pleasant expression darkened for a moment at my reminder of the ménage à trois I'd organized, and then cleared just as fast, fading back into that Prince Charming, fake smile he'd utilized his whole life to present the *right* image. "We both made mistakes, it's okay. I forgive you. I just want us to work through this—"

"Well, I don't," I snapped and Aaron's pale blue-gray eyes widened as his jaw clenched. "I didn't make a mistake, *you did*, I happened to have a great time yesterday with Brad and Cody. You know, Cody can do this little thing with his tongue—"

Aaron's hand hit the door frame and his face was cold and hard. Gone was the sweet guy-next-door image he portrayed, like it would fool me. "Enough," he said carefully and I squared my shoulders, darting a glance back to where Liv had poked her head around the living room door and waving her back. "You know that what we have is special, baby. Taylor was just... a quick fuck. A stupid mistake. She couldn't keep her legs closed if she tried."

I wrinkled my nose in distaste, did he even hear how he sounded? I wasn't sure if I'd ever been in love with Aaron but I knew that whatever it was he felt... it wasn't love. Or it was a love so twisted that it might as well have been hate.

I stepped forward and his eyes lit up as I got close, tilting my head up so I could see into his eyes before I took another drag of smoke. "Get out."

Aaron frowned. "Jamie—" he said warningly and I laughed, my lips almost brushing his as I let him look his fill, let him see the absolute lack of emotion in my eyes as I regarded him.

"If you come back here to bother me again," I said softly, tapping my joint so that the ash fell on his pristine-white trainers, "I'll cut off your balls and feed them to you." I pressed a cold, unfeeling kiss to his mouth and he flinched. "Have a nice life."

I stepped back and slammed the door shut, breathing hard for a second and then flipping the lock and slipping the deadbolt into place for good measure. Aaron wasn't accustomed to being denied and I was done with his bullshit. What I'd ever seen in him I couldn't say.

"Is everything okay?" Liv asked quietly and my head jerked up, my hand shaking as I raised the zoot to my mouth again. She strode forward and paused before hesitantly wrapping her arms around me. "You are... something else, Jamie."

"Says the girl who led a lesbian revolution at St Agatha's." I smiled, letting loose a shaky breath as I squeezed her gently before letting go. "I don't think I gave you a tour last night," I said, eager to change the subject and uncomfortable with my own vulnerability, "so shall I show you around now?"

Liv's eyes ran over my face before she nodded and I pointed her in the direction of the linen closet, my room, and then our shared bathroom, all with her watching me like a hawk. My room was organized chaos, clothes overflowing from my wardrobe, my guitar resting against my desk and various chokers slung across my dresser. But the sweet orange walls

27

soothed me and I could see that Liv was surprised at the size of the room. The large bed against one wall took up a lot of space but it was a necessity, I liked to starfish.

"The rooms are pretty good sizes," I said and Liv nodded along, "obviously you've already seen the second bedroom but it's only a little smaller than mine."

The shared bathroom seemed almost bare without Taylor's shampoo and make-up cluttering up the space but Liv seemed pleased, it was relatively modern and the water pressure was good. I couldn't have asked for more than that with the budget I'd had to work with.

"What do you study?" Liv asked as we made our way back into the lounge, clearly she'd decided to let me avoid the topic of Aaron for now. I dropped back onto the sofa as I finished my joint and she sat gingerly down beside me and it only hit me just then that I had a virtual stranger sitting in my apartment with me. Thankfully, the weed killed any sort of panic I might have had. I hadn't known Liv for long, but I could tell she was a good person. Trustworthy. Plus, it was hard to be suspicious of someone who looked so... sweet. We'd grabbed her stuff from the temporary housing dorm last night before stumbling our way back to mine. I was pretty sure one or both of us had fallen into a bush but there wasn't any lasting damage, all's well that ends well after all.

Liv tugged nervously at the end of her long hair, her eyes running over the room, before she bent and swept it all up into a messy bun piled on top of her head. My eyes were starting to feel heavy but at least my headache was fading a little, as well as the memory of Aaron's impromptu visit, and I let a relaxed smile slip across my face. I was glad I had cut all my hair off last summer, it was so much easier to manage than when it had been waist-length.

"Um, Jamie?"

My eyes fluttered open and I laughed lightly, poking one of the pink hearts that decorated Liv's PJs. "Sorry, sorry. I study History." Liv nodded a little but her eyes were still darting around, as if trying to take in every detail and commit it to memory. "Hey, relax. This is your place too—if that's what you still want, I mean, if you've changed your mind it's fine." I tried to keep my voice light and turned away to stub out the joint on my favorite tray. I hoped she would stay though. "But, um, yeah. History."

Hanging out with Liv and Kat last night had been the most fun I'd had in, well, a *long* time. I hadn't realized Taylor and I had been missing anything from our friendship until I'd slung my arm Liv and sweet-talked Kat. Things with Taylor were... *had been*, I corrected myself, conditional. Like I'd been balancing on a knife's edge for a while and not realized it until my feet were back on solid ground. This was a fresh start.

"Oh, that's cool." Liv blinked several times, her brown eyes wide and I choked back a laugh.

"Not what you expected?"

"Well, I just—"

I shrugged at her. "Don't worry, I get that a lot. Academia is not a place for women like me."

Liv's mouth dropped open. "What? Did someone actually say that to you?"

"My Professor. He hates my guts and apparently only accepted me on to the course because he thought I was a guy. Easy mistake considering my name is Benjamin."

"He sounds like a dick."

A startled laugh flew out of me and I smirked at her. "You would be right. The only other girls on the course are timid little good girls that hang onto his every word. I'm pretty sure he only accepted them for like, statistics." I waved a new joint at her from the tin under the table in a lazy salute as I sparked it. "What's your major?"

"Communications," she said with a sigh, finally settling against the couch and letting her head fall back. "I know it's a little generic, but I've never really had the chance to think about what *I* want to do. Not seriously anyway. I never even really cared about coming to college but my parents..."

"They're really not talking to you?"

Liv shook her head slightly, teeth biting deeply into her bottom lip. "Luckily I already had access to my trust at 18 otherwise. Well, they'll get over it at some point. Or I will, I guess."

"You will. I don't talk to my mom either." I hadn't really meant to let the last part slip out and I frowned down at the softly smoking remainder of my weed before tapping off the ash. Damned stuff was worse than truth serum.

My phone was still sat on the dining room table from where I'd left it last night and the shrill *ding* of a notification popping in made my ears ring as it was followed by another and then another. I heaved myself up off the sofa as I made for it, freezing and then lowering the zoot from my mouth when I saw what was on the screen.

"Oh my god," I breathed and then laughed in disbelief.

"What is it?" Liv called from the sofa and my eyes burned at the casual concern in her voice. Poor girl, what had she gotten into by being friends with me? The now freshly-branded campus slut.

I held my phone out for her to take and then dragged harshly on the joint before stubbing it out, letting the smoke wreathe my head and obscure my expression as I looked up to the ceiling, blinking away tears of anger. Bastard.

"Shit," Liv said, eyes flying wide as she looked at the picture of me, Brad and Cody that had been anonymously submitted to the campus gossip page on socials. Considering only two people had that photo and one of them had just left my apartment seething with anger, it was a pretty good bet who had posted it. "You're naked in this. Can't you report him?"

"It's not worth the trouble," I said, taking a deep breath and removing the tag from the photo so at least it wouldn't show up on my profile. "Aaron's rich and co-captain of the football team. I'm a history major with no friends and no money. I'm just surprised is all, normally the thought of a scandal would be enough to scare Aaron away. I guess he wanted to hurt me more than he cared about his rep." I laughed and Liv didn't join in, the faint remnant of my hangover throbbed through my temples and I rubbed at them absently, wanting this day to be over despite it only having just begun. "Anyway... I better go get ready. First housemate meal together tonight though?"

I held my breath as I waited for her response. Had she changed her mind? Did she only want to be friends with me when she was drunk?

Liv blinked at me. "You're going to class?"

"Yeah, of course. Why wouldn't I?"

Liv glanced pointedly at my phone and I shrugged. "What's there to be ashamed of really? So some people are going to see my boobs? I had a threesome, it was great and I bet they'll all just be wishing they were me really. I mean, I have a great rack." Liv snorted and the sound loosened some of the tension still swirling through me. "Dinner tonight then?"

Liv smiled and nodded firmly. "Sounds good."

"Well, let's hope I make it through class with Professor Dick alive then." I shot her a saucy wink. "Pray for me?"

31

"I'm sorry, *what?*" My heart was pounding so hard my hands were shaking as I stared up into the flinty eyes of Professor Davis—or Professor Dick, as I was now going to forever be calling him. I had been determined to ignore the stares, to just go to class and then get home. It was a nude. One nude! Yet people were gaping like they'd never seen a pair of boobs before. Or maybe it had more to do with who I was in the photo with? I wasn't really a big sports fangirl, but I knew that a lot of people treated the college athletes like they were gods or something.

"I've had my doubts about you since you joined this class —" *Yes, a fact he'd been oh so subtle about* "—but this is the final straw. You are making a mockery of this department and, as such, you are on probation to be reviewed in three months' time."

I gaped at him, willing the rising flush away from my face. I was *not* embarrassed by this asshole. It was perfectly normal and healthy to enjoy sex and I wasn't going to let Professor Dick make me feel otherwise. "So, just to make it absolutely clear, you're putting me on academic probation for having a threesome?"

Davis threw his hands up into the air, spinning around to walk back to the front of the class. "You are ruining the—"

"Yes, yes, the reputation,.I heard you the first time. What I *don't* understand is why you're bringing this up in the middle of class," I said pointedly as my classmates' eyes ping-ponged back and forth between us, expressions ranging from pity to amusement. "Also, do you really think I'm the only one in this room having some fun? Nick practically has an orgy at his frat house every weekend!"

"*Nick* does not advertise that fact on social media!"

"Oh, I get it, you're blaming me for being a victim of revenge porn?" I'd never been particularly good at 'respecting' authority, especially when that authority was being wielded by a sexist pig looking for any reason to screw me over. For a second I toyed with the idea of reporting him, as Nick frequently suggested, but Davis had something worse than money or a high-brow reputation, he had *influence*. My other professors took their cues from him, he had tenure and he ran the entire history department, so while they weren't outwardly awful, they didn't speak up for me either. Nor would they if I brought this to the higher faculty—I would be alone. I could stick it out until graduation.

Davis' face flushed red, making an interesting contrast with his white hair. "This is not up for debate or discussion. You're only making this worse for yourself. I think that's quite enough for today, hm?" He snatched up his briefcase, stuffed his papers inside and swept out of the room while I scowled. It was more than a shame, really. I loved history, I'd always found it fascinating, but since having Davis as our third-year professor some of the joy had started to trickle out of the subject. He'd had it in for me as soon as he'd seen me and realized that *Benjamin* was a girl, and not one of his carefully selected sweet little damsels either.

There was only awkward silence for a couple of minutes and then slowly chatter began to creep back in as people left the room, more than one gaze darting to me and then away. I knew Aaron was an ass, but I hadn't expected him to forward-on the photo of me in bed with his brother and best friend to what felt like the entire student body. Still, I couldn't say I was sorry for showing him the door earlier.

A heavy hand fell on my shoulder and I looked up tiredly to find Nick peering down at me. I sighed. "Can you believe this?"

Nick shrugged. "Yeah, kinda. He's always had it out for you. You should—"

"I know, I know." I waved him off as I stood up and shoved

my notebook and laptop into my bag. Nick had been on at me for ages to complain about Professor Davis, but some part of *head of the department* and *tenured to boot* always seemed to be conveniently forgotten whenever he brought it up. "Why would they believe me over him? Why would they even care? He's not really breaking any rules by disliking me."

"Maybe," Nick said, dark eyes running over my face carefully, "but he would definitely be breaking some rules if he had put you on probation based on discrimination."

I paused half-way down the steps to the exit. "What do you mean?"

"Well, he was talking to someone when I arrived, before you got here." He ran a hand across his shaved head and then over his stubble and I followed the movement with my eyes before raising an eyebrow. Nick was always confident, self-assured. He never seemed worried. Not like this. "He wasn't only mad about the photo of you with Brad and Chad."

"Cody," I corrected absently and Nick sucked on his teeth lightly and I couldn't help my laugh. He was right, big difference.

"There was also a photo of you with your arm around some girl."

"So?"

"Your tongue was in her mouth."

"Oh. Okay?"

He sighed and began walking to the door again while I trailed behind him. "So I think a school literally named after a famous lesbian might have an issue with him not liking you kissing a girl."

"It's still my word against his. Look, it's fine. I'll cool things off, be on my best behavior, and just ride out this probation in time for graduation in the summer."

Nick laughed and it echoed around the empty hall. "Sure."

"What?"

"The idea of you behaving. You won't last five minutes, so you better come up with a better plan than that if you really don't want to report him."

I patted his chiseled cheek and sighed enviously. "Why do you have such a good face?"

He smirked as he pushed open the door to the corridor. "God loves me."

"You're definitely proof that god loves the gays," I joked and he grinned before it faded quickly.

"Look, I mean it. Davis could really make life difficult for you, you know I'll support you if you decide to come forward."

"I know, I appreciate it. Honestly."

"But you're not going to do it." He smiled ruefully before ruffling my hair and I spluttered as I tried to rearrange my bangs. "Just find yourself a nice, wholesome guy with a good rep and date him for the next few months. Unless you're with the girl?"

I snorted. "No, she just needed rescuing."

"Ahhh and you were only too happy to provide your tongue as aid, I see."

"Jamie," a low voice called and something in my stomach flipped.

Nick gave a low whistle and winked. "Looks like you've got a good candidate here with Mr. Clark Kent." I swatted at him as I saw a figure approaching out of the corner of my eye. "I'll see you later." Nick grinned and left me to the wolves.

I turned slowly and swept my face blank of any emotion as I took him in. Ryan Sommers. Co-captain of the football team, possibly the sexiest person to ever exist, and strictly off-limits. Or, well, he had been when I was dating Aaron anyway. I let the tiniest hint of a smirk tilt up my mouth as he approached, steps sure and confident, denim eyes fixed on me.

35

"Ry," I said, my smirk transforming into a fully-fledged smile as he stopped next to me and leaned back against the wall next to the lecture hall door. "What's up?"

The corridor felt too small with him standing in it, like he had sucked out all the air and left only heat. His eyes traced over my outfit and that fire moved through me, tightening my nipples and stoking my blood. It was heady, having something forbidden finally within reach, to finally be allowed to *want*.

"Just thought I'd stop and say hi," he said and his voice was sinful. I'd often avoided talking to him when I was with Aaron because that voice... it did things to me. "I couldn't help overhearing—you need some help with your Professor?"

I wanted to focus, I wanted him to leave or to stay, I wasn't sure yet—all I could think about was his voice saying *Do you always open the door in your panties, Jamie?*

I wrangled my hormones back under control. Was a revenge threesome not enough rebound sex to get back at, and over, Aaron? "Ah, I'm good but thanks." *What am I saying?* I may have hated Professor Dick, but a career in academia was what I'd wanted for so long and it would happen over Davis' dead body. If Ryan could help me get things back on track...

He took a step closer and his cologne washed over me pleasantly, smelling faintly of apples and something dark. "Date me for the three months. I have a stellar rep, straight As..." and then he said the one thing he knew was my weakness, "it'll drive Aaron crazy."

I bit back the smile that tried to crawl free. "What would you be getting out of it? Is this because you've seen the photo?"

Ryan raised an eyebrow and his lopsided smile was cute and more than a little cocky. "Pretty sure I saw a lot more than what was in that photo when you opened the door," he pointed out with a slight tinge of pink sweeping across his cheeks. "Anyway, do I really need more of a reason than pissing off your ex-boyfriend?"

I folded my arms across my chest and didn't miss the way his gaze dropped down to my chest and the dark lacy fringe framing my boobs. "Maybe."

"How about this?" he said, stepping closer again until his chest brushed mine and his head bent as his mouth brushed my ear. "Aaron's a dick and he never deserved you. You need my help."

I scoffed. "I don't *need*—"

Soft lips brushed against my akin and a hot breath sent shivers racing through me. "Okay, I'll rephrase. You *want* my help. Maybe you even want me." He pulled back and his eyes roved over my face, dropping to my mouth and my head felt woozy. Was I still high? Was that why he was affecting me like this?

I cut through the sudden tension with a laugh and Ry pressed a finger to my lips, mouth twitching with amusement as if he could see me fighting the urge to pull the tip into my mouth.

"Why not?" he reasoned, stepping back at last and I sucked in a quick, desperate breath. "It's win-win. You get your Professor off your back, get to have a little fun with me *and* you get Aaron back for sharing that photo of you with everyone on the football team."

I should have said no. I should have laughed him off like this was one big joke, but I'd never played it safe before—why should I start now? "This doesn't mean I'll sleep with you."

"Of course," Ryan said with what looked suspiciously like triumph coloring his grin.

I narrowed my eyes at him before nodding, glancing down at my phone and cursing at the notifications blowing up my socials. It made this decision even easier.

"Then let's do this," I said and held out my hand to strike the deal. Ryan slid his fingers between mine and tugged me closer. "Meet me at Cocoa and Rum at noon tomorrow and we can discuss the details."

"Can't wait."

CHAPTER FIVE

IDFC - BLACKBEAR

COCOA & RUM WAS ALREADY PACKED WHEN I ARRIVED with the early lunch-time crowd but I easily picked out Ryan's dark hair sitting at a table by the window. He looked up and grinned when he found my eyes already on him and I bit my lip, wondering for the millionth time if I was making a mistake coming here—yet another thing I had to blame Aaron and Taylor for. I'd never really been one to second guess myself. Never had the luxury, I'd always had to decide what to do on my own and just do it, letting the chips fall where they may. But now I found myself questioning everything—was this the right move? Was my top too low-cut? Was that guy on the street staring at me or just enjoying a stroll through town? Had I said the wrong thing to Liv at dinner last night? It was, frankly, beyond irritating that those two clowns had shook me up enough for me to have my confidence knocked. So I did the only thing I could: faked it.

Ryan had two coffees already sitting in front of him and I looked at them longingly as I slid out the chair opposite him.

He pushed one over and grinned. "Here. You look like you need this."

My lip twitched and I bit down on a smile, not sure if he deserved it yet. "Are you kickstarting negotiations by telling me I look like shit?"

Ry laughed, pushing a floppy bit of dark hair off of his face as he grinned from over his coffee mug. "No, I just didn't want any drool to escape your mouth. I got it for you anyway."

"Thanks," I said, taking a long drag of the iced coffee and smothering a groan. It was warm-ish outside and the cold drink was sweating lightly around the plastic cup. I paused as the flavors rolled over my tongue and raised an eyebrow. "You know my order?"

Ryan shrugged but a small smirk played over his mouth. "You were over at the house all the time guzzling those things, it wasn't hard to remember." And yet Aaron had never seemed to be able to. "So what exactly are we here to negotiate? I mean, I think I've already proved within like five minutes of your time that I'd make a great boyfriend."

"*Fake* boyfriend," I stressed and he shrugged.

"Sure, if that's what you want."

I looked at him sharply and he smiled casually, like the words weren't some kind of declaration. "I'm not going to sleep with you."

"Sure," he repeated and I huffed out an annoyed breath, taking another sip of coffee to give myself a second of composure.

"No kissing. Or touching."

"Am I supposed to be your boyfriend or your brother?" he said pointedly and I nodded grudgingly.

"Fine, but only in public."

A slow grin curled at Ry's mouth as he sat back in his chair, stretching his arms over his head and drawing my gaze down to the small slither of skin now on display that hinted at hard muscles. My eyes flew back up as he cleared his throat lightly and I tried not to blush. "Does that mean you're planning on being with me not in public?"

"Not if I can avoid it," I said sweetly and he laughed under his breath, reaching out and tugging one of my hands away from my coffee cup and then holding it in his, heedless of the wet condensation from the drink. "What are you doing?"

"We're in public, aren't we?"

I frowned at his smirk and bit my cheek as his thumb began stroking taunting circles into my skin. "Yes, but we're in the midst of negotiations still." I tugged my hand firmly out of his and ignored the girl whispering too-loudly at the table nearest ours about whether I was trying to make my way through the entire football team.

"What else is there to negotiate?" Ryan asked, leaning forward again and staring into my eyes so deeply that I felt uncomfortable. Sure, I was attractive and not humble enough to pretend otherwise and so people sometimes liked to look at me, but this felt different. Like he was trying to peer inside my brain and see what made me tick.

"Appearances," I said smoothly, blinking and taking the opportunity to shoot a glare at the perky red-head who had been gossiping to her friend about me. Actually, she sort of looked like one of the sorority girls Taylor hung out with, which would explain a lot about her dislike. "Parties, class, whatever. We need to be seen together."

"Okay," he said easily and I stared at him. I'd been expecting a little backlash about how much effort this was going to cost him but he seemed to genuinely not mind.

"Okay?"

"Yes?" Ryan drank some more of his coffee, eying me over

41

the rim. "It's not exactly a hardship for me to be seen with a beautiful girl."

"A beautiful girl who recently had a sex scandal and dated your co-captain?"

He shrugged. "We both know you don't care about the scandal beyond getting your professor off your back and as far as Aaron is concerned... Well, don't be."

"He thinks we're going to get back together."

"Then let's show him how wrong he is," Ryan said in a low voice that had something tightening in my stomach and I nodded, not trusting my voice.

"Then we're agreed," he said as he set his mug down. "Public appearances, no kissing or touching in private, no sex..." he let the words hang there as if hoping I might suddenly change my mind before finishing, "...and Aaron is a dick."

I smiled. "Sounds about right."

"Then I think we need to seal the deal in the traditional way," Ry said, standing up and offering me his hand. I raised a brow but took it as I stood, grateful I'd opted to wear jeans and didn't have a skirt to smooth back into place. He stepped forward and cupped my jaw in one large hand, the warmth making my skin tingle as he lowered his mouth to mine. It was nothing more than an extended peck really but it made me wonder what a *real* kiss from Ryan might feel like. His mouth was soft but firm and he nipped lightly at my bottom lip before he pulled away and I gasped, not expecting him to take the kiss in that direction.

"How is that the traditional way?" I said quietly and I knew to outsiders we probably looked every part the couple, murmuring sweet nothings to each other, and I wanted to laugh.

"Huh," Ry said as he pulled back but kept a firm grip on

my hand. "I guess I was just thinking about the way they do it on *Supernatural*."

I snorted as he walked with me to the door and stepped out into the sunshine, shielding his eyes with a squint and affording me the chance to watch him without him seeing. I didn't understand how someone who seemed so... *nice* could be semi-friends with Aaron.

"Let me walk you home?" Ryan said and I nodded, expecting him to drop my hand as we walked but he kept it firmly clasped between us and the sensation was new. Other than sex, Aaron and I hadn't been hugely touchy-feely. Neither of us tended to cuddle after sex and we definitely hadn't walked around holding hands, hadn't really needed to. If you were seen with Aaron it was pretty clear that you were *with* him, but Ry just seemed to want to hold my hand because he liked it.

"Has Aaron pissed you off recently or something?" I asked and Ryan gave a short laugh as we walked through the trees.

"When hasn't he pissed me off?"

"I just meant..."

"I know what you meant. I'm happy to make your ex jealous, Jamie." He pulled us to a stop as his eyes met mine and then dropped to my mouth. "More than happy."

"Because you hate him?" I said, ignoring the way my heart thudded a little harder than usual.

"Because he was an asshole to you and deserves everything that's coming to him."

"I didn't realize you cared." I laughed, intending to only tease him but Ry shot me a look I couldn't work out, murmuring something too low for me to hear.

We walked in silence for a while, taking in the trees that were becoming green again and letting the birdsong fill the air between us. It was surprisingly comfortable, the fresh air, the warmth of his hand in mine, the *lightness* of it all. I hadn't even realized I'd been feeling so heavy.

I nudged us in the direction of my apartment and Ry let me lead without question. It was only a short walk from *Cocoa & Rum* to mine and I found myself wishing I lived just a little further away. I stopped outside and nodded to the metal door that would let me into the apartments above the street and Ryan smiled ruefully.

"Text me your schedule and I'll meet you after class when I can," Ry said and I smiled, glad he had been the one to breach the quiet.

I nodded and took his phone from his hand, inputting my number quickly and handing it back. Something about holding other people's phones freaked me out. I wasn't a germaphobe but it just felt icky.

"Sounds good," I said and turned away to head inside when he said my name and I found my lips suddenly on his again. This time it felt more like a real kiss, devouring and hungry and breathless as Ry's tongue swept over mine and my hands tightened instinctively on his shoulders. He pulled away and I stared at him with wide eyes.

"We're still in public," he reminded me and then grinned as he walked away, leaving me outside trying to calm the racing of my heart.

CHAPTER SIX

DRAMATIC - CAT & CALMELL

I'D SPENT THE PAST TWO WEEKS WORKING ON THIS presentation for Davis' class and I knew now more than ever I needed to nail it. My specialism was women throughout history, it was always my focus and the historical lens that I used for my assignments, so I'd thought I'd choose something apt for both the college and my own interests for the project— Radclyffe Hall. Specifically, her novel *The Well of Loneliness* seeing as we were currently dissecting the war and its ripples throughout society in class. It was a great book and *hello* the college was named after her, what better way for me to show my school spirit? At what point my desire for college pep dissolved into a shouting match in the middle of class, I wasn't sure. Possibly around the time that Davis interrupted me mid-way through my speech to call my topic 'an embarrassment' and to further lecture me on banned books, which of course, *The Well of Loneliness* had been because it featured lesbians. Happy lesbians, specifically. If what Nick had told me the other day was anything to go by, then maybe Davis really did have an issue with anything sapphic.

I cut him off before he could continue telling me the ramifications this presentation was going to have on my grade. "Do you have a problem with lesbians?" Davis choked and the class fell silent, Nick's eyes were wide and he frantically shook his head at me, clearly feeling that this wasn't the time or place for this discussion. I smiled tightly. "No?" I asked when Davis remained silent. "What about women in general?" More silence. "My presentation is perfectly valid in its relation to the subject of war and I think the book itself sheds interesting light on the way war affected women and society. Of course, if you think Radclyffe Hall's work is reductive then maybe you can go and tell the board exactly why that is—maybe even provide them with an alternative namesake for the college?"

The room was quiet and Davis was bone white, either from shock or anger I couldn't tell. I flicked through the last few slides without commentary and looked out over the class before I moved away. "If anyone has any questions or wants to see the rest of the slides let me know. Thanks for your time."

It was probably going to bite me in the ass. But what was the point in me spending time and energy on a project I had truly enjoyed *and* had crushed only to be stopped half-way because of some derogatory bullshit? If Professor Dick wanted to hate me, fine. But getting in the way of my learning? Forcing the class to conform to his biased bullshit? I wasn't going to just sit back and take that, even if it did get me kicked off the course.

I sat back down next to Nick and he gave me a grudging smile, as if to say he'd hated that I'd done it but was proud of me at the same time. I shrugged lightly and blinked when the lights flashed back on, I guess we were done presenting after the mini-meltdown that had just occurred.

I shoved my laptop back into my bag and avoided the eyes of the class as I walked out. Davis didn't stop me, didn't even look at me, and a kernel of dread took root as I imagined all the ways he was going to use this against me. He couldn't kick me out for this alone, not least because I was right and he wouldn't want to attract attention to it, but he would find a way to twist it, of that I had no doubt.

Nick fell behind as I charged down the stairs of the lecture hall and out the door, drowning in both anger and a helplessness that left me blind to everything else until I collided with a very hard, warm chest and nearly went sprawling.

"Hey," a familiar voice called me back, gripping my forearms to prevent me from falling to the ground, and I looked up into blue eyes that somehow steadied me. "Are you alright?" I forced a nod and Ryan frowned, hands loosening on my arms as he instead moved them to my shoulders and he bent his head down towards me. "Take a breath," he said and I did, then took another when he told me to do it again. By my fourth, the anger had receded and the tears starting to burn in my eyes had faded. "What happened?"

I blew out another breath for good measure and then started walking before the rest of the class started leaving through the doors behind us. "I got into it with my Professor when he cut-off my presentation mid-way through."

Ryan frowned. "Aren't you supposed to be winning him over?"

My hands curled into fists as I whirled on him. "This isn't about *me,* it's about him trying to warp fucking history with his bigoted—"

A hand clapped over my mouth and I glared in outrage, ignoring the swooping sensation in my stomach. I reined in my first instinct to bite Ryan's hand and knew he had been right to stop me from ranting when Davis walked past, eyes flicking between me and Ryan before he hurried away.

"He'll get what's coming to him eventually," Ry said when

he released his hand from my mouth. "But for what it's worth, I'm sorry."

"It's okay." I sighed. "At least he saw us together. I wasn't expecting you to meet me so soon after Saturday, can't keep away?"

"Never could," he said and I turned that over in my mind, wondering what it meant as Ry changed the subject. "If you want, you can do the presentation for an audience of one?"

I blinked at him, letting out a small laugh before I realized he was serious. "What?"

"You didn't get to finish, right?" Ryan grinned cockily, "I don't like to leave anyone feeling unsatisfied."

I rolled my eyes but let the comment slide. "You don't have to—"

"I want to," he said, slipping his hand into mine and laughing when I jumped. My classmates started to pour past us, Nick waggling his eyebrows when he saw who now held my hand, and then the whispers kicked up again.

"*I heard she had an orgy—*"

"*Can you believe* she *cheated on Aaron?*"

"*So fucking stuck up, imagine lecturing the lecturer—*"

"Shut the fuck up," Ryan said loudly and a few wide eyes ran over him standing at my side as a quick hush descended. If there was anyone the fangirls worshiped more than Aaron... A few people lingered close-by, mostly girls, waiting to see if any more drama unfolded and Ryan looked directly at them, mouth tight and jaw clenched. "Fuck off."

I snorted and the girls practically fled, Ryan steered us in the direction of the doors and I dropped my eyes to the death grip he had on my hand. "Am I supposed to be impressed?"

He frowned at me, not bothering to answer. "Is it always like that?"

"Only recently." I shrugged and his frown deepened,

clearing only a little as the fresh air hit us. "You know, there's not really anyone around right now, you can let go of my hand."

The frown disappeared as he grinned, letting go of my fingers and slinging an arm around my shoulders instead, tucking me in close to his side. "Is this better? If you wanted to cuddle you only had to say so."

I rolled my eyes but didn't bother pulling away, he'd only find some other way to irritate me.

"So?" he said after the silence stretched on.

"What?" I asked, looking up at him in confusion and breathing in the scent of warm apples, like he'd been baking or something. It wasn't fair that he smelled so... delicious. I wanted to shake myself and Ryan stared down at me like he'd said something, grinning a little when I remained quiet.

"I *said,* aren't you going to tell me your presentation?"

He had to be joking, right? Ryan brushed my bangs out of my eyes and raised an eyebrow like he was waiting. I hesitantly began talking, recounting my intro and background of the book and the war, glancing up at him every so often to see if he was actually paying attention or just humoring me. His dark brows were furrowed as he listened to me speak and we strolled aimlessly around the park, neither of us ready to head home yet.

"And this book was banned?" he said and I nodded.

"It's starting to happen again in the US where books that disagree with the status quo get banned."

"I had no idea," he said and it was clearly something that bothered him as he bit his lip and glanced at me. "I hope you don't think I'm stupid."

I laughed. "I mean you *are* a jock."

"I study psychology," he pointed out and I blinked, because I honestly hadn't known. I was starting to realize that I was kind of self-absorbed. But hey, at least I knew it, right?

"Well, I don't actually think you're stupid," I said and Ryan smiled crookedly as he sat down on a bench under a big tree, the sunlight filtering through so it wasn't in our eyes.

"Tell me more," he prompted and my mouth went dry. I could count on one hand the amount of times someone had ever asked me to tell them *more* about history. Once, when someone wanted to cheat off of me for an exam. Second... Ry.

My phone vibrated and I glanced down at it, glad to give myself a moment to sort out what I was feeling, and any peacefulness that had started to flow immediately withered and died inside me.

UNKNOWN: Benji, baby, how are things? You know I love you, I'm sorry I haven't been around much but tell me when you're free and we can meet up. I've missed my girl.

A sick feeling started in my stomach and clawed its way up my throat. There was only one person I knew who called me Benji and I had nothing to say to her. How she'd even found my number I wasn't sure. I opted to ignore it, not wanting to encourage her, if she messaged again then I'd reply mostly to stop her from turning up here out of the blue. That would be the last thing I needed with this mess going on.

"Everything okay?" Ryan asked, eyes assessing the rapid change in my mood and I nodded.

Suddenly I wanted nothing more than to be alone with my thoughts for a while. I hated that she had this effect on me, the familiar mix of anger, sadness and guilt. She was my *mother,* what kind of person felt that way when their mom texted?

"Yeah, I just need to get going, I told Liv I'd hang out with her today," I lied and Ryan nodded easily.

"Sure, do you want me to walk you back?" he asked, standing with me and reaching for my hand.

I pulled away with a strained smile. "No thanks, I'm good." I gave him a nod and he bit his lip but gave a half-hearted wave as I walked away. It was for the best, I couldn't let us become too comfortable, couldn't let myself be vulnerable like that right now. It had been a mistake with Aaron and Taylor and it would be a mistake with Ryan. He wanted to piss off Aaron and maybe play white knight. Fine. It didn't need to be more than that. We could have a little fun and keep things at a distance, I was tired of people wiggling their way into my heart and crushing it from the inside.

I rifled through my bag until I found the black protective tub, popped open the lid and pulled out a zoot. I just needed my thoughts to be quiet for a while. I lit it with one hand while I walked, inhaling to keep the fire burning before the light breeze could snuff it out. I was trying to be more respectful of Liv and smoke outside of the apartment. She said she didn't mind but I could tell she didn't like the smell.

I finished the joint just before I reached the downstairs door to the apartment and stubbed it out on the brick wall next to it. My brain had a pleasant haze and my eyes felt heavy. I hoped Liv was out because I wasn't really in the mood for conversation. I just wanted to put on my baggiest tee, crash out on the sofa and binge watch *Vampire Diaries* while I devoured a bag of chips.

I was mid-way through doing exactly that when Liv walked in, calling out a quick *hello* that I reciprocated blearily. I'd somehow made it through four episodes and Liv walked in, flinching at the fleshy sound as Damon ripped out some poor dude's heart.

"Hey," she said again as she settled next to me and I patted the top of her head. "I know I said I'd cook tonight but I kind of fancy take-out."

I waved my hand airily as my stomach grumbled, the chips hadn't been enough to satiate the munchies. "Pizza?" I asked and she grinned.

"Sounds perfect."

Normally, Liv cooked and I cleaned. That was the deal. Mostly because I both hated to cook and seriously sucked at it. Like, I could manage toast but even that usually wound up burnt. Liv placed the order while I called out toppings and then we sat and waited.

"So..." she said and I snuggled deeper into the corner of the sofa, keeping my eyes fixed on the screen. "You seem kinda... sad."

"Maybe this is just my personality," I mumbled and Liv pinched my arm. "Ow, okay, what?"

"What's on your mind?" she insisted and I groaned.

"My mom texted me today and I think Ryan is hot." I could tell that Liv was baffled on multiple levels so I sighed, knowing I needed to talk more to elaborate. She'd only had the bare minimum details from me on Friday evening and I hadn't seen her to fill her in on Saturday's coffee date yet. "Ryan is Aaron's co-captain and currently my fake boyfriend to get Professor Dick to ease off me because of the probation and he has the added bonus of pissing off Aaron. My mom is an addict and I hate it when she texts because she's normally looking to relieve her guilt or get some cash."

Liv hummed, nodding her head slowly. "Your life is like a movie."

"Can't wait for the credits," I mumbled and she sighed, moving closer and spooning me from the side.

"It'll all work out," she reassured me, and in Liv's calm and collected voice I almost believed it too. "But for now, I want more details on this Ryan guy."

I laughed and she grinned as I peeked up at her from beneath the hood of the blanket I'd found on the sofa. I was pretty sure it was Liv's but she didn't seem to mind. Just tucked the hood in closer around my head as we lamented the perfection of the Salvatore brothers.

CHAPTER SEVEN

R U MINE? - ARCTIC MONKEYS

I'D SPENT MOST OF THE WEEK DODGING SORORITY girls out for my blood, trying not to antagonize Davis further and meeting up with Ry just enough to maintain our ruse. I'd met him after his psych class yesterday and we'd walked to *Cocoa & Rum* together for coffee, which would have been fine had Taylor not been in there waiting for her order. Her presence had quickly dampened any sort of heat that might have been kindling between Ryan and me, though maybe I should have been thanking her for killing the buzz before I could get in too deep.

I'd been lounging on the couch for the past hour, pretty much just staring into space while I avoided working on the essay that was due very imminently. It was hard to have motivation to do any work when Davis was likely to fail me just on principle. My phone buzzed from across the room and I happily ignored it. I'd had to pare back a lot of my socials recently thanks to Aaron, the jackass, people apparently couldn't get enough of my naked picture. Who knew? But there were only so many *Hey beautiful* DMs I could take. My mom hadn't messaged again since Monday and I'd felt a horrible relief at the fact and then a surge of guilt for good measure. My phone vibrated twice more against the dining room table propped in the corner near the kitchen and I sighed, heaving myself up to grab it. The first two alerts were promo emails for *The Box* but the third...

Ryan: So what are you wearing?

I huffed a laugh and threw my phone down onto the sofa just as Liv walked in, arms full of textbooks.

"Hot date?" I called as she set them down onto the wooden dining table that stood in the corner of the room just outside of the kitchen.

She threw me a look as they thumped down. "Oh yes, my ideal Friday night involves staying in with these hotties."

I hummed *Livin' La Vida Loca* as I picked up my phone again and peered down at Ry's message. Three small dots appeared and a grin pricked at my mouth as I waited.

Ryan: The black set from last week?

I snorted and ignored the heat rising from my cheeks as I impatiently brushed my bangs out of my eyes.

Jamie: I fed those to the fire.

. . .

Ryan: So... you're naked then?

Jamie: Wouldn't you like to know.

Liv flicked through her textbook and sighed, whatever she was reading clearly not interesting in the least. I shook my weed box at her and she rolled her eyes.

"I'm good, thanks."

"Suit yourself," I said cheerfully as I took out my red grinder and promptly dropped it—empty, thankfully—when my phone buzzed again.

"Who's messaging you?" Liv raised her eyebrows as she took in my blush. "It's not Aaron, is it?"

I recoiled. "What? No. Why would I get back with him after he leaked a nude photo of me all over the internet?"

She shrugged. "People do dumb stuff for love."

I wrinkled my nose, unsure that what Aaron and I'd had could really be considered *love*. My phone buzzed with another reminder and I bit my lip. "Um, it's Ryan."

Ryan: You're right. I would.

Jamie: Nudes are reserved for non-fake boyfriends.

Ryan: Who's faking?

. . .

I cleared my throat as I read his message again, unsure how to respond and so instead locked my phone.

Liv's eyes widened at whatever she saw on my face before she laughed. "This is going to be messy."

"That's sort of the point," I said, annoyed. "It'll piss Aaron off, plus I told you what Professor Dick said—my reputation needs a little TLC."

"I just hope you know what you're doing," she said quietly and I glanced down at my phone again as it buzzed against my thigh.

"Come on, put down those textbooks."

"What?" Liv said, startled when I strode over and tugged one out of her hand. "Why?"

I grinned at her. "It's Friday night and we've been invited to a party."

Liv protested half-heartedly for a couple of minutes before giving in and heading to her room to change. It was funny how quickly the room across the hall had become Liv's in my head, clearly I'd been ready to move on from Taylor for a while and it had taken my brain a beat to catch up with my subconscious. Or maybe it was all about Liv—we just seemed to click. It had been surprisingly fun having her here this past week and I was definitely relieved, what could have been a disastrous drunken offer has actually turned out to be a pretty sweet deal. Plus, she'd offered to help me redecorate the apartment this weekend and I couldn't wait to get the new color on.

After a break-up some people liked to dye their hair or get a tattoo—I got drunk, laid, and then I liked to decorate. Not necessarily in that order. Part of the motivation this time was definitely that Aaron had originally helped me paint this place, but it was time for something new anyway.

"Do you think this is okay?" Liv called as she strode out of her room in a hot pink mini skirt and floaty baby pink top that tied around her neck. I grinned and hooted at her, it was girly but she rocked it.

"*Yes*, oh my god I love it."

"It's not too... pink?"

I finished pulling on my boots and smiled. "Oh, it definitely is, but like, in the best way. You look great, don't worry."

"I've just never been to a frat party before so I don't know what the vibe is."

"Drunk and horny," I supplied, touching up my deep purple lipstick in the hallway mirror and tucking my dark bob behind my ears to show-off the rows of gold earrings I'd put in. "Trust me, there'll be a mix of people there."

"Including your ex?"

I glanced at Liv in the mirror, her mouth was pinched and her hands were clasped tightly in front of her like maybe she was remembering the tense encounter with Aaron last week. I put the lid on the lipstick with a sharp click and kissed her on the cheek, leaving a purple lip-mark. "There, now you look edgy."

She reached up and touched the mark. "Are you nervous to see him again?"

"Nervous?" I took in my tight black velvet skater dress, fishnets and docs and met Liv's gaze in the mirror. "Not at all."

Everyone wanted to look good when they saw their ex again for the first time, and Aaron had ruined that for me by turning up here unexpectedly, but tonight... hopefully I'd skipped past *good* and Aaron would eat his fucking heart out.

There was a bass pounding so hard that the walls seemed to shake and as it pulsed through my body I felt myself relax. Academia was where my future lay, but music was what had always called to me. I had taught myself guitar when I was a teenager, mostly just so I could have an accompaniment when I sang, but I quickly learned from my mother of all people that dreams were just that. If I wanted to go somewhere, make something of myself and my future, I needed a serious career. That's what my history degree was for me—stability, security, the chance to have the life I'd always dreamed of. So there was no chance in hell I was letting Professor Dick put that at risk.

Liv fussed with the hem of her skirt as I pushed open the door to the party, it was frat-boy-brown, the kind of basic tan that all school buildings adopted—neutral—which was ridiculous considering we were at a school that claimed to care about nurturing individuality and the arts. I slapped Liv's hands away from her skirt and gave her a comforting smile.

"You're a boss ass bitch. Nobody in there is worth worrying about. Trust me." I should know, this party had made up a part of my weekly routine when I'd been dating Aaron. During peak season it was their after-game blow out but post-season, like today, was usually wildest as it was the last chance to get crazy before they had to focus again for their final games. Plus, the big competitive matches had all been done within our first semester so there was less reason for restraint. There wasn't a huge amount of difference between pre-season Aaron and the Aaron who was supposed to be 'keeping things chill'. Mostly that meant that he swapped coke for weed or xannys.

There was a row of girls sitting up the stairs directly opposite the door as we walked in—part of the sorority I'd left Taylor in the hands of—and they shot me dirty looks as I moved past them. I smiled sweetly and blew a kiss to Brad and Cody when I spied them in the hallway that led to the kitchen.

The place reeked of beer, sweat, and marijuana already and a haze was in the air that made Liv look like something out of a dream as she wafted through the smoke and batted her amber eyes at a girl across the room. A warm hand snagged my waist and I inhaled deeply as the scent of Ryan's cologne surrounded me. I spun to face him and let my eyes move up his body in appreciation before coming to his face where he looked like he was holding in a laugh.

"Hey Ben," he said and his voice was deep enough that it carried past the shrill noise of whatever the boys standing by the aux had picked to skank to. I winced, I hated Skrillex.

"Jamie," I corrected absently as my eyes found my ex-bff across the room. She was wearing cut off booty shorts and her boobs practically hung out as she ground against a sorority girl in an attempt to get the attention of the guy sitting next to them. Aaron.

Ry slid a hand under my chin and tugged my eyes back to his before pressing a searing kiss to my mouth that left me dizzy. "What—"

"Public, remember?" he murmured and my gut twisted in something that felt surprisingly close to disappointment but I just smiled and introduced Ryan to Olivia.

"I need a drink," Liv muttered and I couldn't help but agree.

"Shots," I directed at Ryan and he nodded in the direction of the kitchen before following us through. I poured Liv a small shot of sourz and she sipped it gingerly before smacking her lips in appreciation. I laughed. "You're not supposed to taste it." She shrugged and I poured us each two shots of vodka and we slammed them back one after the other while Ryan watched.

"None for you?" I asked, raising my eyebrow and licking a drop of vodka off of my pink plastic shot glass. His eyes dropped to my mouth and I bit my lip.

"Nah, somebody has to be sharp for tomorrow's practice and it's definitely not going to be Aaron considering the amount of coke I saw him do earlier."

I rolled my eyes but wasn't really surprised. Liv, on the other hand, looked absolutely scandalized. "You dated this guy?"

I shrugged. "I like to party."

"So do I," she said slightly defensively and I poured us another shot, clicking them together before throwing them down just as Nick walked into the room.

"Well, looky what the cat dragged in," he purred and I pulled him in for a quick kiss on the cheek and introduced him to Liv and Ryan. "Oh! This is your mystery girl, I heard Jamie slipped you quite the tongue the other night."

Color filled Liv's face and Ry sent me a look as if to say, *Really?* I responded with an eyebrow wiggle and pressed myself against his side as Taylor walked into the kitchen, spotted me and sniffed haughtily as she knocked into Nick reaching for the plastic cups.

Liv recovered well, not everyone could adjust to Nick's occasionally crass humour so quickly, and sank her hand onto her hip as she pursed her mouth. "I can't believe you already have a gay black friend, here I thought I was special."

Nick laughed. "You can join the rainbow hon, Jamie is only slightly less gay than me."

Ryan looked like he didn't know quite what to make of this conversational turn and Liv looked... confused? It was hard to place the look on her face as her wide eyes turned to me and she took a step closer. "Really?"

I slapped at Nick's shoulder. "I'm definitely not as gay as you Nick, otherwise Ryan wouldn't have anything I'm interested in."

Taylor finally spoke up, like I'd been waiting for her to do. "Oh well, that's not hard. You've fucked, what—half the football team now? You're not exactly picky."

I smiled and Liv relaxed the tense grip on her shot glass

before the cheap plastic could break. "Opposed to you, Taylor? Oh right, I forgot. Your type is other people's boyfriends."

Taylor scowled and Nick whistled. Liv opened her mouth like she was going to respond but was cut-off as the person I'd been both looking forward to and dreading seeing walked into the kitchen and stopped short, taking in the arm that I now had firmly hooked in Ry's.

There it was. The look I'd been waiting for. The rage, maybe a little betrayal, crossing those blandly handsome features. The pop of his jaw as he strode closer to us, the clench of his fists, the way the air around him seemed to crackle as if his rage was a tangible thing. Like I was a prize to be fought over.

I turned my back to him as he got close enough to speak and instead leaned into Ryan. A small grin curled Ry's bottom lip, that sloppy smile more attractive than Aaron's carefully polished looks by a mile. Ryan didn't look up from my lips, running his tongue lightly across his mouth before saying calmly, "Hey, man."

A hot hand clamped onto my forearm and I gasped, whirling around to face my ex and shrugging his arm off me ineffectively. Another hand, strong with a pale scar running across the index finger to his wrist, grasped Aaron's and prised it off slowly. Ryan's expression didn't change, as though the action required little to no effort.

"When a woman recoils from your touch, you should let go."

My eyes met Ryan's and I got lost in the pool of blue for a moment, letting Aaron stew for longer. Like a bad dog, I didn't want to give him any attention. Ryan was steady, calm and maybe a little smug where Aaron was seething. Liv leaned back against the faux granite countertops, sipping at another shot of vodka and I pulled a face at her. Why couldn't she just swallow the things like a normal person? Who wanted to actually taste their vodka? Not me, that was for sure.

"Ryan," Taylor cooed, trying to wedge her way between us as she pressed perfectly manicured nails to his chest so hard they left ripples in his dark shirt, "you could do so much better than these damaged goods."

"Like you?" Liv snorted and I grinned, glad she had my back.

"Who even are you?" Taylor snarled, spinning around so fast her blonde hair whipped across Ry's face. "Just another slut, I'm guessing. Did Jamie fuck you too? You guys could form a club!" She clapped sarcastically and only Ryan's hand sliding firmly around my waist stopped me from ripping her hair out.

"Academic probation," he whispered as he pressed his mouth to my neck, trailing kisses up to my ear and biting the lobe punishingly.

"Oh." I let out a deep breath and decided to ignore Taylor in favor of finally acknowledging my ex, knowing that denying her any attention would hurt her vanity more than me plowing a fist into her mouth. I ran my nose against Ry's cheek, teasing a kiss at the corner of his mouth before flicking a disinterested look over at Aaron. "It's you."

Aaron's nostrils flared and his eyes were like hard blocks of ice, the blue looked cheap and faded next to Ryan's deep denim tones. "Really man? You're banging my girlfriend?"

"Ex," I corrected helpfully and pressed my chest against Ryan's from the side as I looked up at him, effectively pushing Taylor out of the way and she left the room in a huff. Good job too, this tiny room was becoming crowded.

"What the fuck are you doing here with him?" Aaron barked and I fought back a laugh. "I don't want you two together."

"Hmm," I said, tapping a finger against my chin as I reached out and accepted a shot from Liv with my other hand. "That's strange." The alcohol burned all the way down, setting my veins humming.

"What?" Aaron snapped, mouth a flat, white line, like a bloodless slash in his face.

"I'm just really struggling to remember when I asked you for your fucking opinion." I turned and gave him a wide, sweet smile, the one I used to use when I sucked his dick just the way he liked, and he heaved in a breath that sounded like a grunt as Liv snorted and Nick muttered a prayer. Ryan slid an arm around my waist and I moved my body back against his. "Now, if you'd be so kind—get out of our fucking way. I think Taylor went in that direction when she stomped out of here. You guys are close, right? I'm sure she'll give you some of the attention you so clearly need."

I mouthed *blue balls* at Liv and she grinned as she linked her arm with Nick's and I slid my hand into Ryan's as we collectively elbowed our way past my ex. A smug smile caught at my mouth as I saw Aaron's enraged face in my head over and over. Ryan didn't even look at Aaron, just let us lead as we made our way back to the main room where the music was loudest.

Someone with some taste had finally taken the aux off of the freshmen new recruits and I moved my hips to Doja's *Woman*, grabbing onto Liv's hips and encouraging her to move when she stayed standing still. Nick shook his ass and Liv relaxed a bit more, laughing.

Ryan dropped down into an armchair close by and I felt his eyes on every inch of my skin as I moved to the beat, like I danced just for him. Liv held tightly onto the plastic red cup of drink she'd made in the kitchen as she bobbed her head to the music, eyes darting back and forth between me and Ry.

I pulled the joint I'd pre-rolled before we arrived out from behind my ear and lit it with the hot pink lighter I'd tucked into my boot, smirking as I sank toward the ground in an exaggerated squat when the music changed to *Drop it like it's hot*. Ryan followed my movement with his eyes and heat sped through me as I looked up at him from the ground. It was the worst tease, to act as if he were mine. Like I was his, to touch, kiss... fuck.

Usually I liked to be in control, but there was something about being on my knees with Ryan above me that had my breaths coming a little faster.

I exhaled smoke while I danced and watched it curl around the ends of his dark brown hair, slightly longer on the top, and wanted to follow it with my fingers. I tried to remind myself that this was pretend. That I just needed to piss off Aaron and be seen with someone responsible that would improve my reputation. But the longer I looked at Ry all I could think about were his earlier words—*Who's faking?*

Liv's eyes flicked to the doorway behind us and she gave me a slight nod. I didn't even look back, just moved closer to Ryan and draped myself across his lap, ignoring the daggers Taylor was glaring at me. I dragged the joint and exhaled before offering it to him, torturing myself just a little as I watched his lips ghost over the same spot mine had been. It was okay though, I reasoned, this was all part of the act. It was okay for me to seem infatuated with Ryan, because Aaron had walked in through the door and his gaze had zeroed in on us almost instantly.

Ryan flicked ash into a nearby tray and let one arm settle around my waist, his large hand falling mid-thigh below the hem of my skirt and stroking upwards lightly. Aaron had seemingly forced his gaze from us and well... that was not going to do. I wanted him to hurt just as much as he'd hurt me. I wanted to drive him feral with jealousy. *I wanted to be wanted.*

I let my body relax against Ryan's and hummed along to some generic pop song as I moved my mouth closer to his skin. Ryan's gaze caught and locked with mine before my mouth grazed the outer shell of his ear, traveling down lightly until I took the lobe between my teeth and tugged, a response to his own teasing earlier. I watched the pulse in his neck jump and that fascinated me more than anything, so I pressed my lips to that too and then trailed open mouth kisses down his neck, leaving a collection of red-purple lip prints that made him look well-fucked. This felt like crossing a line, but with the weed wreathing my brain and the taste of him in my mouth, I couldn't remember why that would be a bad idea.

I pulled the joint out from between his lips as I sat up, now fully in his lap with my skirt spread wide around me so that only my tights and his jeans separated our bodies. His hands ran up my calves above my boots to cup the back of my thighs and their warmth made me shiver. I kept myself lifted off his lap slightly, not wanting to take this too far. This was just teasing, Aaron was the only one who needed to believe this was for real.

I swayed my hips in time to the music and linked my arms around Ry's neck, fingers tangling in his silky hair, eyes locked on his. His gaze flickered just once, warning me that someone was coming over and I didn't need to guess who. My fingers curled around Ryan's chin and I tugged lightly until he could see only me, then I slowly pressed fully against him, chests flush, his jeans slightly scratchy against my inner thighs as my mouth brushed his once, twice.

"Jamie," Liv called too late as I found myself dumped on the floor. Aaron stood over the armchair and Ryan, blood smeared on his fist. Ryan grinned, his mouth a lazy sprawl as he spat blood and stood. He had a good inch or two on Aaron and that filled me with a strange sense of satisfaction as the bass pounding through the room heightened the tension. Two guys who had been standing near a beer pong set-up were trying to push past the small crowd that was forming, one with a shock of baby blue hair and the other with broody dark eyes, and Ry shot them a look so I guessed he knew them.

I picked myself up from the floor, using Liv's hand as leverage, and made sure my skirt was covering everything. I wasn't typically a violent person, I preferred to use words as weapons generally—however, I did have a few exceptions and being dumped on the floor like yesterday's trash was one of them. Ry clearly noticed the glint of murder in my eyes and shook his head, I took a step forward and he sighed.

"Thanks for hitting me first, asshole," Ry smiled grimly and I paused, "and if you ever lay a hand on *my* girl again I'll beat the fuck out of you." His words were clipped and his eyes were shadowed in the darkness of the room and in that moment, I believed him.

"Sure man, if you want my sloppy seconds then go ahead. I mean, she's good enough in the sack—my brother can attest to that too, right Brad? Or was it the photo? You liked what you saw, huh?" Taylor cackled like Aaron had said something brilliantly funny and I narrowed my eyes but couldn't help my smile as Aaron dismissively brushed away the hand Taylor was attempting to run across his chest. "If I'd known how clingy *you* were going to be I never would have fucked you," Aaron said and for a second, real, genuine hurt flickered over Taylor's face before she flounced away. "Then again," he said, turning back to Ryan whose jaw looked like it could break at any moment from the tension lining his face, "Jamie was always better in bed anyway. But hey, you've seen the picture. Maybe she'll convince you to do a wholeass movie."

He laughed and it felt like the pit dropped out of my

stomach. I shouldn't care what he thought. He was a scumbag and a cheater and an *asshole* but I couldn't hide my flinch when he looked me up and down as if he alone could determine my worth and said, "Slut."

Up until that moment, I didn't think Ryan had actually planned on hitting him back. Not until he saw that tiny, minuscule flinch cross my face. Ry glanced around to see where his friends were and, seeing them struggling to get to us, he smiled and struck faster than I could believe. His hand slammed into Aaron's face and my ex groaned, clutching it as Ryan stood over him, clenching his hands like one punch hadn't been enough to satisfy him.

The blue haired guy reached us first, grabbing for Aaron and hauling him away before he could retaliate—or maybe before Ryan could inflict any more damage. Blood stained my ex's pressed blue shirt, marring that faux-perfect image he presented. To me, the bloodstains felt more accurate anyway.

The dark-eyed brooder grabbed me and Ry, pushing us in the direction of the kitchen while Ryan massaged his hand. I shot Nick a look to keep an eye on Liv and he nodded before I was pushed around the corner and stumbled as I found myself pressed against the countertop with Ryan at my front and the kitchen blessedly empty.

"I'm sorry he hit you," I said as soon as the door closed, "and that you hit him back. It's not what you signed up for." I tried for a smile to ease the anger still lining his face. "Thought your rep was supposed to be stellar?"

"It was until I got involved with you," Ryan drawled with a slow chuckle. "Don't worry about it."

"Um, so can you let me up now?" I mumbled and felt his laugh rumble through my chest.

"If that's what you want," he said and moved away to the other side of the small kitchen.

I raised a brow. "Why wouldn't it be?"

"Oh, no reason," he said, taking a step closer, footstep echoing on the tiled floor. His face hit a beam of light coming in from the window and my eyes fell to the perfect imprints of my lips on his neck. "It just seemed like you might be enjoying yourself out there."

I snorted. "Yeah that was kind of the point."

Ryan huffed a short laugh. "Are you really going to play dumb?" He closed the small distance between us until we were breathing the same air and hoisted me up onto the counter so our eyes were level. He stepped between my legs and I shivered as his warmth ghosted across my skin.

"You're kind of handsy," I said breathlessly and he hummed a little in assent.

"I think you like it," he said in a whisper that raised the hairs on my skin as my body came to life with awareness. "I think," he brushed one hand over my knee, "you like it a lot."

My mind had gone blank at the sensation of his heat on my skin, his fingers stroking distracting little circles so deftly that I wondered if he was even aware he was doing it. When I made no move to push him away he ran his hand slightly higher and I let out a short breath that *might* have been a pant and his lips ghosted across mine in a barely-there kiss.

"You're wrong," I finally managed to mumble, reason trying to claw its way to the forefront of my mind. "It's just pretend and we're in private now. So no kissing, touching, anything." I rambled, pressing a hand to his chest and feeling the thud of his heart against my palm but instead of pushing him away I seemed only able to draw him closer.

"You're telling me," Ryan said, mouth moving lower and brushing the skin of my neck while his hand stroked higher on my leg and I instinctively tipped my head to offer him better access, "that if I pushed your panties to the side right now I wouldn't find you soaked for me?"

A small gasp left me as his finger brushed the very edge of those panties and my mind ran wild with what could happen, where this could go if I let it. But would it be a mistake? I needed him for three months, until my probation was over. Was what would likely be very good sex worth making things awkward?

I grabbed his hand by the wrist and looked up at him, forcing my eyes to focus on his and not the mouth that was mere breaths away from mine.

"That's what I'm telling you," I said and he smiled lightly. "Is this why you offered to help me? I told you already it doesn't mean I'll fuck you."

Ryan stepped away, his hand falling to his side and the moment lost. "I offered to help you because Aaron's a prick."

My throat felt tight and I cleared it lightly before saying, "Okay."

It was just light enough in the room that I could see his eyebrow rise. "Okay?"

I huffed in irritation. "Yes, okay. What did you expect me to say? This fake arrangement is helpful and that's all."

"If that's what you want then fine, but you know as well as I do that you're either mine or you're not. You can dance around it all you want."

I slid off the counter and stared up at him, the decision made only because he'd forced my hand and I wasn't good with ultimatums. "Then I'm not."

CHAPTER EIGHT

DONE FOR ME - CHARLIE PUTH, KEHLANI

R YAN HAD TEXTED ME THREE TIMES BY THE TIME I'D woken up on Saturday afternoon, hungover. Again. I wasn't really sure what to make of the way he'd acted last night, hitting Aaron when he'd seen how much he had hurt me with his words, cornering me in the kitchen as if he couldn't stop himself from touching me. I groaned, rolling over and scrubbing a hand roughly over my face as I rubbed my eyes into oblivion. Why couldn't my life just be simple? Liv would probably have said that I brought it on myself. She likely wasn't wrong.

Ryan: Aaron had a fat lip when I saw him this morning lol

Ryan: Are you pissed at me or just asleep? Because technically I didn't break any rules, we were at a public party

. . .

My eyes burned like they had sand in them as I stared at the texts and blinked furiously, swearing when I noticed smeared mascara on the back of my hand. No wonder they felt so awful, I'd gone to sleep in my make-up again. My phone vibrated in my hand and I stopped the smirk from taking over my face as I saw Ryan's latest message.

Ryan: Coffee?

I wasn't sure how to take it that he'd clearly been waiting for the little 'read' icon to appear next to his messages. Fake boyfriends didn't need to be quite that dedicated. *You know as well as I do that you're either mine or you're not.* I shook the words out of my head. I wasn't Ryan's, I wasn't Aaron's. I belonged only to myself. I clicked back off the messages and saw my mom's text, still sitting unanswered in my inbox, before quickly tapping back on Ryan's name. Better to get any awkwardness out of the way and just bite the proverbial, smoking-hot bullet.

Jamie: You're buying. Call it a broke-the-rules kiss tax.

I rolled my legs out of bed with a thump, half of my body still reluctant to leave the warmth of my bed, and decided it was time to tackle the mess of my face. Liv glanced up at me as I opened my door, making her way to her room across from mine with a cup of coffee in hand. She winced as she took in the state of me—she looked nothing short of stunning, of course. I bet *she* took her make-up off before bed.

"You look like I feel," Liv said and I winced as I swallowed, my tongue feeling thick in my mouth. Fuck, how much had I drunk last night?

"Gee, thanks." I yawned and then suddenly remembered *why* I felt so awful. We'd left the party not long after I'd left the kitchen, Ryan and I having made our point to Aaron and Taylor and successfully teased ourselves, apparently. Liv and I had decided to keep the party going once we'd got home. "How come you don't look like you drank a third of the bottle of tequila last night?"

Liv grinned, her brown skin practically glowing. "I can handle my booze better than you I guess."

I flipped her off and headed into our shared bathroom, attacking my face, teeth and body vigorously until I felt a little more human when I re-emerged. The smell of Liv's coffee still lingered in the air and my mouth watered, Ry had better bring the goods or our fake relationship would be over before it fake-began.

Ryan: downstairs

I threw the phone back down onto the bed after texting him a quick 'okay' and reached for my favorite pair of sweats. I hesitated with one leg inside, should I be dressing up more to see my 'boyfriend'? Would people think it was weird for me not to put in more effort? I frowned before tugging them on stroppily and pairing them with a cropped tee. *Who gives a fuck?*

I called a quick goodbye to Liv as I toed on my shoes and left, the thought of the waiting coffee making me hurry. I spotted Ryan's dark hair first as he leaned against the wall of the building next to mine, keeping the entryway clear as he held the two coffee cups in his hands protectively. Then he turned around and I gasped, coffee forgotten as I rushed over and took in the bruising across his cheekbone.

"Hey," he said easily, smiling as if it didn't hurt—which I couldn't imagine to be the case considering the deep purple that blossomed there. Ry held out a coffee to me and I stepped closer to him, my fingertips brushing across the bruise until he flinched and I snapped my hand back to my chest. "Here," he said, waving the coffee my way again. "Cute sweats."

Other than the bruising, he looked unfairly refreshed. Though, if I was remembering rightly he hadn't exactly had a lot to drink, just a few tokes of my joint... My eyes dropped to his mouth before I cleared my throat lightly and looked up at the blue sky. It was such a nice day and it made me feel a thousand times worse as my eyes throbbed in time with my pulse.

Ry fell into step next to me as I took my coffee and immediately sipped it, hissing at the way it burned my tongue but desperate for it all the same. I looked up at Ryan again as we walked and darted my eyes away as he met my gaze.

"Thanks," I finally said and raised the coffee awkwardly in my hand in a weird *cheers* that made Ryan bite his lip on a grin. "So last night was..."

He snorted. "You're telling me." Ryan frowned as he looked out over the green as we walked towards it. "I don't think Aaron is going to let this go."

"Taylor either," I admitted and then shrugged.

"I guess that means the deal still stands then." I could hear the amusement in his voice without looking and suddenly the warmth of him at my side felt like more of a temptation than a comfort.

"Sure," I said easily, clamping down on my emotions tightly, "but nothing has changed."

"Right," he agreed, nodding for emphasis as he moved in front of me and spun to face me as we walked. "Except that you want me."

I snorted. "Cocky much?"

Ry's blue eyes flicked over my shoulder and a grin tugged at his mouth, my stomach flipped uncomfortably as he stepped closer. "Not cocky, no. Just not an idiot."

Then he kissed me. It was nothing like the teasing nips or the occasional chaste pecks he'd given me in coffee shops when we were on our public outings. No, this was sweeping, his arms full of me and my mouth full of him, his scent tangling with mine as his tongue swept across my tongue and a low groan rumbled out of him that I was seconds away from echoing when he pulled back.

"What—I—" I gaped at him, breathless and desperate not to show it as my thoughts fogged with the sweet, fruity scent of him. He let me slide from his arms slowly, as if reluctant and my brain took longer than it should have to find its footing again. *Why did he do that? Did he want more? Did he want* me? My hands slid down across his chest as I jerked myself away, trying to ignore the feel of him under my fingers. Ryan bit down on one kiss-reddened lip and nodded behind me.

"Saw Brad and Cody over there," he said and I swiveled my head around to look, disappointment crowding my insides when I spotted them walking just a little behind us in running gear. "We have to sell this, right?" I promptly shut the feeling down—this was what I wanted, why should I feel disappointed? I didn't want to date Ryan fucking Sommers. *But maybe you want to fuck him*, a small voice taunted in my mind and I drained the last of my coffee in a huff, eager to wash the taste of him out of my mouth.

"You okay?" Ryan asked as I stomped over to a trash can and dumped the disposable cup. Other than the slight mussing of his hair where my hands had run through it, he looked entirely cool and collected and a burn of anger stung my skin as I flushed.

"Fine," I bit out, unsure if I was angrier at myself or him and willing my stupid heart to slow down as the back of his hand brushed against mine while we walked.

"So, you and Liv," Ryan started when the silence between us clearly stretched too taut for him and surprised me with his line of thinking, "you're just friends?"

"Yes," I said firmly. "Don't let Taylor mess with your head."

"I just didn't know—"

"That I like girls too? Why? Is that a problem?" I couldn't keep the snap from my voice, wishing I'd never bothered to get out of my bed today.

"No," he said with a casual shrug. "I just thought it might be the sort of thing a fake-boyfriend might know about his fake-girlfriend."

I relaxed fractionally. "You want to know about when I first got my period too?"

Ryan snorted. "I'd say you're clearly not a morning person but it's the afternoon."

I chose not to answer, instead nudging us back in the direction of *Cocoa & Rum,* if Ryan had any hope of surviving the walk back to my apartment then I would need more caffeine. A lot of it. My phone buzzed and I glanced down at it long enough to see another notification tagging me in my own nude. I locked my phone again and let out a deep breath. Ryan, wisely, chose to remain quiet and I was grateful—mostly because I didn't *actually* want him to hate me and he likely would if I had to hold a conversation right now. I had a bad tendency to say what I wanted and then obsess over it unhealthily later.

My fingers itched for my guitar, needing the cool slide of

strings beneath my fingers, bruisingly pinching as I coaxed whatever pretty sounds I could make out of it with my limited skill. I needed to taste the lyrics on my tongue and fucking scream until I couldn't remember Aaron or Taylor or my mom or the taste of Ryan still lingering in my mouth.

"Want me to send you a photo of Aaron's busted mouth?" Ry said at last, eyes seeming darker now than they had been a moment ago, as if my anger upset him too.

I let a vicious smile sweep over my mouth as I laughed and nodded. Bastard.

CHAPTER NINE

BETTER NOW - POST MALONE

I WAS IRRITABLE. USUALLY I WAS PRETTY EASY GOING, the exceptions being when I was PMSing, my mother called and... when I was frustrated. Sexually. *Stupid fucking Ryan.*

I attacked another piece of skirting with my paintbrush and Liv hummed to herself across the room where she was covering the sofa with sheets to protect it from spatter. I'd chosen the most violent shade of pink I could find for redecorating after seeing Ryan yesterday, still pissed off about the way things had gone down at the party the other night and then his unexpectedly movie-good kiss. Plus my thoughts had been swimming in endless circles about what Aaron had said to me at the party, which didn't improve my mood any.

Aaron was an asshole. Had I just ignored that while we had been dating? Or was he usually just nicer around me? I huffed as I dipped my brush again.

In the end Liv had talked me down from the monstrous color, instead suggesting a much more refined and elegant shade of baby pink—or *blush,* as the tin claimed.

Liv winced as I slapped on more paint, clearly worrying

about the hardwood flooring but I was pretty sure I'd managed to cover it all beneath me. Unfortunately, my foul mood couldn't be solved quite so easily.

I had already used my vibrator twice and it had barely done anything to take the edge off, all I could think about was Ry's stupid hands on my skin, the way he had tasted on my tongue. Maybe I had made a bigger mistake in not fucking him than I would have in sleeping with him. Did that even make sense? Was my brain so steeped in a sex-craze that it wasn't even coherent anymore?

I sighed, maybe I needed to use the roller on the wall to let out some frustration. A knock sounded from the front door and I shot Liv a questioning look but she just shrugged. The people who had my address were a very small list and two of them definitely wouldn't be coming around any time soon—so if Liv wasn't expecting anyone it had to either be Kat or a neighbor.

I plodded through the hall, wiping my paint smeared hands on the holey, rough t-shirt I'd stuck on just for painting. I'd opted for bike shorts, it tended to get hot in the apartment and painting made me sweaty anyway. It was a choice I regretted as soon as I opened my front door to the three ridiculously gorgeous guys stood there waiting, taking me in from my messy hair to the pink paint smeared on my kneecap.

My body instantly perked up at Ry's crooked smile and stayed on high alert as I recognised the blue-haired hottie from the other night and his broody friend next to him.

"What are you doing here?"

Ry leaned against the doorway, his blue eyes surprisingly warm and the bruise on his face from Aaron's fist had already started to lighten to a green that should have been off-putting but just made his brown hair look deeper. "You really do have the warmest greeting, Jamie." He grinned but I just folded my arms across my chest, glaring. Ryan sighed. "We were invited."

"You most certainly were fucking not."

"Actually..." Liv said from behind me and I whirled on her with wide eyes. *Traitor.* "Well, you were becoming unbearable!" she whisper-shouted at me. "I swear your left eye was twitching and your vibrator is not as quiet as you think—you clearly like him."

"I don't even know him!" I whispered back just as furiously, ignoring the boys still stood on the threshold, unsure of whether they should come in or not. "How did you even get his number?"

"Well here's your chance," Liv said smugly and stopped whispering. "And get his number? I looked him up on FacePage like a normal person, or at least, like any person who doesn't currently have to avoid social media because of their leaked nudes." I huffed and Liv smirked. "So just get it over with and screw already. The tension is making me break out."

Ryan's friends chuckled and I shot them a glare as I turned around. "Well? Are you coming in or not?" Ryan's grin widened as they walked in and Broody shut the door behind them. "I hope you don't mind getting messy."

"Not at all," Ryan said in a low voice as he followed Liv into the living room. I ignored the thrill his words sent through me and handed out rollers and brushes to the boys before connecting my phone to the bluetooth speaker sitting on top of one of the sheet-covered tables and turned the volume up so I didn't have to talk.

Doja Cat was interrupted by yet another social media notification plinking through the room at triple the normal volume and I winced. Ry glanced up at my phone from where it sat near him and he frowned. "What the fuck is this?"

I rolled my eyes, striding over and snatching the phone

from his grip. "Hello? Ever heard of privacy?" I frowned over at Liv, this was all her fault, and she dutifully ignored me as she painted clean lines around the outlets in the wall.

"Yeah and normally I'm all for it, but it's pretty hard to ignore the massive dick-pic blowing up my girlfriend's screen." A muscle in his jaw popped and I shook my head, re-focusing and then choking on my spit when what he'd said registered.

"I'm sorry, *what?*" Pink paint dripped onto my leg from my brush and I cursed as I set it down on top of a sheet.

"I said there was a massive co—"

"I'm not your girlfriend," I said, narrowing my eyes and knowing I needed to nip this in the bud. Was he just trying to piss me off or was he serious?

Ryan stepped closer, clasping my chin in one warm hand and tugging my face up to meet his eyes as he murmured, "Oh, so you didn't agree to date me?"

"That's different—"

"And you *didn't* kiss me back at that party?"

"It doesn't count when it's a fake kiss." I folded my arms across my chest and ignored the way Blue, Broody and Liv were watching us and pretending not to.

"That's easily rectified," Ry said, mouth tugging up on one side in a way that was entirely too captivating, so I turned away and scooped up my brush as I walked back to my wall.

"Are you ever going to actually introduce your friends? Or should I continue to refer to them as Blue and Broody?" I said into the tense silence a minute later.

A short laugh echoed from the wall closest to me and I glanced up to see Blue grinning. "I'm Broody, right?"

I smirked and shook my head as Broody—well, brooded. He had dark eyes and long black hair that fell over his forehead and full lips that seemed to be in a perpetual frown, saved only by his cute chin dimple. I'd noticed the way his eyes had followed Liv around the room and knew he was going to be in for some disappointment when he realized she didn't play for his team.

Blue, on the other hand, was like a ray of positivity, his hair was short and the color of a light summer sky. He had a range of piercings, the most interesting of which was a black bar with an arrow's head tip that went through his bottom lip.

"I don't get a nickname?" Ryan stuck out his bottom lip and I flicked a bit of paint his way and Liv tutted.

"Oh, I have one for you, but it's not made for polite company." Blue let out a roar of laughter and I couldn't hold in my own chuckle, his laugh was that infectious. "Seriously Blue, what are you doing hanging out with these two?"

"You really don't know?" he asked, raising an eyebrow and shooting incredulous looks at the two boys. "We're all on the football team."

"You are?"

"You dated the co-captain of the football team and don't know who the rest of the team members are?" Liv asked and the boys all stared at me alongside her.

"Well it's not like we ever really hung out—"

"Except for the after parties? And pre-season parties? And—"

"Okaaay." I huffed. "I never paid much attention. Better?"

"Oh yeah." Liv laughed. "Definitely."

"So..." I trailed off, hoping they would finally feel some pity and clue me in. Surprisingly, it was Broody who did.

"I'm Xander and this is Kit. I'm pretty sure you and Ry are already acquainted." Xander smirked and I scowled.

"What do you guys study?" Liv asked and Xander's eyes seemed to focus on her with a laser-like intensity.

"Art," Kit called and yeah, I could have called that. "Graphic design, specifically."

"Psychology." Ry smirked at me like he was psychoanalyzing me—and let's be real, it didn't look too good, did it? Revenge threesome, angry ex, hateful professor, weird sort-of-relationship with ex's rival... It probably all added up to Mommy Issues, which was nothing I didn't already know.

"History," Xander said, shooting me an accusatory glance that made me bite my lip. *Fuck.* He was in my class? That meant he'd witnessed Professor Dick's meltdown the other day *and* I was possibly the most ignorant person on Earth to not have recognized him—but how was I supposed to pay attention to every single person in that class?

"Oh, haha, yeah same," I said lightly and he frowned. Okay, so clearly he knew me. Excellent. I turned back to the wall and swapped my brush for a roller, dipping it into the paint and sweeping it across the wall in large arcs.

"So, why the need to re-decorate?" Kit called, his perky voice somehow soothing where I'd expected to find it grating.

"Part of my post-break-up ritual," I explained, "plus Aaron helped paint this room with me when I first moved in."

"Gotcha," Kit sounded like he was smiling and when I glanced up he was. "The pink is a nice touch."

"You should have seen the color she had picked out before." Liv laughed and the two of them started chatting as their corners met up. Ryan moved closer to me and I didn't look up as he got close enough to touch.

"Your wall done already?" I said lightly and felt the air stir when he laughed like I'd said something funny. He didn't elaborate further, just added his roller to mine and helped me cover the wall in *blush,* evening out the places where I'd done a shoddy job without comment. He stood slightly behind me and off to the right and his arm brushed mine as he reached up towards the ceiling with the roller to the spots I couldn't quite reach.

We were done so fast that I blinked and then we moved onto Liv and Kit's wall, seeing as they were both now standing and chatting rather than painting while Xander looked on as if he wanted to join in but didn't know what to say.

"So what color would you give me if we broke up?" Ryan said, mouth curling into that grin that invited me to laugh along as he nodded to the wall we were focused on.

"Well," I said sweetly, "redecoration is reserved for break-ups and we are *not* dating."

"If that's what you want," he said with a light shrug and my eyes fixed on a sprinkle of pink paint that had landed on the edge of his jaw. It was what I wanted, right? I narrowed my eyes, damn psychology majors worming their way into your head, making you second guess perfectly rational decisions—like *not* to sleep with the guy you're semi-fake-dating. "Or," he continued, pretending not to notice my glare, "you could go on a date with me. A real date."

"Why?" I said, honestly confused. Sure, there was an attraction between us and yes, it was satisfying that pretending to date Ryan pissed off Aaron, but beyond that what did he have to gain?

"Because it's what people typically tend to do when they like someone."

"And *you* like *me*?" I snorted and shot Liv a look as if to say *can you believe this guy?* But she just raised an imperious eyebrow and suddenly I was even more unsure of what to do— what did I have to lose? Or maybe more importantly, why did I feel like everything was a game, with winners and tallies and a quid pro quo?

"I've always liked you," Ryan said, his small lopsided smile evolving into a fully-fledged grin. "How about Wednesday night? I could pick you up—"

"I'm busy," I said automatically and a little hurt flashed across Ryan's face, slanting his eyebrows and tightening his jaw.

"Right," he said and we painted in silence after that. I hadn't realized how easy it had felt before until suddenly tension was all I could feel between us, raising the hair on my arms.

"Ryan, I—"

"You know, I think I actually have to take off. I forgot there was something I needed to do this afternoon." Without once looking at me, Ry set down his roller into a nearby tray of paint and left with a nod in Liv's direction.

CHAPTER TEN

I SEE RED - EVERYBODY LOVES AN OUTLAW

"So tell me again why you couldn't go out on a date with him?" Liv settled into her seat at our booth in *The Box* on Monday night and raised her perfectly shaped eyebrows at me over the rim of the cocktail she'd retrieved from the bar.

"Like I already *said*—I'm busy."

Kat looked between the two of us knowingly and I shot her a look. She knew exactly why I was busy every Wednesday night and teased me mercilessly about my resolute dedication.

"You're busy the whole night?" Liv's mouth screwed up on one side and I sighed, better to get this over with than let her speculate something crazy. The girl had one hell of an imagination.

"I sing."

"You what?" She blinked, clearly not expecting that answer and Kat cackled into her rum and coke.

"Every Wednesday night." I huffed, rubbing my temples and gulping back some of my *Sex on the Beach*. "I come here for open mic night. It's non-negotiable."

Liv's big brown eyes were wide and then a delighted smile

took over her face. "Oh my gosh! I didn't know you wanted to be a singer!"

I could tell she was about to start gushing so I shook my head. "What? I don't. I just like to sing."

Kat grinned, slinging an arm around my shoulder and winking at Liv across from us. "So you could miss one night then?"

I frowned. "I don't miss open mic night. Ever."

Kat shrugged lightly, turning back to her drink. "Okay, it's true that you're somewhat of a regular, but going out with Ryan—"

"—isn't going to happen." I finished for her. "It's not a big deal, okay? It's just my favorite way to let loose."

In truth, other than weed and partying, it was the only *respectable* way I let loose. Talking about my love for music felt awkward. Like, why would I need to drop into casual conversation that I sang? But being on the stage, even just the tiny one that *The Box* used, there was nothing between me and my emotions. It was therapeutic and maybe a little raw, but that's what I loved about it. It was the truth, whole and unbridled.

Liv looked set to argue with me when Kat gasped and we both looked at her in alarm. Kat spun to me and started fluffing my hair, smoothing my brows, and I slapped her frantic hands away.

"Are you having a psychotic break?" I said, still trying to fight her off.

"What? No! Aaron just walked in."

My heart thudded painfully and I buried the feeling, *bastard*. "So?"

"*So*, everyone knows it's a competition when you break up with someone to see who looks the most adjusted."

I looked at Kat incredulously, she thought smoothing my

eyebrows was going to make me look well-adjusted to the fact that my boyfriend fucked my best friend? "Well, I did sleep with Brad and Cody, if that doesn't scream well-adjusted I don't know what does." Liv snorted and I couldn't help my grin. "Yeah, okay, I hear how that sounded."

"What should we do?" Kat gripped my arm, her eyes still on the group of guys that had walked in. I could see Aaron's blond head in the center and I rolled my eyes. Kat loved drama—creating it, hearing about it, it was all good to her. Aaron walked past our table and I could feel his gaze on my skin as latent anger sent a flush through me. He hesitated as he walked by, as if not sure whether to say something or not, and I ignored him.

Instead I smiled at Kat tightly. "If we ignore it, the lack of attention might shrivel its balls." Liv let out a breath as Aaron walked on and I patted her hand across from me. Other than when he was on something, Aaron wasn't the type of guy who liked to make a scene—he cared far too much about his reputation. It's why I had been so surprised that he'd shared that photo of me. Sure it looked bad for me, but the scandal it caused him? I hadn't thought the preppy little good boy would have the guts. Aaron never had liked getting his hands dirty.

I sucked the last of my cocktail through the straw and then stood, the alcohol making my legs tingle. "I'm going to go pee, back in a sec." Kat scooted out so I could leave the booth and settled back down into conversation with Liv as I made my way past the bar to the ladies restroom at the back and pushed through the door. I felt... odd, seeing Aaron. I was going to have to get used to it—campus was small and I had now apparently befriended some of the football team thanks to Ryan. We were bound to run into each other, so it was in my best interest to let my resentment go. Or, at least, to pretend that he didn't exist.

The latter, I decided with a smirk as I rinsed my hands and dried them off on a couple paper towels.

Logically speaking, what Aaron and I had wasn't special. The sex had been mediocre, he had been self-absorbed and then, well, he slept with Taylor. I'd give him one thing—the guy knew how to party.

I stopped short as I came around the corner of the bar and saw Aaron with his hands on the table of our booth, leaning towards Liv with a charming grin on his face. He looked up and smirked when he saw me, leaning down and whispering something in Liv's ear and then sauntering away. My hands curled into fists. I didn't know what he was up to, but I didn't like it.

"What's going on?" I asked as I got back to Kat and Liv, both unusually quiet. "What did that asshole want?"

"Um," Kat said, eyes flicking around the room in an effort to avoid looking at me. Her eyes fixed on the big pitcher of beer she'd ordered that was being brought over, relief passing over her face.

"He asked me out," Liv said and she looked scared, mouth pinched and hands white knuckled around her glass.

"Are you alright?" I squatted down next to her and placed a hand on her arm as I peered up at her. She let out a deep breath, her eyes running over me as she nodded.

"I'm okay. You're not... mad?"

Suddenly her apprehension made a lot more sense. Our friendship was relatively new but it felt like I'd known her forever—of course she was worried I might be mad. Especially since, from what she'd told me, it sounded like she'd dealt with a lot of Mean-Girl culture at her last school.

I grinned at her as I stood up. "Oh, I'm mad, but not at you. I'm sorry he bothered you." I raised an eyebrow at a very relieved looking Kat, "What? Did you think I was going to blow up at her?" Kat opened her mouth and then shut it, offering up only a guilty smile. I blew out a breath and grabbed her pitcher. "Can I borrow this?"

Without waiting for a response, I swept it up and walked in the direction of the table of boys where Aaron was currently sitting. Fortunately, he was at the end of the booth. Good. It would make this easier.

He looked up as I walked over, blue eyes glinting in the low-light, and smiled at me triumphantly. "I knew you'd come back to me Jamie. I forgive you, I knew you still wanted me—"

I dumped the pitcher over his head, the foamy beer flattening his hair under the deluge and leaving him sputtering as his friends fell silent. He stared up at me in complete shock, his eyelashes clumped together from moisture and his blue pressed button-down now flimsy and soaked.

"What the fuck are you—"

"No," I said simply. "What the fuck are *you* doing? Fucking one of my best friends not enough? Thought you'd try for another?" The bar felt eerily silent as everyone listened in and his football bros looked away awkwardly. "I mean, I can tit-tat you again if that's what you want?" I pointed at the friend of his sitting closest. "How about you, big boy? Think you can handle this?"

Aaron stood up abruptly, leaning close to me and my nose wrinkled at the pungent smell of beer mixing with his aftershave. "What is your problem?"

"You," I said and set the empty pitcher down on their table. "I thought the message would have been clear, but you never were the quickest to catch on so let me spell it out for you: Don't talk to me. Don't look at me. Don't even *think* about contacting my friends. I'd say have a nice life but I'd be lying."

I whirled on my feet and strode away, feeling the anger and tension drain away and leaving me feeling only tired. Ugh, if Professor Dick got word of this... I was on thin fucking ice.

Liv's eyes were wide as I got back to the booth and I gave her a small smile. Kat looked somewhat mournfully at her beer and I narrowed my eyes at her, she'd deserved a little payback too for thinking I was going to go apeshit on Liv and she knew it.

"I think I love you," Liv said, still staring at Aaron's booth as his friends grabbed napkins from the bar and Aaron attempted to ring out his hair.

"Oh sure, it feels good now," I told her, "but I'm already on probation for my behavior and reputation so..."

"It'll be fine," Kat said reassuringly, apparently deciding to get over her lost drink. "I don't see how your professor could find out."

"You'd be surprised," I said and then sighed as I spotted Billy the manager heading our way. "Anyway I think I'd better leave before Billy kicks me out. I'll see you back at the apartment?"

Liv nodded and I blew them both kisses as I left, feeling somewhat numb, like I'd lost something I hadn't even wanted. My eyes blurred with unexpected tears as I pushed through the door to the outside and I bit down on the inside of my cheeks, willing them away as the cool air hit me.

"Hey," a low voice said as a warm hand caught my elbow. I looked up in surprise and blinked at Ryan.

"Where did you come from?" I stared at him in confusion, my eyes caught on the light dusting of stubble on his jaw as his hand slid down my arm before letting go.

"One of the guys texted me when they got here and saw you, they thought there might be some trouble and..." His eyes took in my still-wet eyes and flushed cheeks. "Well, I'm guessing they were right."

"Why would they message you?"

Ryan rolled his eyes. "I think we put out a pretty strong indicator that we were together at Aaron's party. Why wouldn't they message me? What happened in there?"

I pulled away from him and shook my head. "Nothing, I'm just heading home."

He paused, looking out over the dark park and streets and then stepped back from the entrance to *The Box*. "I'll walk you."

"You don't need to—"

"I want to."

He didn't say anything else, just began walking and I hurried to his side with a huff. It was only a short walk to my apartment but something about the crisp, quiet, night air was more soothing than any words Ryan might have said. He seemed to sense this as he stayed quiet, letting me sort through my thoughts as we walked.

I felt... alone. I looked up at the sky as our feet found the familiar trail between buildings that led to my apartment. Clouds fogged the sky, blocking out any view of the stars, and I jumped when Ryan's hand found mine. His fingers were warm and large between mine and I shivered a little at the sensation. Maybe not-so alone, then.

I tugged him to a stop in the darkness of the alley closest to my apartment and I could just about make out his features as he turned to me in confusion. My heart quickened as I stepped closer. I wanted warmth and touch and, just for tonight, not to be alone. Maybe it wasn't fair, but right now I needed him.

Ry's hand slid from my hand to my waist as he held me away from his body. "Jamie—"

"I need you," I whispered, so quietly the sound might not

have existed. But Ryan heard. His other hand found my jaw and he tipped my face up, bringing his lips to mine tentatively and I bit his bottom lip. I didn't need tenderness. Not now. Not tonight.

He understood. His kiss became bruising, heat and savagery as his tongue found mine, stroking and licking moans from my mouth. I pulled away, breathless, and let my hands stroke down his chest as I sank to the floor.

Ryan cursed but it sounded like a prayer as his fingers wound into my hair and I couldn't help but wonder how they might feel in other places. I tugged at the button on his jeans, relieved he wasn't wearing a belt. I didn't have the patience for them on the best of days, but tonight more than ever.

This was crossing a line between us but I couldn't bring myself to care. I needed this and I thought Ryan might have needed it too. He was already hard and sprang free, bobbing in front of my face as I slid his zipper down.

"Are you sure this is a good idea?" Ryan said quietly, he turned his head both ways, checking to see if anybody was around and I wrapped my hand around him, pumping slowly until his eyes instead found the sky as his head fell back. He gave a small groan and I tightened my grip as I leaned in for an experimental lick of his head. He tasted sweet and smoky and I pressed kisses to the long length of him. Ryan swallowed, the strong line of this throat looking erotic in the dark, and his eyes found mine as my tongue wet his tip.

A sharp pant left him and a wicked grin curved my mouth. My toes were cold and my legs ached as I squatted in front of him but it was the heat between my legs that was the most distracting thing as I wrapped my mouth around him and swirled my tongue over his slit. His hand tightened in my hair and a thrill swept through me as my pussy clenched involuntarily. I looked up at him as I took him further into my mouth, sliding up and over him, licking my way up his shaft and torturing him with sloppy kisses to the underside of his tip.

"Jamie," he panted and I let out a *Mmm* around him as I increased my pace. He was right, there would be time for teasing later. For now, I wanted him spilling on my tongue, down my throat.

Ry's hips flexed as he pumped into my mouth with a groan, he tugged on my hair and gasped when I moaned around his cock. I worked him faster, hollowing out my cheeks as I took him in deep, gagging a little as he hit the back of my throat. Footsteps sounded, echoing in the distance and Ryan tensed until I flicked my tongue over his head twice and he came with a hoarse shout that sent satisfaction thrumming through me.

I pulled off of him with a wet sound that had a blush rising to my cheeks. Ryan swayed slightly as his blood returned to his head and away from his dick, his eyes fluttered open and were warm and dazed when they met mine.

The footsteps sounded closer and Ryan glanced to the left before zipping himself back up and grabbing my hand. We started walking again and he snuck glances at me until we got to the door that led to the stairwell for my building. The motion-sensor light outside flicked on and I winced at the bright glare.

"Do you want to talk about it?" Ryan said, letting go of my hand and leaning against the brick wall beside the doorway. Everything about him looked relaxed, sated, except for the tightness around his mouth and I wondered what he was thinking that had him anxiously awaiting my response.

I knew what he meant. He wanted to talk about us but I honestly didn't know what to tell him. Yes, I wanted him. And yes, in that moment I'd needed him. But I'd just got out of a relationship and immediately getting into another just didn't feel like the right thing to do. So instead, I gave him the answer to his earlier question.

"There's not much to say. Aaron came to *The Box*. He hit on Olivia when I went to the restroom. I dumped a pitcher of beer on his head, cussed him out, then left before Billy could ban me from the bar."

Surprise and then amusement flared in Ry's eyes and he let out a short laugh. "You poured your drink on him?"

"It wasn't my drink, it was Kat's. But yeah, right over his head."

He gave me his trademark crooked smile. "Remind me to never piss you off."

I smiled in response and the silence ticked on for a second too long, we shifted awkwardly on our feet and I was about to head inside when he spoke again.

"Come over tomorrow," Ryan said it quickly, like he wanted to get the words out before he could change his mind.

"What for?" I said warily, I didn't want to hurt his feelings but I didn't feel like a date was in the cards right now. Possibly something more casual but... Ry didn't strike me as a casual kind of guy. He wasn't as uptight and straight-laced as Aaron (well, as Aaron appeared on the surface anyway) but he wasn't exactly a player either.

"Revenge," Ryan said in a tone that said he knew I wouldn't be able to resist. "I'm not sure a pitcher of beer really covers it, do you?"

"Well, I did also proposition one of his friends."

Ryan frowned. "Which one?" he growled and I raised an eyebrow, not deeming that to be worth answering. Like I'd have known any of their names anyway. Ry shook his head, smiling at me. "Never mind. Just, come over tomorrow afternoon."

The truth was, he'd piqued my interest... and he knew it. "Okay."

"Okay," Ryan said with a smug grin. I rolled my eyes as I walked past him and opened the door to the stairs.

"God, what is this, a John Green movie?" I muttered and Ryan laughed as the door started to close.

"It was a book first!" he called after me and I waved a hand at him as I made my way up the stairs to the first-floor apartments and my door, hiding the smile I knew he'd never let me live down.

CHAPTER ELEVEN

DIRTY THOUGHTS - CHLOE ADAMS

THE WALK TO AARON'S—ALSO RYAN'S—WAS hauntingly familiar and unease settled in my stomach as I walked, second guessing myself and what might be about to happen. There was every chance we were going to have sex and I couldn't pretend that I wasn't craving that—craving *him*—more than I cared to admit.

I almost walked straight past her without realizing and it wasn't until Taylor wrapped her skinny fingers around my wrist that I drew up short and shrugged her off. She looked like she'd lost a little weight, her blonde hair framing her slim face a little more fully than before, and her eyes gleamed with a manic light that told me she was on something. I took a step away from her, disgusted that this was the low she'd sank to over a guy like Aaron.

"Watch it, bitch," Taylor hissed and I rolled my eyes.

"You grabbed me." I raised an eyebrow and Taylor chewed frantically on the gum in her mouth, the wet sound grating on my nerves.

"This is your fault. Aaron won't even speak to me while he's chasing your golden fucking pussy." Taylor's blue eyes darted about and I blew out a low breath. What the fuck had she taken? "Watch your fucking back."

I raised my hands placatingly but my voice was ice cold. "You can have him, you deserve each other. Stay out of my way and I'll stay out of yours." I quickly brushed past her, ignoring the hand she swept out in an effort to claw my face off. Well, at least she had distracted me from my nerves even if she was acting totally unhinged. I hurried away and didn't look back as I heard her continue to rant and rave in the middle of the pathway through the trees.

I drew close to Ryan's and texted him to say I was nearly outside, not wanting to get stuck in one place if Taylor decided to follow me, and he sent me a thumbs up that I spent too long staring at as I wondered what was about to go down.

I wasn't sure what Ryan's idea of revenge was going to look like—did he want to trash Aaron's room? Fill it with foam? The truth was, I didn't know Ryan that well yet and wasn't sure how his brain worked.

But just in case his head worked anything close to how mine did, I'd dressed nicely. My bra and panties were a red lacy set that matched my nails, and I'd shaved. Everywhere.

Ry pulled open the door after a couple of seconds and my brain short circuited at the amount of skin on display. Maybe Ryan's idea of revenge wasn't so far from my own at all.

"Hey," he said, sweet grin completely at odds with the sinfulness that was Ryan Sommers shirtless. Like, I'd known he was ripped—he was co-captain of the football team and they had a pretty strict workout regimen—but the way the muscles of his skin bunched and relaxed as he led me inside and closed the door behind me had my mind whirling with possibility.

"Hi," I said finally, licking my lips. It was weird being here with just Ryan. More often than not Aaron had come to my place but we'd still spent a fair amount of time together here, occasionally with his roommates. Two of which I'd now slept with and the third... well, we'd see.

"Drink?" Ryan called as he strode to their communal kitchen with me on his heels.

"Tequila?" I muttered and Ryan poked his head back out of the kitchen, nearly colliding with me and I swallowed hard as I took a step back.

"What?"

"Oh, just water please."

"Sure," he said with a smile and I couldn't keep my eyes above his waist as he turned to grab a glass from the top cupboard, stretching upwards, and I bit my lip. Things had always been a little strained between me and Ryan in the past – at least on my side anyway. He was unfairly attractive and he was *funny*. Most of Aaron's friends were either druggies or jocks more interested in sports than talking with their captain's girlfriend. Then I'd met Ryan.

I'd expected about as much from him as I had Aaron's other team mates. So when he'd made me laugh at Aaron's expense the first time we'd been introduced I'd slapped a shocked hand over my mouth and Aaron had glared first at me and then at Ryan. I'd opted to stay clear of him from that moment on. Yet here we were, alone in the house Ry shared with my ex-boyfriend. It was like the past and the present were colliding in a way that made it impossible to deny my attraction any longer.

I mean, sure, there was the odd time when Ry's face may have replaced the faceless fantasy guy's when I'd been busy with my vibrator—but we couldn't control our fantasies, right? Plus,

I'd never acted on them. Unlike Aaron, I wasn't a cheater and I didn't really see the issue with being attracted to someone else, we all had little crushes from time to time. Though admittedly, I hadn't expected Aaron's crush to be on my best friend. Asshole.

Ryan handed me my water and I nodded in thanks, gaze drawn to the water dotting his flat stomach and the dark hair on his chest. He noticed my gaze and cursed when he glanced down. "I don't know how I do it, I swear I can't use a sink without spraying the water everywhere."

I gave a laugh that sounded strangled as he wiped himself down with the towel, coasting it along the hard lines until my tongue felt too big for my mouth and my throat too dry. I took a sip from my water as I watched him, practically draining the glass. I wasn't vain. Ryan simply looked that good.

Wait.

I glanced up and found Ryan's eyes on me, a small smirk playing around his mouth and he bit his bottom lip when our eyes met.

"What are you doing?" I rasped.

"I don't know what you mean," he said, throwing the towel back into the kitchen and folding his arms across his chest. He grinned when my eyes dropped to his biceps.

"What am I doing here, Ry?" I asked, trying to distract myself and stop my hormones from taking over as I set my glass down on the breakfast bar.

"I told you, revenge," he said it so matter of factly that I laughed.

"That kind of encompasses a lot and I'm really not down for murder. Orange is not my color."

He grinned broadly, his eyes soft and warm as he took in my tight jeans and lacy vest top. "I was thinking something a little less bloody, though I'm hoping that you'll still be screaming."

Was that hot or creepy? Yes, I decided. Ryan's low-slung jeans, balancing precariously on his hips, and happy trail leading somewhere very interesting were probably largely to blame for that thought process.

"That's a little cocky," I said, stepping closer, "the only one I remember coming close to screaming recently is you."

I saw the deep breath he took and was relieved when he moved toward me, the skin of his chest brushing against my top. "Well, maybe we should rectify that."

God, I loved it when guys used big words. I wasn't sure Aaron even knew how to spell *rectify*.

I let Ryan take my hand and tug me through the hallway and up the stairs. Their place wasn't as nice as my apartment but it was surprisingly well-maintained. The walls were beige and the gray carpet looked a little worn, but generally they kept it pretty clean. I'd heard that Cody was a bit of a neat freak, so maybe that was the reason it didn't look as bad as the frat house —there hadn't even been any dishes in the sink (something Liv was constantly on at me about).

"Why do you live here again?" I asked as we neared the top of the staircase. It had been bothering me for a while—there was clearly no love lost between Ryan and Aaron, so why had he opted to live with him?

"Someone needed to keep an eye on my co-captain."

"And it had to be you?"

"If not me, then who?"

I fell silent, thinking that over, and only spoke up when we strode past Ryan's door. "Wait, where are we going?" I knew exactly whose room was whose, having spent time in Aaron's and Brad's, and Cody had walked out of the room in the center of the hall to come to Brad's room when I'd launched my plan of seduction a couple of weeks ago. So Ryan's room had to have been the one we'd just walked past. "Aren't we going to your room?"

"No."

I looked at him in confusion, where were we going then? The bathroom? I mean, I liked shower sex just fine but god knew what state their bathroom was in and I'd spent longer than I cared to admit on my hair and make-up today.

We walked past the L-shaped corner that led to the bathroom and instead stopped outside of Aaron's room opposite.

"Ry—"

He opened the door and I closed my mouth, wracking my brain to remember Aaron's schedule. I was pretty sure he was in class on Tuesday afternoons until at least four. I followed Ryan in cautiously and felt a little weird standing in Aaron's bedroom without him there.

"You know what will really piss him off?"

Aaron's room looked pretty much the same as it always had: a pile of clothes on his desk chair, laptop thrown on his bed, football gear in a heap on the floor by the window. The air smelled faintly of beer and aftershave and I smirked when I looked about and saw the shirt Aaron had been wearing last night thrown on the floor, stiff with dried beer.

Ryan closed the door behind me and tugged me to him, walking me backwards until my back was against the door.

"Ry, why are we in here?"

"I told you," he said, leaning in and pressing a kiss to my neck. I gasped as he followed it with another, open-mouthed kiss, tongue gently stroking the skin there as his hand slid over my waist and down over my ass. "I'm going to make you scream."

"Here?" I said breathlessly as his hands ghosted their way

under my shirt and the warmth of his hands made my nipples tighten as he squeezed my breasts.

"Unless you have a problem with that?" he said, pulling back and looking into my eyes. My breathing felt uneven as I considered him before looping my hands around his neck and pressing my lips to his. We kissed in a frenzy, Ry's mouth claiming mine, branding me with his heat and want and I responded just as eagerly. "We've got a bit of time before Aaron gets home, so I'm going to taste you right here and you're going to watch. Don't you dare look away." His body pressed against mine and I gasped as his erection nudged me, Ry laughed darkly. "Look at what you do to me."

He stepped back and slid the hem of my shirt up and over my head, swearing softly as he took in the red sheer cups and my skin pebbled at the loss of his warmth. He moved close again and pressed his mouth to my chest, kissing down to my breasts before reaching behind me and deftly unhooking my bra with one hand. "Love this," he said as he vigorously threw it down, "but I need you bare for me."

His words left me aching and my head fell back against the door as his mouth found one hard nipple, licking and then sucking hard while his hand massaged the other. He bit down lightly and I gasped, arching my spine, wanting more, needing more.

"Now these," Ry said as his hand felt the button on my jeans, "are going to be a little more tricky. Wish you'd worn a skirt."

"My ass looks better in these," I said breathlessly as his mouth found my skin again.

"Disagree," he mumbled, tongue curling around the other nipple and leaving me wanting when he pulled away, "your ass looks good in everything." He slapped it lightly and the small sting made me laugh as Ryan kissed the sound away.

He got my jeans to my calves and I huffed in frustration, trying to maneuver my legs a little more open. Ry's eyes lit on the matching sheer red panties and he wet his lips as he grabbed the fabric covering my pussy and shoved it to one side. "Matching," he said hoarsely before giving me a cocky grin, "good to know where your head was at when you were getting dressed this morning."

I chuckled and tugged him closer by his waistband, pulling him into a dirty kiss that left us panting into each other's mouths. Ryan's hand slid up my thigh, stroking those maddening circles into my skin until I was almost going out of my skin with need. *Just a little higher...* I writhed against him and he grinned.

"Need something, Jamie?"

I grabbed his hand and moved it where I wanted and his eyes slipped closed as he felt how wet I was for him. Two fingers slid over my clit, rolling it between them and I let out a noise I might have been embarrassed about if it hadn't felt so good. Ry knew what he was doing, that was for sure. He let me writhe for him a moment more before sinking one of his large fingers inside me and I panted as he held it there without moving while he lowered his head back to my breasts. Ryan pulled the finger out and stroked lightly at my folds while he licked my nipple, torturing me slowly as he skirted around my entrance.

"Ryan—" I cut myself off as he sank back into me and instead tried to work myself against his hand.

"No, that's not going to do it," he whispered into my ear, biting the lobe lightly and then thrusting two fingers inside me instead, rocking his hand back and forth in a slow motion that had me begging for more. "No?" he said, amused as I tried desperately to fuck myself on his fingers. "How about this?" Ry pulled the fingers out and sucked on the first and then the other. "So sweet," he murmured as he moved to the floor in front of me. This wasn't something Aaron had ever wanted to do to me, in fact, it had mostly always been about *him*. Ryan looked only too eager, his eyes fixed on the bare wetness in front of him as he bit his lip. "Is this okay?"

I nodded shakily, my breath held as he moved closer to my pussy and pressed a long, hot kiss to my clit. I moaned as he pressed against me more firmly and lavished me with long licks to my center before sliding one finger deep inside me again. He wasn't teasing now, his finger set a steady, throbbing pace that had me tightening around him as his tongue brought me closer to the edge. I threaded my fingers through Ryan's dark hair and pressed one hand back against the door to Aaron's bedroom and he pressed his mouth deeper into my pussy. God this had been a good idea. It turned out that I liked the way Ry's brain worked. His fingers pumped into me and I moved my hips in time, wanting the friction, the room was quiet other than my gasps and the sound of my wetness against Ryan's mouth.

His tongue moved over me again as he sucked my clit and suddenly I was coming undone around his mouth, begging for more. I breathed heavily, slumped slightly against the door as Ryan stood up. His mouth was wet and he licked his lips, his eyes looking darker than usual as he took in my flushed skin and mussed hair.

"That was..." I didn't really have words. I'd never been put first like that before. Sure, I'd had guys and girls that were eager to please, though generally the girls paid a little more attention to what you were enjoying and how to repeat it. But I'd never been *worshiped* like that before.

"—only the beginning," Ry said, smirking as I stared at him.

"I–I don't know if I can come again—"

"Oh, you'll come for me," he said, brushing a thumb over one still-hard nipple and sending a bolt of pleasure directly to my groin. "I promised you'd scream and I like to keep my promises."

He kissed my mouth slowly, deeply and I moaned but pulled away, not enjoying the taste of myself on his tongue, and he smiled and nodded as if he understood somehow. One hand smoothed over my breast and my overly-sensitized skin tingled at the contact, his fingers plucked and squeezed at my nipples and the warmth at my core quickly became an inferno again. He dipped his fingers into my pussy and I moved my hips against him until he chuckled. "I told you."

Yeah, he had.

He spun me around until my bare front pressed against Aaron's door and his hands slid over my ass as he squeezed it and spread my cheeks, tugging at my center in a way that had me bending over, showing him what I wanted. I looked at him over my shoulder and Ryan's eyes smoldered at me as he pressed himself against my ass and my dampness rocked against his jean-clad body.

"Take off your pants," I demanded and he laughed quietly but complied, the sound of the zipper somehow erotic and I looked back to find him fisting his cock as he looked at me, a bead of pre-cum at his tip. It had been too dark for me to see it last night when I'd been on my knees in the alley, but I had felt how big it was in my mouth and hands. It didn't disappoint, he was thick and long with a slight curve, flushed pink and peach. Ryan gave a breathy groan before reaching into his pocket for a foil packet that crackled when he unwrapped it and then slid the condom on.

Ry nudged at my entrance, sliding himself against my wetness as I braced myself against the bedroom door, already rocking my hips lightly at the barest touch of him. He pressed his head into me and I gasped, ready for the delicious stretch and drag that I knew he would give me.

"How do you want this to go?" he asked, voice tight from effort as he moved shallowly inside me. "Hard or—"

"Hard," I interrupted, "fuck me hard, Ry."

The low groan he let out had my blood singing as he slid into me in one long thrust that had me crying out. He gyrated his hips before pulling out and slamming back in again, building up a bruising pace that quickly had me moaning his name as I gasped. Our bodies rocked together and I needed *more*.

Ryan seemed to agree and pressed me flat against the door with a quick, "Like this?" so there was no space between our bodies and I nodded hurriedly as his cock sped in and out of me, rattling the door and creating a tightness that had my body coiling—

"What the *fuck*," someone on the other side of the door shouted and my heart jumped in fright before I laughed. Aaron. I pressed myself back against Ryan even harder, was it wrong that I was wetter knowing that Aaron was outside having to listen to me get fucked in his bedroom? Ryan laughed as if he'd noticed and then slid one hand around my front to stroke me as he pushed into me hard, the smooth drag of him sending sparks through my body. I held onto the door as I jolted with the force of his cock driving in, short pants of "Oh, oh, *oh*," exhaling rapidly as I built towards a crescendo bigger than the last.

Aaron raged on the other side of the door, his fist beating against the wood and the adrenaline tightened my nipples, heightening my senses until all I could feel was Ryan's hands on my body, his cock inside me as it twitched in pleasure.

"Faster," I demanded and Ryan moaned my name as he obeyed.

"Jamie what the fuck are you—"

I tuned Aaron out as Ry hit just the right spot, hit it again and again until all I could do was shout until my voice was hoarse as my pussy clenched around him and my orgasm fell over me.

"That's right," Ryan groaned as he came, "scream for me, Jamie."

And I did, enthusiastically, both because *I felt fucking good* and to make sure Aaron got the message that I wasn't his—would never be his again.

CHAPTER TWELVE

BELLYACHE - BILLIE EILISH

I panted against the door for a second as Ry pulled out, the grin on his face when I turned around matched my own as he tied off the condom and chucked it in the bin in the corner of the room. He passed me my bra and I hooked it on and fixed my bottoms while Ry zipped up his pants. The door flew open with a smack and Aaron's body took up the doorway.

"Ever heard of knocking?" I quipped as Aaron bulldozed in and he practically snarled at me like a wild dog. I looked him up and down disinterestedly as I pulled on my vest top. "Ew."

Ryan snorted and Aaron's gaze flew to him and then darted back and forth between us, as if assessing whether or not we had actually had sex in there. I raised an eyebrow and held out a hand to Ryan who smirked as he grasped it.

"What's wrong Aaron? Need another picture to understand what just happened?" I probably shouldn't have baited him quite as much as I did, but I couldn't resist. He infuriated me like possibly nobody else. He shoved his way forward, shoulders back and jaw jutting forward—that should have been my first alarm bell. He was on something and there was no telling what limits *this* Aaron had. It was a pattern of behavior more than familiar from my childhood. Why had I ever dated him? Oh, right. Mommy issues.

Ry caught Aaron before he could get up in my face and I tugged him away. It was time to go, before things got violent. Aaron said nothing, just let us leave and then slammed the door behind us and I breathed out a sigh of relief, a grin tugging at my mouth.

"So listen, about Wednesday..."

I blinked at Ryan in confusion, did he think that I was somehow magically un-busy just because we'd had sex? Or did he really think that I'd made up an excuse last time he'd asked?

"Ry, I'm really sorry but I wasn't lying before. I really am busy Wednesday."

"Oh," he said, his smile dimmed slightly but he nodded. "Yeah sure I get it. What about Thursday night?"

"I just got out of a relationship," I said carefully, "and I like you, things are fun. But I don't think I'm ready to date again yet. It's too soon."

"I don't think you can really call what you and Aaron had a relationship," Ryan said with a roll of his eyes. "At best you seemed like fuck buddies who sometimes hung out."

"Great, thanks for mansplaining my own relationship to me," I said sharply and pushed past him to get to the stairs, walking down them without a word as I heard him sigh heavily.

"I'm sorry, I didn't mean it like that. I just meant that he didn't treat you right and—"

"And what? You think you'll do better?" Well, maybe he was right, but that still didn't mean I was looking for a relationship. "Look, you're fun Ry and under different circumstances well, things would be different." He chuckled and I rolled my eyes. "I just mean that now is not the time okay?"

"So, to be clear, you want me to act like we're a couple for the sake of your professor and maybe even fool around when it suits you—but you don't want to be official?" His jaw was tight and he ran his hand over it as he watched me.

"Yeah that pretty much sums it up," I said, a brief flare of guilt making me wince a little as I said it. But I'd told him what I needed up front before I'd slept with him. He didn't get to act like I'd somehow tricked him. "And if you remember, I specifically said this arrangement didn't mean I'd sleep with you. You're the one who initiated that."

"Oh, I guess I imagined the public blowjob then."

Okay. Point.

"I'm not ready to date, Ry. If you want out, then fine. Just say so."

He said nothing, blue eyes burning with some emotion I couldn't name, and he didn't stop me as I walked out the door.

"Please tell me you're joking," I said to Nick on Wednesday afternoon after our lecture. I'd filled him in on everything that had gone down since the party, feeling a little bad that I hadn't checked in with him recently, and he'd laughed himself breathless when I'd told him about the beer I'd dumped on Aaron's head.

Things had been radio silent from Ryan since he'd wildly fucked me against Aaron's bedroom door and I didn't know if that was because he was pissed at me or if he was giving me space. If it was the former then I was screwed.

"I can't believe he didn't include you in the email," Nick said, leaning against the wall outside of the classroom. "Well, actually I kind of can because that's why I thought I'd mention it to you. That guy is such a snake."

A department mixer. *This Friday.* And I needed my goody-goody date at my side to help me look wholesome and domesticated. Worse, Professor Dick was clearly done messing around because the mixer was attendance mandatory and if I had missed it as he'd intended then it would have been a big mark against me. Maybe even enough to get me suspended seeing as I was already on probation.

"Will you forward me the email please?" I turned towards the double doors that would lead us back outside and stopped. Taylor stood there, smiling at me with big, red, overlined lips. She squealed and hurried forward, throwing her arms around me and I choked on the overly floral scent of her perfume until she released me. What the fuck? How messed up had she been yesterday? Did she seriously not remember threatening me?

"Jay-Jay! I can't believe I've run into you, I've missed you." Her blue eyes were heavily lined, like she'd been out the night before and hadn't bothered to take off her make-up and had instead filled in the gaps.

"I'm sure you've missed Aaron more." I stepped back from her, wrinkling my nose in distaste. "Wow, seriously? It's barely one in the afternoon and you're wasted?" Did she even attempt to be sober anymore?

Nick let out a low whistle but didn't intervene and Taylor looked him up and down openly sneering. "Found yourself another new boy toy already? You and Ry not working out?"

"She wishes," Nick rumbled, purposefully pulling me closer and I fought off a wave of irritation at the sound of Ryan's name in her mouth.

"You know I couldn't handle you, baby," I said and Nick's lips twitched as he fought off a laugh.

"God, you're *sick*. First that girl from the bar and now him?

What is it, like, a fetish?" Taylor's hands were balled at her side and I was in too much shock to respond straight away. Who were these people I'd been associating with?

"You're vile," I said at last when my voice finally recovered. My hands balled into fists at my side but Nick gave me a minute shake of his head. He was right, Taylor wasn't worth getting kicked out. "Don't come anywhere near me, or Nick or Liv, or I'll report your racist-ass to the school board."

Taylor snorted and rolled her eyes, flouncing away on a cloud of dead flowers and floaty blonde hair. I turned to Nick, taking in the tight set to his jaw as he attempted to smile.

"Are you alright?"

Nick's smile dropped. "You really know how to pick 'em, Jamie."

"I'm sorry," I said as we walked out of the doors into the hesitant sunshine. "Do you want to report her? I'll come with you as a witness."

He shook his head. "It's not worth it, trust me."

"Are you sure?"

"I am," he smiled again and this time it felt firmer. "I'll forward on that email to you but you better start thinking about how you're going to get Ryan to come."

I shrugged as we headed in the direction of *Cocoa & Rum* for our usual post-class coffee. "I don't *need* him there. I mean, sure it would make things easier if it looked like I had a clean, wholesome rep but I'll just be—"

"—on your best behavior. Right." Nick laughed and shook his head. "Davis is not pulling his punches babe, I'm not sure there's enough best behavior in the world for him to drop this."

Maybe he was right, but it didn't seem fair and I was going to jump through all the necessary hoops because I wanted to be on this course. I wanted my secure job in academia and I wanted the life my mother never gave me. So Davis was going to have to suck it up.

Cocoa & Rum was busy when we walked in, the lunch time rush leaving the barista looking harried behind the counter until someone else arrived to help her out. I squinted at the familiar blue head—*was that...?*

"Hey, what can I get you?" Kit said, grinning when he realized who was in front of him. "Oh hey, Jamie! How're things?"

"Um, okay thanks. I didn't know you worked here?"

"I just started yesterday," he said and then his eyes flicked behind me and he smiled. "Hey, Nick."

I blinked, looking between the two of them. "You guys know each other?"

"Oh yeah," Kit said while Nick laughed. "We're in the same club."

"Ah, cool." I said awkwardly, feeling like I was missing something. I placed our coffee order and then moved further along the counter to wait, the crowd was dying down now so I had the perfect opportunity to test the waters. "So Kit, have you seen Ry lately?"

"You mean, is Ry still sulking that he asked you out and you said no?" Kit threw me a devious grin that revealed a flash of silver from what had to be a tongue piercing. "Nah, he's all good."

"Really?" I felt my shoulders relax and I raised an eyebrow at Nick who shrugged back.

"Yeah, I mean he's still mopey because he's obviously super into you. But he was wearing jeans and not sweats the last time I saw him so that's a good sign."

Ryan was 'super into' me? I mean, he obviously liked me—you can't fuck someone as well as he had without caring about them a little bit—but I'd thought it was more of a passing flirtation, not actual *like*.

Kit slid our coffees over and I smiled at him, he nodded and we left the coffee shop silently. I was stuck in my thoughts, re-analyzing every conversation between me and Ryan. I supposed it was a good indicator of his feelings that we'd already slept together and he still wanted to take me out. Maybe I'd been a bit too quick to shoot him down.

Nick nudged me and I looked up from the stare-a-thon I had going on with the sidewalk to see Ryan approaching. I started to smile, raised my hand to wave and then the people in front of him moved and I saw who he was laughing with.

She was tall, legs a mile long and gently waving sleek blonde hair that reached her waist. Her bright blue eyes practically sparkled as she gazed at Ryan and something ugly reared its head in my chest when he grinned back at her. It looked unrestrained, easy, no complicated exes or revenge plans. Just fun, adoration.

Nick saw the change in my expression as I dropped my hand and he winced. "Uh-oh."

I snapped my head to look at him. "What?"

"Nothing," he said quickly, adjusting his bag across his shoulder. "This looks like it's about to get super awkward though so I'm just going to—"

I grabbed his hand and glowered. He wasn't going anywhere.

Ryan looked up and saw first me and then Nick, his smile wavering as we came to a stop opposite each other.

Nick broke the silence first as the blonde's eyes flicked back and forth between us. "Hey man, I'm Kit's friend Nick."

Ryan relaxed, as if that were some sort of secret code and I threw Nick a questioning look that he ignored. "Oh right, I thought I recognized you. You were at the party the other night too, right? How're things?"

I ignored his question in favor of a smile that probably looked more like a threat than a greeting. "Aren't you going to introduce your friend?"

Ryan gave me an odd look, like he couldn't figure out what my problem was, and smiled at the elegant woman standing next to him. Up close I could see the depth of her blue eyes, they tugged at my memory but I was certain I'd never met her before. "Yeah, sorry, this is Bryn. Bryn, this is Jamie a... friend."

Wow. He'd really pulled out the F word. I smiled tightly at her and she beamed back, immediately coming over and pressing a kiss to my cheek and I stood there, confused and a little surprised. Maybe slightly aroused too, which was annoying because I couldn't even blame Ryan for liking her. Bryn was gorgeous in a very put-together way. *Liv would like her,* I mused.

"Nice to meet you," she said, stepping back and kissing Ryan on the cheek too. "Thanks for meeting me, Ry. I'm going to go in and find Kit."

Ry nodded and she headed inside. Nick cleared his throat awkwardly and turned to me. "Um, yeah so I've really got to get going." He nodded at Ryan and then practically ran away. I narrowed my eyes at Nick's retreating figure. Coward.

"Yeah I should probably let you get back to Bryn," I said into the silence as I brushed past Ryan, gasping when one large hand closed around my bicep and tugged me to a stop. He peered into my face, brows furrowed before smoothing as he grinned.

"Benjamin Silver, are you *jealous?*"

I spluttered. "Jealous? I–No, why would I be jealous? I'm just Jamie, your *friend.*" I wasn't jealous. Not really. I was just... annoyed that he'd been on at me about this date he wanted me to go on, when really he was already pursuing something else. Or maybe he was never that interested and Bryn was just his latest fixation.

Ryan laughed and the deep sound made me blush. "You *are* jealous." Then he laughed some more until I tugged on my arm furiously, trying to leave, and he cut himself off abruptly. "Bryn is Kit's sister."

"Cool, keeping it in the family, huh? Sweet." Fucking Kit, he hadn't thought to mention this oh, ten minutes ago?

"Kit's *very gay* sister." Ryan grinned. "She's more inclined to date you than me."

I blinked, ceasing any attempt to pull my arm free. "Then why were you meeting her?"

"I was just walking her here to meet Kit, there's someone on her course bothering her or something so I agreed to meet her after her lecture and walk her here."

Oh. So not only was he not interested in Bryn, he was a fucking saint now too?

"Oh," was all I said and he smirked.

"Yeah," he replied and dropped my arm. I immediately missed his warmth and shivered a little as my eyes dropped to his mouth. "It's good to know you care, though," Ryan said and immediately ruined the moment.

I bristled. "I never said I didn't care."

"You also never said you did," he pointed out and my mouth dropped open.

"Oh my god, what are you? Four?"

"That might have been better for you—more familiar if Aaron is anything to go by—you might even have been able to walk properly the next day." Ry fought off a smile, finally giving in at the look of horror I was likely wearing. I *wasn't* limping. Sure, he had a big dick. Yay for him, but did he think I couldn't handle it? Was this his idea of flirting? If so, it was only working about ten percent. Maybe fifteen.

"I'm going to pretend you didn't just say that," I said as I tried not to grind my teeth and instead changed the subject. "My department is hosting a mixer on Friday that I was conveniently left off of the invite chain for. I need a date." Nick was right, Davis wasn't going to go gently and I needed all the help I could get if I wanted to stay on the course—which I did. There wasn't anything more important to me.

"Are you asking or demanding?" Ryan raised an eyebrow imperiously but the heat in his eyes said he wouldn't mind if I were being a little bossy.

"Both." I smirked. "Will you come or not?"

"Don't threaten me with a good time." He grinned and I shook my head as I turned away to head home.

"So fucking cheesy," I muttered and he laughed.

CHAPTER THIRTEEN

SO HIGH - DOJA CAT X HIGH ENOUGH K.FLAY

ONE OF THE THINGS I LOVED THE MOST ABOUT MUSIC was the ability to take a song and make it new. The way everyone could hear something slightly different in the sounds or interpret the lyrics in a different way.

It was one of the reasons I'd started doing open mic nights. At first I'd just watched, cheering on the people brave enough to get on the stage. Then, after much prodding from Taylor of all people, I'd decided to do it myself. What did I have to lose really? I mean, there was always the chance of getting booed off the stage, but that hadn't happened to me yet and I was a regular at *The Box* on open mic night. Sometimes I brought my guitar to accompany me, sometimes one of the guys who ran the evening would accompany me on piano, I'd used backing tracks in the past but I hated how tinny they sounded—plus, if I was doing an original arrangement then it made it hard to use a recorded track I hadn't made myself.

Liv had insisted on coming with me tonight, she'd said she'd never been to an open mic before and plus, she'd said, "I can't really imagine what your singing voice is like, so no way am I missing this." To be honest, I wasn't sure why I'd kept my love for singing from her. It wasn't a secret, really, but it did feel like I was letting someone see into the heart of me—everything from the song I chose to the way I sang it... it was vulnerable. Oddly enough, it felt easier to be that way in a room full of strangers than with people I actually knew and liked.

In the end I'd just rolled my eyes at her and invited her along. It was sweet that she wanted to come, but she could easily just keep an ear out when I was in the shower. My best performances were done on high heat with my shampoo bottle mic.

Kat was working tonight which wasn't unusual, they often got her to fill in on a Wednesday as it was one of their more popular nights and I knew she needed the extra cash. Kat's living situation was the only thing she *didn't* like to gossip about and I knew better than to ask after the first time she'd bit my head off. Stubborn and proud, if I so much as covered the bill for her at dinner she glared.

There was a pretty good crowd tonight, maybe forty or so people, but it often built up as the night went on so it was better to have a middle slot—something the staff usually accommodated for me because I was here every week.

I didn't like to drink alcohol before singing so I only grabbed a water as Liv ordered some fruity cocktail that was the house special and Kat winked at us from the other end of the bar. If she was lucky then maybe she was on the early shift and could hang out once she was finished – for the time being she could keep Liv company well enough though.

"Jamie!" Billy called as he saw me sitting at the bar with Liv, his eyes were wide and his skinny hands clutched his chest in apparent relief. "Our usual opener hasn't turned up and we need to get going. Do you think you could...?"

Oh god, opening? There was pretty much nothing as nerve

wracking, it set the precedent for the whole night – you were either the most memorable or quickly forgotten about if what followed was better. Not that I was really here to be remembered, this was more of a catharsis for me, but I still didn't want anyone to hate my performance. Nerves kindled in my belly and my hands shook unexpectedly. I hadn't had pre-show jitters for a while.

"I don't know Billy, you know I prefer to go in the middle—"

"Please?" He interrupted, mopping at the sweat on his forehead with a handkerchief and honestly I hadn't known people still carried those. "You owe me for the other night."

Fuck. I knew that pitcher of beer was going to come back and haunt me.

"Fine," I muttered, standing up and signaling to Kat to keep an eye out for Liv.

There wasn't much of a backstage area, just a seat next to the few steps on the side of the stage that led to the center. I placed my water down on the seat and took my guitar out of its case. I wasn't really that great with instruments in general, but I could play enough to give myself a decent accompaniment and that was all I really needed.

I generally preferred to stand when I sang, so I ignored the chair on the stage and instead slid my guitar strap over my shoulder so I could still play. The lights dimmed a little and a short cheer went out. I gave no intro, just strummed the first chord and lost myself as the sound echoed out over the people drinking and chatting. Some stared up at me expectantly, others played pool or were making out in semi-dark booths. I put them all out of my head and sang the opening to my arrangement of Doja's *So High*.

The crowd quieted as I sang and the two stage lights *The Box* had were in my eyes, making the faces look like shining stars and I was relieved I couldn't see their expressions as my thumb skipped over a string it wasn't supposed to. Something about going first today had me more nervous and on edge than usual. Normally I could lose myself to sensation, relaxing and just singing. Today felt a little different. It might also have been that I'd spent ages on making this arrangement work and I hoped it paid off. Instead of singing the chorus to Doja I hit a slightly discordant chord and sang the hook for *High Enough*, melding the songs together.

A whoop sounded and that was all the encouragement I needed. I sank into the words—I'd picked the songs for more than just their compatibility for a remix. It felt like it had never been clearer to me that some addictions could be more dangerous than drugs. People were often one of the hardest things to be hooked on.

My thoughts turned first to Aaron, then Ryan and settled finally on my mother as I finished my song. She probably knew more than anyone about addiction—she'd tried it all and it wasn't a life I wanted to be a part of. Ironic then that I had ended up with Aaron, who was just as much of a mess as my mom, and Taylor who seemed to be high all the time lately. I'd lost count of the times that Aaron had shown up to meet me, blue eyes fogged with whatever he'd taken that day and I'd just gone along with it. Hindsight, I guess, was a bitch.

I had half-expected Liv to rush up to me after I got off the stage—she was generally a pretty peppy person and while that might have grated on me coming from anyone else, I actually respected her more for going through what she had and still being unfalteringly positive. I glanced about for her as I grabbed my water but couldn't make her out through the crowd of people jostling at the bar. Kat looked flustered, her normally neat hair had curls escaping from her careful bun and when she caught my gaze she gave me a helpless look. Clearly she didn't know where Liv had got to either.

Before I could make my way back to the last spot I'd seen her, a well-dressed man stepped into my path and I stopped before I crashed into him.

"Sorry," he said with a smile that showed even, white teeth. "Didn't mean to almost knock you over. I just wanted to say I loved your cover, you have a great voice."

I smiled at him, he looked a little older than me but still young, maybe mid-late twenties. His shirt collar was unbuttoned and his jeans were tight, he looked like he'd stopped in at the bar after a long day selling houses or something.

"Thanks so much, I appreciate it. Sorry, I've got to go and find my friend." I gave him another polite smile before moving around him to search for Liv. She should have been easy to spot, pink seemed to be her signature color and today she had been wearing a pink velvet mini dress—complete with matching choker. There was actually a lot of color in her wardrobe and it seemed like a deliberate choice, like maybe she hadn't even had the freedom to pick out her own clothes before, or maybe not the balls. Either way, I was happy for her. It was funny really, we should have been polar opposites—my wardrobe was more grunge than girly and I generally gravitated more towards red, black and purple than pink. Yet, we clicked. I guessed we balanced each other out.

I spotted a flash of hot pink and hurried in that direction, finally spotting Liv near the restroom. Her color was high in her cheeks but the rest of her face was completely drained, leaving her normally bronzed skin ashy. I sat my cup of water down on the bar and bit my lip as my eyes found hers.. She'd swept her hair into a half-up style that was trendy and some asshole had a hold of her high pony. I didn't recognize him, so

I'd guess he wasn't a regular, but his biceps were large and his face was leering as he leaned closer to her. Couldn't we have just one night out without some stupid motherfucker getting handsy?

The guy didn't even notice me approach, but thankfully Liv did and a look of relief so strong it almost made me cry passed across her face. I quickly thrust forward before he could notice me, stepping hard on the inside of his foot and felt my chunky platform squash something that I hoped hurt. The guy yelled and let go of Liv's hair, stumbling slightly and *holy shit*. How was this guy still getting served? He stank to high heaven.

His face turned red and spittle formed at the corners of his mouth as he spun to me just as a large hand grabbed him and a body maneuvered between us. I stumbled back a step, grabbing for Liv's hand and holding her to me while she shook. Button-down had a hold of the guy's shoulder and had pressed him back against the wall outside of the restroom entrance.

Xander's broad back stood between them and Liv and me. I wasn't sure what to make of his sudden appearance. It looked like maybe button-down had followed me over, which was a little weird, or maybe he had just simply been in the right place at the right time. Xander though... I wondered if maybe he had been keeping an eye on Liv. If so, he'd done a pretty shitty job if he was only just stepping in.

I threw a quick glance around the bar to see if Ryan was there too but couldn't see him or Kit's signature blue hair, a strong surge of relief filling me when I became certain Ry wasn't there hearing me sing. I wasn't sure where we'd left things earlier but I was fairly sure he wasn't mad at me anymore. Mostly. Still, whether he'd show up to the mixer on Friday remained to be seen.

"It's alright," I murmured to Liv, nonsensical words to soothe her as she trembled in my arms. "Thanks for your help,"

I said to the guys, "I take it you can let the manager know what happened? I need to get her home."

Xander turned to us, brown eyes soft on Liv as he nodded and brushed a strand of hair out of her face and cupped her jaw. "You're safe. We won't let anyone hurt you, okay?"

It was probably the most words I'd heard Xander say in a row and Liv seemed shocked as she stared at him and slowly nodded. Her shaking had stopped at least and I let go of her body but held onto her hand tightly as I gave one last look of thanks to the guys before heading past the bar to leave.

I waved for Kat's attention and gestured toward the door so that she knew we were leaving. Luckily I still had my guitar slung over my shoulder so we could head straight out. I supposed in a pinch it would have made a good weapon, but more than anything it made me sad that we had to think about everyday objects so clinically, everything reduced to two columns: *could save my life* and *useless*.

I could see Kat talking to Billy behind the bar and his eyes rose to us in concern. For all his quirks, he took care of the people on his premises and I knew that asshole wouldn't be back here again. Ever. Billy nodded at Kat and she threw down her apron and pushed through the tables to meet us.

"What happened?" she said and I let Liv explain as we strode for the door, the cool air outside barely registering. *The Box* had always felt like a safe space for me and I hated that some drunk idiot had managed to take some of that security away, but more than anything I wanted Liv to be okay. I should have told Billy I couldn't do the opening slot. Kat should have kept a better eye on her. But we just hadn't expected it to get so busy so fast, it normally wasn't really crowded until at least eight-thirty—but there was no excuse. If we had done more then maybe he wouldn't have gone after Liv.

"Stop," Liv said as we passed under a street light.

"What? What's wrong?" I said, my eyes jumping to her immediately.

"It's okay, I'm okay. But I can tell you're not."

"Me?" I looked at her incredulously, my jaw slack with shock. "You're the one who—"

"Yeah and I can practically feel the heat waves coming from your brain right now as you think about everything you could have done differently. Don't. I'm fine, we're all fine, and you helped me." Liv looked away, her voice soft as she blinked moisture from her eyes rapidly, "Nobody from my life before would have done what you did. You put yourself at risk for me and I'm grateful, I just wish you weren't in that position to begin with."

I sighed and tucked her under one arm and Kat under the other as we made our way back to the apartment. "You're impossibly sweet, Olivia. Now shut up and let us take care of you."

The rooms were dark in the apartment when we walked in, so we moved around and turned on all the lights, checking each room as a group until we all felt relaxed enough to settle in for the night. I lent Kat some oversized PJs and we set-up camp in the lounge, turning on *Pirates of the Caribbean* and stuffing ourselves with popcorn until we dozed off, wrapped together on the couch. It was good to have friends.

"Jamie? Kat?" Liv whispered softly in the blue light from the TV.

"Yeah?" we whispered in unison.

"Thank you."

CHAPTER FOURTEEN

I FEEL LIKE I'M DROWNING - TWO FEET

COCOA & RUM'S FUNCTION ROOM WAS ABSOLUTELY packed by the time I made it to the department mixer on Friday. I'd borrowed a pretty pale pink dress from Liv, more subdued than anything I had in my own closet, and she'd used her straighteners to smooth the usually jagged ends of my hair into a sleek look. Honestly, if Ryan did show up he might not even recognize me. I hated these events, they inevitably held one every year for everyone who was on the History course to give us a chance to 'network'. Why I needed to know some scraggly-ass freshman I wasn't sure.

I tried to pay a little attention to who was around me as I attempted to delicately shrug off the tiny jacket Liv had also loaned me—it was definitely for fashion rather than practicality but I was absolutely sweltering. Warm hands fell on my bare shoulders and smoothed down my arms, disentangling the jacket before tugging me around.

I smiled up at Ryan, feeling more than a little relief that I wasn't lingering in the corner by myself any more, cursing my inattentiveness in class that led to me knowing nobody but Nick. And Xander, too, I supposed. "You came."

His lopsided smile appeared and he tucked my arm into his as he moved to my side and looked out at the room. "I told you I would."

"I know, I just..."

"Wasn't sure you believed me." He rolled his eyes.

I gave him a slightly sheepish smile in response. Ryan was thoughtful, kind and smart and he was present. Aaron would have likely checked his phone at least twice during just this conversation if it had been him here with me instead of Ry.

"So," he said looking around, presumably for Xander, and I took the chance to dip my gaze and check out the gray blazer and jeans he was working. Ry made stuffy academia look *good*. "Point out all your friends and we can go and say hi."

I raised an eyebrow and followed his gaze around the room until I saw Nick by the refreshments. "Look, there's Nick."

"I've already met Nick," Ry said and I laughed sharply.

"Yeah, well, not all of us have a massive friend group."

"Fair enough," he said and nudged my side lightly, "that's okay. Do you want to go over and say hi?"

"Sure," I muttered, friendship (or my lack thereof) was somewhat of a sore subject for me. Especially since I'd lost both Taylor and Aaron, but I'd gained Liv and Ry and that was more than enough. I'd even become closer to Kat—really, Aaron had done me a favor. "Oh hey," I said as we made our way across the room, my uncomfortably low, sensible wedges making an annoying *clack* against the hardwood floors. "What was all that about the other day with Nick and Kit? I felt like I was missing something."

Ryan chuckled and slid me a smirk. "I think I'd rather let you figure it out yourself, you're going to kick yourself later."

I sighed and looked longingly at the glasses of some kind of punch at the table, just far enough away from the laptop sitting there that it wasn't a hazard. This was already unbearable and we hadn't even run into—

"Well, well, Miss Silver. Glad to see you could join us." Professor Dick's grin stretched grotesquely over his face like his skin was too tight and I gave him an equally painful smile as Nick spotted us and closed the remaining distance.

"Oh yes," I said stiffly, "I was so *pleased* to receive an invitation. Wouldn't have missed this for the world." Stilted silence fell between us and Nick hesitated on the threshold of our conversation before spinning around and heading for Xander by the drinks. Traitor.

Davis' cold eyes burned into me like he was trying to dismantle my soul and I grit my teeth as he opened his mouth but huffed in surprise instead when Ry thrust out his hand.

"Ryan Sommers," he said with what had to have been his best charming smile because even I was feeling a little gooey at the edges. "I'm here with Jamie, it's nice to meet you." Wow. So Ryan was apparently a smooth talker—*note taken.*

"Ah yes." Professor Dick's eyes lightened as they took in Ryan. "Likewise. I've heard good things about you from Deborah King, the Psych department?"

Ryan laughed and nodded. "I'm glad. I'm the co-captain of the football team too."

I nudged him in the ribs, not sure if Davis liked jocks, but Professor Dick smiled. "Ah, brains as well as brawn then." Right. It was just me that he hated. I bit my tongue in frustration and smiled politely as his eyes flicked back to me and his expression soured. "Well, do enjoy the mixer. You never know when you might need to rely on a new connection."

The threat was clear. He wasn't impressed and he was watching me closer than ever, desperate to get rid of me. I didn't like people! So sue me. But just because I didn't really know the names of many (or any) of my classmates didn't make me a bad student. Maybe a bad human, but this wasn't a philosophy major so why should Davis have cared?

I gave him a stiff nod and moved past him to where Nick and Xander were watching by the canapes. Nick winced as I got close enough to smack his arm. "You little traitor."

"I'm sorry Jay, the vibes between you guys were... nasty." Nick shuddered and Xander nodded solemnly while I rolled my eyes.

"Whatever, this fucking sucks, my shoes are hurting my feet and my bra is too small," I whined rubbing the center of my chest, hidden by the high neck on the dress I'd borrowed.

"Why is your bra too small?" Ryan asked, looking perkier now that the conversation revolved around my breasts.

"Because I borrowed it from Liv, I didn't have anything strapless for this dress." Ry looked mystified and I just waved a hand at him in agitation.

"How is Olivia?" Xander asked, his low voice taking me aback for a moment. "We spoke to Billy after you left and he kicked that guy out, Max stayed with me to report what happened. Nice guy." Xander spoke in clipped sentences that felt vaguely threatening despite his relaxed posture. I'd thought he was broody before but maybe he was just serious. I shot Ryan a quick look but Xander continued talking. "Did you know he was a record producer?"

"He what?" My mouth fell open and Xander looked away uncomfortably as all the attention was diverted to him. Oh my *god.* Max had to be button-down. Which meant that button-down was a record producer. A *record producer* had liked my voice!

"Who is this Max guy? What are you guys talking about?" Ryan frowned, his smile fading as he looked to Nick who shrugged back.

"*The Box,*" Xander supplied. "I went there for a date on Wednesday night and saw some asshole grab Olivia by her hair."

"*What?*" Ryan and Nick both gaped and I winced. "Why didn't you say anything?" Ryan asked, brows pulled together as his hands found my arms again, running his fingers up and down until I caught them in my own to avoid the tendrils of heat he was stirring.

"I didn't think it concerned you," I said casually and Ryan's face darkened in a way that had my mouth drying and heart skipping.

"It definitely," he said leaning in close to my ear, "concerns me."

I swallowed hard. "Well, I'm fine and Liv is fine. I'll tell her you asked about her, Xander."

He nodded his thanks and Nick cleared his throat.

"What?" I asked with a sigh and he pouted.

"Why wasn't I invited? Did it not occur to you that most drunk guys won't mess with you if there's a guy around?"

I rolled my eyes but smiled a little. "You have a standing invitation, doll. And I don't need you to protect me." One of the things I liked most about Nick was that he didn't beat around the bush and he didn't let grudges fester—he was honest and upfront and I appreciated that a lot.

Nick looked slightly mollified but I narrowed my eyes when Xander snorted a laugh. "I'll say. You should have seen the way she charged in and stepped on that guy's in-step." Ry's jaw tightened and I widened my eyes at Xander, but he obviously didn't understand or didn't care about the daggers I was shooting his way because he continued, "If you'd just checked you would have seen me coming over to help, but nope! Honestly it's a wonder he still had a working foot afterwards because damn those heels were big—"

Ryan's patience snapped and he took my arm in his hands,

gently but firmly tugging me away, the look in his eyes warning me not to argue.

"What?" I hissed at him when he finally stopped in the slightly darker corridor leading to the restrooms.

"I don't like the thought of you getting hurt," he said, blue eyes absolutely serious for once, "I especially don't like the thought that you didn't tell me about any of this."

"You're not my keeper," I said, folding my arms across my chest and taking a step back from him. Ryan followed until I was pressed to the wall and his chest was flush with mine, his arms rising to pen me on either side.

"Maybe I want to be," he whispered and I closed my eyes, as if when I opened them his words wouldn't still be lingering in the air between us. "Why didn't you tell me?" he asked quietly and I bit my lip.

"I just didn't think to even mention it. I didn't know you'd care." God knows I hadn't told Aaron every detail of my day, let alone my life.

Ry stared at me blankly and then pushed away from the wall, his eyes never leaving mine.

"Okay," he said slowly. "So, I'm thinking about getting a coffee."

"What? Now?"

"Yeah," he said, raising an eyebrow. "Want to come?"

A date. Sort of. More of a peace offering than anything else. Casual enough to not blur things between us but also enough to indicate just a little something more. I couldn't have been at the mixer for more than half-hour but at least Davis had seen me and I'd wandered around a bit. I could probably sneak away early. *Who am I kidding?* Davis had been watching me like a hawk since I'd arrived and I knew that even this small absence was surely being noted.

I released a deep breath and shook off the lingering tension with a small smile.

"If Davis catches me leaving early it won't be pretty," I said apologetically and Ryan's mouth tugged up into a half smile even as his shoulders slumped. "Rain check?"

"Sure," he said and then held out his hand for me to take as we moved back towards the group. I curled my fingers around his and let his warmth ease into me before he tugged me to a gentle stop. "But next time something crazy goes down... tell me, okay? I'm not some asshole who only wants to get in your panties. I'm not Aaron, and even if we're faking this I hope you know that—"

I couldn't resist. I pressed my lips to his, sinking my fingers into his soft hair and bringing his face down to meet mine as his words cut-off abruptly. I did know. For whatever reason, Ryan Sommers cared about me.

"Okay," I agreed breezily as I pulled away, as though this wasn't the next dangerous step on the path of addiction. From the room around the corner I heard a glass being tapped and didn't hold back my eye roll. I loved history and wanted to be a part of academia, whether that was teaching or researching, I didn't mind, but sometimes the pretentiousness was too much. *Stuffy men in equally stuffy suits,* I thought as we rounded the bend and saw people gathering near the back of the room where the projector that was usually used for quiz nights had been set-up.

I smothered a yawn. I wasn't a hugely sociable person, not for these kind of events anyway, but this was easily the worst part of these mixers: the shakedown. Professor Dick cleared his throat and the remaining chatter faded away, not that any of us except the newbies needed to hear him. We'd all heard this speech a hundred times. First, he would wax poetic about the amazing staff and department, then he would beg for volunteers for whatever events they had planned for the rest of the year. Then, for any of the donors present, he would talk about what the department needed—usually funding for trips, showcases and whatever else they could come up with to grab a little more cash.

"Thank you all for coming. It's such a pleasure to see your faces once more, though for some of you this will, of course, be your last mixer with us." Davis paused as if waiting for tears or some other melodrama and frowned at the stony silence of the group. He hit the small presenter's button in his hand to move onto the next slide, "Anyway, I've put together this small presentation to—"

His words were drowned out by gasps and I felt the blood drain from my face as I stared up at the screen.

I didn't know how he thought he'd get away with this, or what his fucking game was but there was no way this would be allowed. People would speak up, surely, head of department or no.

Because that was my own flushed and sweaty face beaming up from the screen, squashed between Brad and Cody's, with a good amount of boob showing too. Was this even legal?

Heads began to turn my way and Professor Davis glanced back at the screen behind him, doing a phony double-take that made me see red. Asshole. Nobody could be buying this. I flicked my eyes around the room and saw a few hands pressed to mouths and then the muttering started: *slut* and *heard she cheated on her ex* and *she's here with another guy! How many does she have?*

Ryan took my numb hand in his as Davis began to splutter apologies, but all I could hear was the crescendo of whispers rising.

It was hard, being driven and confident. I liked sex, I liked my body and I wasn't afraid to put myself out there.

Unfortunately, all of those things weren't necessarily attributes that the outdated world of academia favored. Davis must have truly hated me to be going to these extremes though. I just hadn't imagined he could be so direct, so... public.

I stopped short of the exit that Ryan had been guiding me to and his brows furrowed in concern as he watched my jaw work. "What is it?"

"It's not Davis' style."

"What?" Ryan's voice rose in confusion but he didn't stop me as I spun around and raked my eyes across the room.

"He hates spectacle even more than he hates me. Besides, he didn't even know I would be here so how would he have known to include that picture in his slides? I just don't see how he benefits."

"What are you saying?" Ry threaded his fingers through mine and pressed a quick kiss to the side of my head, clearly just relieved that I wasn't a bawling mess right now. It was tempting, but by this point nobody in the room was saying anything that hadn't already been said to me via social media. Some people had even got a hold of my cell number and had sent me all sorts of hate —fans of Aaron's from the football team I had assumed. In the end, Liv had taken my phone off of me so I wouldn't have to see them popping up.

"I'm saying," I said as my eyes paused on a familiar blonde head, "that he didn't do this. But I think I know who did."

Ryan followed my eyes and grabbed my arm before I could walk over. "She's not worth it. Your professor is already out for blood and you giving her a smackdown isn't going to help."

I let his words wash over me as I kept my gaze fixed on the girl across the room. I took a deep breath in and held it and then took another. Tried to let my anger and, okay, a little hurt, fade away as I watched Taylor laughing in the doorway to the kitchens. There was a dark-haired girl at her side that I vaguely recognized from the sorority house I'd sent Taylor to the day I'd kicked her out. I was guessing she had been responsible for sneaking my ex-bff in here and letting her edit the presentation that had been left sitting in the open on Davis' laptop until he was ready to give his speech.

"You're right," I said, relaxing the balled-up fists my hands had curled into. "Let's get out of here. I'm so fucking done."

Ryan helped me shrug back into my mini jacket and then held my face between his hands as he looked into my eyes before letting go, "How about that coffee?"

Taylor looked up from the doorway and her eyes met mine, she looked pointedly at my face on the screen and then back to me with a shit-eating grin. Rage boiled through me and I glared at her from across the room. It wasn't bad enough that she'd gone behind my back and slept with my boyfriend, but then she'd lied about it and now she was—what? Exposing me? I threw back my head and laughed lightly, Ryan's lips curved up in response and Taylor's face soured as I blew her a kiss and grabbed Ry's hand. She'd done me a favor. The irony wasn't lost on me that by trying to hurt me, she'd only really helped push me into the arms of someone who genuinely cared.

"Coffee sounds great."

CHAPTER FIFTEEN

SAY SO - DOJA CAT

WE FELL INTO A STEADY RHYTHM OVER THE NEXT TWO weeks. Coffee on Tuesdays after class, pizza on Fridays with Liv, Kat and Ry's friends too. I wasn't sure what we were, exactly. Dating? It didn't feel gooey enough for that, though Ryan continued to flirt outrageously with me at any given opportunity. It really just felt a lot like friendship, which wasn't something I'd ever anticipated finding this close to graduation.

I sat down in *Cocoa & Rum* and Ryan blinked up from his phone blearily, bloodshot eyes focusing in on the coffees I set down on the table between us.

"I was just texting you," he said with a relaxed smile and my stomach tightened in response. Liv had got me a new SIM for my phone in the end. It wasn't like it had been a huge hassle, all of the people that needed to have my new number were either living with me or people I saw on a regular basis anyway. Ry and I spent a lot of our time texting. His course and the football team demanded a lot more of his time than my studies did of me, but the silly little flirty check-ins that came through each day made me smile.

"You look awful," I said in lieu of a greeting and he rolled his eyes.

"Gee, thanks."

"I mean it," I reached out and placed a hand on his for a second, blushing and quickly pulling it back when he glanced down. "What's wrong?"

"Nothing," he said with a sigh, grabbing the coffee and taking a long sip, eyes closing in bliss as he swallowed. "I was just up late finishing an essay."

"Leaving it to the last minute?" I smirked. "How very unlike my academically fastidious friend."

Ryan laughed and bit his lip. "Good word." His eyes darted to the counter where the barista was calling out another order for collection before they settled back on me. "Is that what we are then, Jamie? Friends?"

"What else would we be?" It was the closest we'd come to any sort of *define the relationship* discussion and I wasn't sure how he felt. Sure, he was stupidly hot and yes, we'd previously hooked up. But that had been weeks ago and he hadn't made another move since, seeming content to be patient.

Ry's smile drooped slightly before he seemed to catch himself and said cheerily, "Friends, right. Of course. Sounds good!" I raised an eyebrow at his unconvincingly chipper display and he groaned, burying his head in his hands and slumping forward against the table. "I like being friends with you Jamie, really, I do."

"But?" I asked, my palms started to sweat where they were clasped around my hot coffee and I felt a little sick waiting for him to finish his sentence. It was one of the things I admired about Ryan, when he knew what he wanted, he didn't hold back. Except with me, apparently.

He peeked up at me from where his head lay on the table, took a deep breath and sat up, looking directly at me. Even with his blood shot eyes and rumpled dark hair, he was still gorgeous. "Look, I've been trying to give you time and I wanted us to get to know each other better. I know you had just got out of a relationship, but it's been a few weeks now and—"

"Ryan—"

He waved me off. "But it's time for me to say this and for you to hear it and whatever you want to do with this information is okay, okay?" He was breathing hard and I said nothing, just waited. "I love being your friend, Jamie."

Was that it? "But?"

"But I want more."

My breath shuddered out of me and I gripped my coffee cup a little harder than necessary, relief swirling through me, and really that told me all I needed to know. If I hadn't wanted something with Ryan, then I wouldn't have been feeling so relieved that he'd finally told me what he wanted. What I thought I wanted too.

"Okay," I said easily and his eyebrows shot up, like he'd said this to me with every expectation of being shot down. I laughed. "I like you. This might be a disaster but I'm willing to try it out."

A smile overtook his face and he reached for my hand, bringing it to his lips and sending a small pulse of desire through me. "A date, then," he declared and I smirked. "A real one this time, not this in-between thing we've had going on."

It was dumb to feel nervous when I'd been getting coffee with Ryan by myself for the past few weeks, and yet there it was. A small tendril of nervous anticipation coiling in my stomach, sending butterflies through my body and making my heart beat just a little harder as I nodded.

Ryan grinned, choosing to ignore the blush staining my cheeks. "So how have things been with Davis?"

I sighed and shrugged. "Same as usual really." In fact, class had been not-awful. Since the fiasco at the mixer, Professor Dick seemed to have adopted the mentality that if he didn't talk to or look at me, then I didn't exist. And honestly, I preferred it that way. My phone sounded a little *bing* from my bag and I fished it out as Ryan took another sip of his drink, trying to ignore the dread that automatically accompanied a phone notification now. In the past, it had been because I was dreading my mom reaching out but more recently it was because of the barrage of hate I'd been receiving mainly on socials. People just really hated it when a woman got laid, I guess.

But things with Ryan were good, my mom hadn't reached out since I'd changed my number and it had been a few weeks since the photo had leaked for the second time at the mixer, so the hate was starting to die down. Ryan was reliable, and thoughtful—definitely not qualities Aaron had prioritized. We knew each other's coffee orders and Ry always let me have the last slice of pizza. Maybe I had been kidding myself into thinking that friends were all we had been. Especially when the sex we'd had before... well, you couldn't really have it that good and then just pretend like you didn't know the exact way someone moaned when they came. Casual sex wasn't a problem for me, I could do it and enjoy it just fine. But I hadn't been able to stop thinking about how sex with Ryan had felt. Maybe it was just the additional rush of getting one over on Aaron. I smirked, *guess we'll just have to do it again so I can compare.*

My smile faded as I finally read the notification on the screen. "What the fuck."

Ryan glanced up, frowning as he took in whatever was on my face. "Jamie?"

I clenched my jaw, holding my phone out for him to see. "I should have bitch-slapped her when I had the chance."

Ryan's mouth moved slightly as he read the words in the email, eyes widening in first shock and then narrowing in outrage. "How can they be pursuing this? It didn't even happen on campus."

I re-read the email from the Campus Student Support team when Ryan handed my phone back to me. "A formal complaint is not going to do me any favors for my probation. Hell, maybe that's why I have to go to a hearing for it."

"You think they're taking this more seriously because of the probation?"

I shook my head. "I have no idea. But what am I supposed to tell them? She's claiming I fucking harassed her and that there was a physical altercation between us." I shook my head in disbelief, Taylor was out of her mind. I couldn't believe she hated me so much that she'd decided to formally complain about me to the school. "I mean, if anything, *she's* the one harassing me!" I blew out a long breath and reached for my bag, Ryan relaxed as I pulled something out. "What, did you think I was bailing?"

He shrugged lightly. "I would have just come with you."

I snorted as I took a pre-rolled joint out of my box,."Well, grab your coffee then, I can't smoke this in here."

Ryan stood and followed me out the door, pausing only as I did in order to spark the joint. I slipped it into my mouth and inhaled as I lit it, exhaling a thick cloud of smoke as we continued on through the walkway between the trees that led back to campus.

"What are you going to do?" he asked and I didn't know how to answer. What *was* I going to do? I obviously couldn't let Taylor fuck me over like this, but anything I did would only provide her with some of the currently non-existent evidence she needed for this complaint to go through. I couldn't let that happen. I hadn't put up with Professor Dick for three long years to let Taylor fuck things up for me now.

"I have to be careful about confronting her directly," I said slowly as I dragged the weed, "otherwise she might use it against me at the meeting I have to attend. So I either have to get her to rescind the complaint before the meeting in two weeks or I have to prove that she's full of shit."

"How can I help?" Ryan said and we paused on the corner of the road, one way leading to his house and the other to my apartment.

"I think tit for tat is only fair, right?" I let the beginnings of a wicked smile curl my mouth and Ryan looked intrigued. "I think I need to come to your place."

Something darkened in his eyes and I felt a tug in my core in response. *No,* I told myself sternly, we weren't going there for *that.*

But wouldn't it be fun? A little voice whispered and I shook it off firmly.

"Then let's go," he said and his smile promised trouble.

The boys didn't live too far from campus and we reached the house relatively quickly, finding it empty.

"I don't know when they'll be back," Ry said as we stepped through the door. I didn't bother removing my shoes, we needed to do this and get gone. "So whatever you want to do, we had better hurry."

I liked that he was automatically including himself in this plan, even though I hadn't told him what it entailed yet. My brain felt a little foggy and I stumbled on one of the steps leading to the bedrooms upstairs, Ryan steadying me with a firm hand to my waist.

"Thanks," I said breathlessly and he grinned.

I led us past the rooms until I reached Aaron's, finding it open and empty.

"Round two?" Ryan quipped and I rolled my eyes, I didn't want to make a habit out of fucking in my ex-boyfriend's room.

Aaron's laptop was on his desk for once and I hurried over

to it, typing in the password and breathing a sigh of relief that he hadn't changed it.

"What exactly are you looking for?" Ryan asked as I found the photos app that would be backing up Aaron's phone.

"Leverage," I murmured, "there's no way Taylor's backing out if she's already gone this far. But if I can convince her not to show up..."

"It might hurt her case."

"Yeah," I said as I scrolled back through photos that mostly consisted of shirtless snaps, football selfies and a couple of nudes I'd sent him a couple of months ago alongside the one of me, Brad and Cody. I swiftly deleted them and Ryan remained wisely silent. Aaron had a thing for photos. It was partially why I'd chosen to break the news to him in the way that I had—I wasn't sure if it was a fetish or not, but he'd asked for nudes at least three times a week (not that I'd always provided). So if he had been asking me for nudes... I scrolled back a little further, searching. I doubted that what I'd seen between Taylor and Aaron had been a one-time thing, which meant—"Got it."

Blonde hair piled high on her head and perky tits pressed up under her arm, Taylor's face stared up at us from Aaron's screen. I felt a little sick as I stared at the undeniable proof that they had been carrying on together for a while. Assholes. I sent the picture over to myself, deleting the message from his laptop afterwards, and then deleted the photos of me from his trash for good measure.

"What exactly are you going to do with that?" Ryan asked, looking a little more wary now.

"I'm going to show it to Taylor," I said and relief passed over his face. I rolled my eyes. "What, you thought I was going to release it? I'm not that much of a dick. But Taylor doesn't know that," I said with a smirk and Ryan chuckled.

"Are you sure about this?"

"No," I admitted, the weed making my lips a little looser than they might otherwise have been. "But I don't know what else to do. Did you know they invite your department heads to these meetings? There's no way Davis is going to speak on my behalf and that's going to look bad enough in itself."

Ryan drew me closer and I held my breath as my head rested against his chest. This was new but I liked it. A lot. "Just don't let her bring you down to her level."

I smiled up at him from beneath his chin. "Don't worry. I'm just going to spook her."

"Blackmail her, you mean."

I shrugged lightly. "Potato, potahto. I'll delete it once the meeting is over."

"Just be careful, okay?" Ryan pulled back and held me at arm's length before pressing a kiss to my forehead. "I don't want you to do something you'll regret."

"Thanks," I said, "but it's fine. I'm just going to tell her not to come to the meeting if she doesn't want a dose of her own medicine."

"No bitch slapping?"

"No," I confirmed and then grinned, "well, not unless she hits me first."

"I suppose I can't ask for more than that." He chuckled.

CHAPTER SIXTEEN

CRAVE YOU - FLIGHT FACILITIES, GISELLE

L IV WAS ALREADY HOME BY THE TIME I WALKED through the door later that evening, still dizzy from the kisses Ryan had pressed to my mouth as we stood at the entrance to the stairwell of my apartment. I wasn't a huge fan of PDA—sex in public not withstanding—but something about having Ryan's hand in my hair, his tongue twining expertly with mine, made any hangups I might usually have had fade away. Especially because everything was *new*. Learning the pattern of each other's breaths, the way he liked to be kissed, that little spot on my neck that made me moan...

Though, other than the physical, I appreciated his ability to go along with my harebrained plans of revenge sex and blackmail—and we'd only been officially together for a day. Did that constitute a keeper?

"Hey," Liv and Kat called and I smiled as I toed off my sneakers. Normally it was only Liv and I for our roommate dinners, we tried to sit down together at least once a week but Liv had a lot of work to do as her course had a couple of prerequisite units that she hadn't covered in her first year at St

Agatha's. Kat often picked up extra shifts at *The Box* and so it became hard for us to find a time that we were all free to eat food and hang out.

I inhaled deeply as I walked into the lounge and threw myself into a chair at the dining table squashed in the corner of the room. Liv was a great cook and it smelled like lasagna throughout the apartment, my mouth watered and my eyes slipped close briefly. Honestly, she was a godsend. I couldn't cook for shit and would likely be living off of ramen noodles if not for Liv.

Kat grinned up at me from the chair opposite. "Your face is all red." She grinned and I choked on the water I'd been sipping from one of the glasses Liv had thoughtfully set out, alongside a pitcher.

"What?" I spluttered and Kat leaned forward with a smug smile taking over her face.

"All here," she said, drawling the words and gesturing to her own mouth and throat before smirking. "Beard burn," she said decisively and I gaped. "Let's hear all about it!"

"All about what?" Liv said as she came in from the kitchen with a dish cradled in her oven gloves and set it down on the table.

"Oh, just how nice the dark wood table pops against the pink you chose," I said quickly and Kat snorted as Liv stripped off the gloves and threw them to one side before starting to dish up the cheesy, saucy goodness to each of us.

"Yeah, right." Kat laughed. "Just look at her Liv! You look like a kid that got caught making out behind the bleachers."

Liv looked up and ran her dark eyes over my face, something in her expression tightening before smoothing out and she laughed. "You look..."

"Well-fucked." Kat grinned toothily and I shooed her away, scooping some lasagna on to a fork as Liv sat down.

"This looks amazing Liv, thank you," I sing-songed and they both stared at me until I sighed, lowering the cheesy morsel. "Ryan and I are officially... something." Then I shoved the food in my mouth and chewed slowly, hoping that might be the end of the questions.

Kat snickered. "Oh hell no, I'm going to need more than that, babe. How big is his dick? Did you guys do it again? Was it good?"

Liv blushed and I speared another piece of lasagna before pointing it at Kat. "I am *not* going to answer any of those questions."

"Are you happy?" Liv said a little more quietly than Kat and I smiled when I glanced at her.

"I mean, we've literally been together for less than twenty-four hours, but yes. He's..."

"Swoony?" Kat suggested and I rolled my eyes.

"I was going to say *nice.*" I bit back a grin and Liv laughed.

"Bo-*ring*," Kat sang and I threw a napkin at her. "I didn't know you'd be into the nice guys, Jamie."

"Well..." I gave her a slow grin as I scooped the last of the gooey pasta from my plate. "He can be nasty too, when he wants to be." Liv groaned and Kat whooped as I laughed and waggled my eyebrows. "Though I do have other news about a different type of nasty." Kat immediately looked focused, ready for whatever gossip was about to come her way, while Liv just looked concerned, perfectly shaped eyebrows drawing together while she watched me.

"Taylor has placed a formal complaint against me with the school." I sighed, slumping forward a little and resting my elbows on the table and fighting back the unexpected memory the action sparked of one of my mom's druggie boyfriends slapping at the skin of my forearms with a metal fork. *Bad manners,* he'd spat, *didn't yo momma ever teach you about no manners?* Clearly it had been a trying day if this was what my brain was giving back to me tonight. "She's saying I harassed her and that I hit her to get her to leave the apartment."

"Did you?" Kat asked, eyes wide, and I shot her a withering look.

"Of course not. Fuck sake, Kat, what do you take me for?"

"Sorry, sorry," she muttered, pink mouth curling down into a small pout, "got lost in the drama for a sec."

I waved her off and Liv placed a hand over mine on the table, as if she could sense I wasn't as okay as I was pretending to be. "What are you going to do?" she asked quietly and I knew that what she was really saying was *How can I help?* and my eyes filled with tears for a second as I saw the same look on Kat's face. How had I got so lucky?

I smiled my thanks and Liv let go of my hand, her cheeks taking on a slightly pink hue as she looked down at her food. "I'm going to blackmail her."

Kat burst out laughing and Liv dropped her fork with a clatter that made me wince.

"Oh," Kat said, "you're serious."

I shrugged. "You know how she leaked my nude the second time? Stuck it right in Davis' presentation slides?"

"Yeah...?" Kat's thick black brows drew together and Liv sucked in a sharp breath. "You're not going to—"

I shook my head. "No, but I suspected I'd find some less than ideal pictures of her on Aaron's laptop. I was right. I'm going to tell her to back off or else."

"You need to be careful," Liv said and I nodded, grateful for her concern—after all, Liv knew more than most how it felt to be burned by an institution you trusted.

"I will," I promised her and then I waved my hands about like I was brushing away invisible mosquitoes. "Anyway, tell me more about you guys. Work? Boys? Girls? Class?"

Liv groaned. "Ugh, don't even mention class to me. Sometimes I wonder why I'm bothering with this degree considering I hate it so much."

"You're only in your second year," I said carefully, Liv was a year younger than me and, unlike me, hadn't waited a year before enrolling in college. So she was a year behind me and Kat, unsure of what she really wanted in life and her studies— her parents had pretty much decided her whole life for her, Liv had explained to me, and it was hard to go from having practically no choice to making all of them. "If you wanted to transfer into something else, maybe something similar, I bet they'd let you transfer your credits because of your... special circumstances." It was unusual to transfer schools mid-way through a semester, but Liv hadn't been given much of a choice, if she didn't complete the make-up work she would end up in summer school, or having to re-sit the year.

Luckily, Liv's parents weren't totally heartless and had given her a hefty trust fund before rinsing their hands free of her, so at least she was able to pay me rent. But she wasn't yet used to the freedom she had, in some ways I envied that. It must feel so weightless, to have every option open to you. *Or very suffocating,* I sighed.

"Liv, honestly, you can do what you want. You can quit altogether and re-enroll elsewhere or on a different course, you have time to figure it out."

Kat nodded, fingers drumming on the table. "If you really hate the course that much then maybe it's not for you."

Liv was nodding slowly but still looked scared and I pecked her on the cheek as I stood and gathered up the plates to carry them into the kitchen.

"What about you, Kat?" I called back as I placed the plates in the sink and started running the tap to rinse them. "Got any spiritual healing you want to confess to while we're all here?"

149

She laughed and Liv snorted. "I confess..." Liv and I fell silent, waiting. "That I need a margarita. Please tell me you have tequila."

I snorted and Liv moved into the kitchen, rummaging for limes for the drinks, and Kat began to dry the plates as I set them on the side. A warm feeling swept over me as I looked over at them and smiled softly.

CHAPTER SEVENTEEN

LOVE ME LAND - ZARA LARSSON

"You are such a bitch," Taylor growled, her entire petite frame practically shaking with tension and anger as I carefully placed my phone back into my front pocket. I'd found her exactly where I'd expected her—at the sorority house. Despite me kicking her out nearly two months ago, I knew Taylor would never have put in the effort to actually find a decent place to stay. Not when she could mooch off of someone else.

"Thank you," I said with a smile and watched the rage on her face heighten. "Next time you decide to plaster *my* nudes all over some public presentation slides, maybe put two seconds of thought into being a little more sneaky about it, huh?"

"I don't know what you're talking about," she said stiffly but the smirk attempting to turn up her mouth spoke volumes. I rolled my eyes, why had I ever been friends with this girl? She was toxic on a good day.

"I'm not here for your excuses. Frankly, I'd rather fuck Aaron again than be here, having to talk to you. But, well, you've made that impossible by submitting this stupid complaint and I honestly don't really understand why."

"Because you're a—"

"Yeah, I'm a bitch. You already said that." I rolled my eyes and Taylor's small frame seemed to vibrate with anger.

"You wrecked my fucking life," she said, voice tight and blue eyes glazed.

"Oh, yeah." I scoffed. "I forgot *you're* the victim here. Never mind the fact that you were the one who fucked my boyfriend—"

"*You didn't deserve him,*" she shrieked and I blinked, frowning at her. To be honest, I wasn't even sure I was angry anymore. Looking at Taylor, seeing the mess of her, I just felt... sad.

"Neither did you," I said, meaning it as a compliment but knowing she probably wouldn't take it that way. "So here's the deal," I said, taking a steadying breath. "Don't show up to the meeting. Don't breathe another word about this to anybody. Better yet, drop the complaint."

Taylor laughed and I held up my hand. It had been a long shot and the truth was, the damage had already been done. It was on my record now.

"And if I come anyway?" Taylor stepped forward, jaw jutting out as we assessed each other.

"Then I'll send this picture, along with an explanation and a few other choice videos from our party days, to your mom and let her deal with you." It was a low blow. Taylor's mom was shockingly strict but stupidly trusting. If she had any idea the sort of shit Taylor was pulling while she was off at college... Well, tuition didn't pay itself.

"Get out," Taylor said in a voice like ice and I smiled cheerily.

"Gladly."

I tugged at my skirt, making sure it was covering everything it was supposed to, as I walked back out of the sorority house. It didn't entirely solve the problem of the upcoming meeting but if she didn't turn up then it would definitely be a point in my favor. The truth was, though it had been a necessary step to getting Taylor to back the hell off, I didn't feel good about it. I had never wanted our friendship to turn out like this, nor mine and Aaron's relationship. I mean, they were both assholes and I was glad that I could finally see that, but I still mourned what could have been and what was. All the memories we had were now tainted by their betrayal. Maybe I should have seen it coming, maybe if I looked back I could have seen the signs, but the truth was that I didn't want to. I didn't want to go through the photos and messages and work out when it might have happened, who might have initiated it. I was better off not knowing. I was moving on. I could only hope they would get over themselves and do the same.

I headed straight for *The Box*, needing to clear my head in the way that only music could give me. I'd been working on an acoustic cover the last few weeks, the song had been stuck in my head and I didn't want to think too much about why exactly that might be.

Kat had the night off and was sitting in a large booth with Liv when I walked in and waved, grabbed a drink from the bar and headed over. I sipped my water innocently as they stared at me.

"Well?" Kat demanded and I snickered. Her need and love of gossip was pretty much unparalleled.

"I'm fine thank you, Kat. How are you?" I said sarcastically and Liv grinned. It looked like they'd had some fun before I'd left the apartment early to talk to Taylor. Kat's make-up was suspiciously pink, pale in the inners and deepening into a hot pink flick lined with some sort of sparkly glitter. Whereas Liv's sweet look had been replaced with a hot smoky eye, gray shimmer and deep red lips completing the look.

"Did you guys dress each other?" I asked and they both laughed.

"We wondered how long it would take you to notice." Liv grinned and I was relieved that she seemed to be having fun. We'd been back here since the night that asshole had grabbed her but we'd made sure that Nick or Kat had been able to come too so that everyone felt comfortable. It wasn't just for Liv either, it was hard to have a good time when you were worried about your friends getting hurt.

"You both look amazing." I grinned and Liv blew me a kiss which made me laugh, she had totally picked that up from me.

"Benjamin," Kat warned and I batted my eyes innocently at her, "do not deflect! How did Taylor take it?"

"Probably missionary, she's a little vanilla."

"*Benjamin!*"

I pouted at Kat as Liv slurped the last of some bright orange concoction in a cocktail glass. "There's nothing wrong with missionary," she said and I nodded formally.

"You're so right, all sex is valid sex." I laughed at the growing look of impatience on Kat's face and Liv joined in. "Okay, okay, it was fine. She was absolutely raging though."

"Do you think she'll come to the meeting?" Liv asked, big brown eyes concerned as she stood to head back to the bar.

I shrugged. "I guess I'll find out."

Kat whistled. "Can't believe you threatened to tell her mom."

"Can't believe she fucked my boyfriend and plastered my post-threesome nude in my professor's slideshow," I countered and Kat coughed to hide a laugh.

The guy on the stage singing a slightly off-key version of *Hey Brother* finished to a smattering of applause and I clapped along idly before standing up and pecking Liv on the cheek as she returned back to her seat. "I'm up. Hope you guys brought enough spare panties to throw for me."

Kat hooted and Liv's eyes burned as she grinned. "Who said we brought *any* panties at all?"

I laughed. "Damn girl!"

Liv's laughter still sounded in my ears as I made my way to the stage and Billy settled at the old piano tucked into the corner behind me. It was a light, worn brown but played beautifully and I knew Billy loved open mic night purely because it meant he got to play for a crowd, even if he was just accompanying someone else.

The first chord sounded and my eyes burned as I blinked back tears. It was like this sometimes, like an emotional unplugging as the last few days hit me or whatever I'd been trying to work through mentally finally eased until I could just *feel* instead of think. This song in particular was deceptively hard, it needed a lot of control and breath work to get from the husky low tones to the sharp high crescendos and I smiled. I loved a challenge.

I sang the opening line, no thoughts ghosting through my mind, just pure exhilaration and joy. I spotted Liv and Kat and grinned, my eyes flicked to the back of the room and I almost choked as I saw a pair of familiar blue eyes locked onto me. Ryan.

My skin felt alive as I sang for him, this song that I knew I'd latched onto because my subconscious wanted me to know I was ready.

My voice turned husky as I sang the pre-chorus bridge of *Love Me Land* and a dark smile unfurled on his face. He licked his lips and I wanted to taste them with my tongue, wanted to taste every inch of him, and Ry leaned forward in his booth as he watched me, like he wanted the exact same.

I shivered beneath the hot lights, remembering how his tongue felt against my wetness as I tried to keep focused. How I hadn't missed a note yet was a miracle. Ryan bit his lip, holding back a grin, clearly seeing my struggle even when nobody else could.

I swayed my hips to the piano, running one hand up the side of my body and reaching it for the ceiling, looking up as I sang the high note. My clothes felt too tight, my underwear was uncomfortably slippery as I finished the song, remembering Ryan's hands bracing against the door above my head while he'd fucked me. It had been brutal, raw and savage, just an explosion of need. I had to wonder if next time he might go a little slower, taunt and tease me with that clever tongue just a little more. The intent expression on his face as I dropped my head and the piano came to a stop suggested that might be the case.

Applause broke out and Liv and Kat hollered for me, I laughed as I placed the microphone back in its stand and headed down the steps. deja vu hit me as I almost collided with a solid, warm chest and looked up to see Button-Down—Max, again.

"Hey." He smiled and I smiled back.

"Hi, sorry I didn't get the chance to thank you the other week for helping my friend. But we appreciated it, really."

"Oh, it's nothing," he said, rubbing the back of his neck awkwardly as his cheeks colored a soft pink. "I actually was hoping to see you again." I raised an eyebrow and he practically choked. "Not because—I mean, not that you're not—" he sighed, rubbing his hand across his brows. "Sorry, let me try this again. I like your voice. I want you to call me so we can discuss getting you in the studio." He held out a white business card that simply said his name and *AZ Records* and I took it numbly. Somehow amidst all the crazy shit that had gone down recently, I'd forgotten one of the most important things Xander had told me—Max was a record producer.

"Wow, I'm so flattered but singing is really something I only do for fun." I felt dizzy and absolutely unsure of what to say.

Max gave me an easy smile. "It'd still be fun, you'd just be getting paid for it." I laughed and he nodded towards the card. "You don't have to decide right now, just think about it and give me a call."

I nodded. "I—sure, thank you."

A shadow fell over us and Ryan's eyes flicked between me and Max as I slipped the business card out of sight. Ry's jaw ticked but he smiled. "Everything okay?"

"Yeah, it's all good thanks. This is Max, he helped Liv and me a few weeks ago."

Recognition dawned in Ryan's eyes and he relaxed slightly. "Oh, right, of course. Thanks again for helping the girls out, man."

"Of course," Max said easily before giving us one more nod and smile before leaving.

"So this is what you do on Wednesday nights," Ryan mused, slipping a hand around my elbow and steering me in the direction of his booth where I could see Liv, Kat, the boys and a familiar blonde waiting.

I shrugged. "It wasn't a secret." Even though it kind of had been.

"But you didn't mention it either."

"I was just..." I sighed and squared my shoulders. "I was worried you might think it was lame."

He stopped just before the booth and cupped my jaw in his hand. "I've never seen anything fucking hotter than you standing on that stage, singing for me." I shivered at his words and he smiled knowingly as he leaned in to whisper, "You're

157

wet for me right now, aren't you?" and my pussy clenched around air.

"Ass," I said faintly and he chuckled as we finally reached the booth. "Hi guys," I said to the group and Liv squealed, jumping up to wrap her arms around me and Ry yielded a step to her. The group called their hellos and I stopped short at the slim, blonde guy who was sitting next to Kit. "I don't think we've met," I said and the guy gave me a polite smile.

"I'm Leo," he said and reached across for a handshake which I accepted with a quick look at Ryan who just grinned. "I've heard a lot about you."

"Oh no," I said drily and Kit cackled. Leo's smile became a fraction warmer as he watched Kit laugh. Interesting.

"What did Max want?" Xander asked from the middle of the booth where he sat wedged between Kit and Liv.

"He was just saying he liked my performance." I mentally cursed Xander, he of the big fucking mouth. "Nice to see you again, Bryn." I quickly changed the subject and sent a smile her way. Kit slung an arm around her shoulders and pressed a smacking kiss to her cheek that made Xander wince. Ryan sat down next to Leo and Kat slid further down the booth on his other side so I could fit on the end.

"Likewise," Bryn said with a sly smile, like she knew exactly why I'd changed topics. "It's so nice to meet you guys, hanging out with the boys all the time gets a little..."

"Annoying?" Kat suggested.

"Tempting?" Kit teased.

"Draining?" I mused and Liv giggled at each of us, prompting Bryn's head to turn her way and smile wolfishly.

"I was going to say noisy," she said diplomatically and Leo snorted into his drink.

"Do you guys all live together?" Kat's eyes lingered on Leo sitting next to her and I caught Liv's eye as we both smirked.

"No," Leo said and Kat blinked at his curt tone.

"I live with Aaron," Ryan said, clearly attempting to rescue his friend. "And Bryn's a recent transfer so she's renting a place up by the mall."

"What do you study?" I asked Bryn and she smiled, pulling her eyes away from Liv with difficulty.

"Law, Leo's on the same course but I've already completed some of the units at my old college."

"Why did you move?" Kat asked and I frowned at her, sometimes her quest for gossip could be a little rude. She was like a dog with a bone.

Bryn caught my frown and waved it off. "I was in California before and I wanted to be closer to Kit. So I transferred."

Kat looked disappointed that the answer wasn't juicier and Liv looked like she was trying not to laugh. I couldn't focus on any of that though, not when Ry's warm palm landed on my thigh just shy of the hem of my mini skirt. My mouth went dry and I glanced up at him quickly to see him absolutely *absorbed* in a conversation with Kit across the booth, meanwhile his fingers stroked higher. I felt flushed, my breath caught in my chest for a second and I coughed when Liv asked if I was okay.

"Yeah, sorry I'm fine," I muttered and saw a little smirk on Ry's face as he nodded at something Kit was saying. Kat seemed to be trying to get Leo to open up and it was like pulling teeth. I caught Bryn's eye and she winked at me, eyes dropping to my lap, before sliding her gaze back to Liv and then raising an eyebrow at me. I knew what she wanted and I gave a soft, exasperated laugh.

"Xander, would you mind grabbing me a drink?" I coughed again for emphasis and then smiled sweetly as he stood and moved to the bar. "Kit. Go with him."

Kit glanced between me and his sister before ruffling her hair and murmuring a quiet, "Behave," that Bryn promptly ignored, reaching for Liv's hand and sliding her along the bench of the booth as soon as the space was clear.

"Hello," she purred and Liv blushed, shooting me a look to say she wasn't sure what to do with this overtly sexual creature before her as Bryn pressed a kiss to her hand. I shrugged lightly and then bit back a gasp as Ry's hand flirted with the edge of my panties.

He leaned closer as if telling me a secret. "I knew you'd be soaked for me."

Xander and Kit came back from the bar and I thanked them for the drink, promptly gulping it down and then wincing. "Is this vodka?"

Kat shuddered. "Don't speak its name. Fucking devil juice."

Xander was glancing between Liv and Bryn with a frown on his face but Kit took it in stride, settling down opposite me and waggling his eyebrows at my flushed face until I kicked his shin beneath the table.

He cursed just as Ryan's fingers pushed aside the material of my panties and slicked one finger up my center, making me gasp. I clenched my hand into his shirt sleeve and he looked at me innocently. I ignored him and turned to Kit as if the gasp had been on his behalf.

"Sorry blue, didn't mean to hit you so hard."

Kit gave me a saucy grin. "I think we both know exactly who's har—"

I kicked him again and Liv glanced between the two of us suspiciously as I gave her a bright smile and decided to turn the tables on him. "How do you know Nick, blue?"

Leo choked on the sip of his drink and I scrunched up my nose when Kit gave a laugh so quiet I wasn't sure anyone else had heard, his eyes were dark as they watched Leo and something tickled the back of my brain as I watched them.

"Ahhh," I said as it finally clicked. "You and Nick, huh?"

Kit grinned as Leo went a little pink, still choking, and Kat thumped him on the back twice. "Just a couple of hookups. He's a great guy."

"That he is," I murmured as Leo finally settled down and that same small smile stayed on Kit's face.

"Where is Nick, anyway?" Kat asked, the gossip-hound in her standing to attention and I blinked several times to focus as I answered.

"I think he said he was on a date," I said faintly and was instantly grateful when the conversation moved on because Ryan's fingers had pressed firmly against my clit and my eyes fluttered shut. My nipples tightened and I let out a ragged breath, shooting him a murderous look that only had him licking his lips as he dragged two fingers down and looked more than smug at the sudden rush of wetness he found. He slid one finger deep and I held still, knowing if I moved even a fraction I would ride his hand right here and not give a shit who saw. He slid out, the small tug shattering any remaining self-control I might have had.

I leaned over like I was going to say something to him, pressing my head close to his ear and biting the lobe before tauntingly licking it and standing up. The chatter flowed around us but Liv looked at me questioningly as I stood and I gave her a reassuring nod.

"I'm going to head out," I said, "performing always makes me tired." I threw Ryan a mocking glance and tried to hide my desire from my face as I saw my wetness glistening on his fingers. "See you guys later."

I strode away from the table, my wide heeled boots clomping familiarly along the floors as I made my way to the door. I'd only reached the first streetlight when Ryan span me around and captured my mouth in a kiss that had me gasping, pressing against him as my tongue teased his.

I pulled away but grabbed a hold of his arm when he made to head in the direction of his house.

"My place is closer," I said and there must have been enough desire in my voice that he decided not to argue, just sucked his bottom lip into his mouth for a second and looked at me like he was debating whether he could last the walk to my apartment.

CHAPTER EIGHTEEN

RIVER - BISHOP BRIGGS, KING KAVALIER

WE SLAMMED INTO THE WALL ON THE INSIDE OF THE apartment door, mouths fused together and my fingers tugging and curling in Ryan's hair as I moaned. One of his hands slid up my leg and the sensation over my fishnets had me gasping. I hooked the leg around his waist and pressed myself against him, rocking lightly until he cursed and shoved himself away from me to close the front door.

I was back in his arms in an instant. Ry lifted me up, mouth sucking at my neck, nipping at my jaw, and buried his hands into my short hair, gripping the strands just hard enough to send a thrill through me. He set me down on my feet and pressed me back against the wall, murmuring to me between bruising kisses.

"This is what I wanted to do to you," he said, sliding a hand up from my waist to pinch demandingly at my nipple through my crop top. "When we were in that hall at the history mixer." He thrust one leg between mine and I ground down on it shamelessly as he stroked my breasts, bit my lip. "I promise we'll go slow at some point." He laughed humorlessly. "But right now I just need to be inside you."

He waited for my breathless nod and then nudged my legs further apart, ripping larger holes into my fishnets as he roughly shoved the material of my panties aside and cupped me. I shuddered, my head falling back as I felt his fingers working me until I dripped for him and he thrust two fingers deep inside.

I reached frantically for his belt buckle as he pumped his hand against me and I rocked my hips up, panting, needing more. I quickly grasped his zipper and slid it down, mouthwatering as he sprang free, already slick at the head. I took him in my hand and felt him jump against me, hot and needy. I pumped him slowly and watched him swallow, desire darkening his eyes as I cried out his name, hovering near the edge, and whimpered when he pulled his fingers away, sucking them clean.

"Tell me what you want," Ry murmured in my ear and I let in a shaky breath as I felt him nudge near my entrance. My eyes flying wide as I remembered one important detail.

"Condom," I said and he laughed.

"Fuck." He sighed and pulled away and I missed his warmth immediately.

"Or..."

"Or?" he said, interest lighting up those blue eyes as he ran them over me, taking in my red well-kissed mouth and rumpled hair.

"I'm on the pill," I said carefully. "I always use a condom, usually, and I get tested regularly."

Ryan moved a step closer and claimed my mouth in a sloppy kiss that had me burning for more. "I'm clean too, if you're sure...?"

"Yes," I groaned as his fingers found my clit. "Now, Ry."

He didn't hesitate, just swept my legs around his waist and

propped me up with the wall as he slid himself inside me in one long thrust while his fingers found my clit again. Rolling the tight bud in a smooth circle, I moaned as he drove into me harder before speeding up until my head bounced off the wall. I didn't even care, not so long as he kept hitting—

"Right there, right there, right *there,*" I gasped and the drag of him against my sensitive inner walls had my toes curling desperately.

"Fuck," Ry panted, fucking me shallowly for a second and I couldn't help but watch as he worked his way back into me deliciously slowly. "You're so hot, so wet..."

His cheeks were flushed and his eyes were heavy and I swept him into a kiss, tongues tangling as we groaned into each other's mouths while he rocked into me. "Anything you want," he moaned, "whatever you need baby, tell me how to make you feel good."

"Let's go to my room," I said and he nodded, easily carrying me across the hall and into my room. His eyes were completely focused on me and I shifted my hips restlessly against him, making his eyes flutter close as a gasp forced its way out of his mouth. "In my drawer, there," I directed and he followed my instructions without question. Not even hesitating when he saw what was inside.

"I'm going to set you down now," he said and I nodded as he slid out of me and laid me down onto the bed. He squeezed the bottle of lube in his hands until a dollop came out onto his finger. "Do you want me to use this on you?" he said, nodding to the purple toy he'd also grabbed from the drawer and I nodded quickly, wanting him back here inside me.

I shifted to the edge of the bed and spread my legs wide, watching as he wet his lips at the sight of me bare and glistening for him.

"Do you want me to fuck you with it while I fuck you?" he

said hoarsely and I nodded again, lifting my hips in invitation and a breath shuddered out of him as he slipped the cold lube over my ass, dipping inside briefly until I moaned. He spread some more lube over the toy and then carefully pressed it inside me, his eyes didn't waver as he watched himself fuck me with the toy.

"Ry," I gasped as he pushed it all the way inside.

"You want more, baby?"

"Yes."

He lined himself up as he worked the toy in and out of my ass, the softly wet sounds seeming loud in the silent room, he slid his cock through my wetness before pressing in his head and I moaned. I tilted my hips up, wanting more, and he obliged. I didn't want to go slow and Ry seemed to agree as he thrust all the way in, mimicking the action with the toy in my ass and I whimpered in pleasure at the twin sensation of being filled. The hand holding the toy faltered as Ryan sped up his pace, fucking me fast and hard and I nudged his hand out of the way. His eyes burned hotter, mouth dropping open as he moaned, watching as the purple dildo sped in and out of me until I was helplessly grinding against it and him, his cock twitching inside of me and I knew he was close.

"I'm not coming," he panted, "until you do." His hand found my clit again, stroking me through the pleasure of his cock and the toy moving in tandem until I was crying out, clenching around him, and he followed me to his own climax.

I let my hand fall away from the toy, letting it thump to the coverlet as Ryan pressed a clumsy kiss to my forehead and then pushed himself away, kicking off his jeans. I dragged myself upright and gave him a small smile. "Make yourself comfortable, I just need to go pee."

He nodded and I padded away to clean myself up, returning in a few minutes to find Ryan curled up in my bed. His eyes opened when he heard me come in and he smiled sleepily. "Hey. Sorry, hope you don't mind."

I rolled my eyes. "Yes, actually, I do mind. That's my side of the bed."

His grin showed his relief and he moved over to the side of the bed closest to the window as I clambered in.

"So... we're doing this then?"

I snickered. "Are you asking me to define the relationship, Ry?"

"Maybe," he said, rolling back to face me, blue eyes soft and hair mussed against the cream bed sheets. "I don't like to share, Jamie."

"Neither do I," I replied and he smirked.

"So it's settled," he pulled me closer and wrapped himself around me. "While we're doing... whatever it is we're doing, I won't see anyone else and neither will you."

"It's a deal," I mumbled into my pillow. It had been a while since I'd shared my bed with anyone but it felt... nice, having Ryan here.

"Jamie?"

"Yeah?"

"Did Max give you his phone number tonight?"

I wanted to laugh at the timing of the question, was jealousy already rearing its ugly head? "Wow, asserting your dominance already?" I rolled over so I could face him and Ryan frowned.

"It's a simple question and I'm not asserting anything, I just... forget it."

I sighed, smoothing a hand over his brow. "Relax. He gave me a business card, he wants me to come to the studio that he works for to do a recording."

Ry sat upright and looked at me with wide eyes. "Fuck, wow. Really? That's amazing!"

"Okay well, don't get excited. I told him no."

His smile faded. "Why?"

"Because I'm not interested in a music career."

Ryan looked at me like I was speaking another language. "But you clearly love music. You were great up there and your voice... Jamie, you're *good*. How can you just walk away from that?"

"It was never the plan! Music is fun, I love it, it helps me feel... it helps me feel. Okay? But I never meant for it to go further than that. History, academia, that's where my future is." I was breathing hard as I stared at him. Ry couldn't understand, but the music world... it was unstable. I wanted, no, *needed* safety, predictability, security. A music career wouldn't give me all that. Singing was a hobby, that was it.

"You have a gift—" Ryan tried and then sighed, crashing back down against the pillows as he saw that I wasn't going to budge. "Okay, fine. Just, promise me you'll at least think about it? It's an amazing opportunity."

"Maybe," I murmured noncommittally and he sighed again but let it drop. Running a hand through my hair as I settled my head against his chest.

"I just don't want you to regret not going for it," he said at last and I reached up and pressed a kiss to his jaw.

"I know," I said. "Thank you."

CHAPTER NINETEEN

IN MY MIND - LYN LAPID

"Hey!" I said breathlessly as I jogged to catch up with Liv and Kat who were waiting outside of the main campus building. Other than a few smaller buildings that were off-shoots of Radclyffe, most classes were held in the big Victorian-inspired building. "Sorry, class let out late."

"That's okay," Liv smiled but it seemed… off. In fact, she'd seemed a little weird ever since Thursday morning when she'd woken up to find Ry in the kitchen making coffee. I'd been meaning to check-in with her about it but had seen surprisingly little of her around the apartment.

"Listen, I'm sorry for not checking with you first before Ryan stayed over the other night. We both accidentally fell asleep."

"It's alright, you don't need to ask. Have whoever you want over," Liv said and she seemed to mean it, so I wasn't sure what else could be bothering her. Of course, I could have just asked but Liv tended to get a little closed off sometimes when there were things that she didn't want to talk about. This felt like one of those times.

So I changed the subject, glancing over to Kat as we made our way through the park. It was sunny out and I sighed as the warmth brushed across my skin. It was nice now, but once late June hit the heat would likely become unbearable. "What happened with you and Leo in the end?" I hadn't had much time to talk with her since Wednesday night either and we tended to reserve Fridays for pizza and girly gossip. Though sometimes Ryan and some of the guys joined us too and it felt good. I was finally one of those girls who had a big friendship group.

"I can't get a read on him," Kat said, brushing a hand through her thick brown hair. She'd added delicate blonde highlights to it last week and the effect was gorgeous, if very nineties. "One minute he's super interested and the next he'll barely say a word to me."

"Um," Liv said and we shared a look.

"Kat, I think there's a chance that Leo's..."

"What?" Kat said, glancing between the two of us.

"Gay," Liv said at the same time that I chimed in with, "In love with Kit."

"Huh," we said in unison again and then laughed. Kat groaned and we schooled our faces into more appropriate looks of sympathy.

"Why wouldn't he just tell me he wasn't interested? He must think I'm such an idiot." Kat bit her lip and stared fixedly ahead.

"Maybe he's not out yet," I said and she nodded slightly. "Or maybe he didn't realize you were being anything but friendly."

Liv stifled a laugh. "Nope, that message was coming across loud and clear. You should have seen her undoing extra buttons on her shirt when she went to the toilet and then came back with her boobs half in his face."

I laughed. "Oh Kat."

She sighed. "I don't know how I get myself into these situations." I shook with barely controlled laughter and avoided looking at Liv, knowing that if I did I'd lose it completely. "Oh hey, who was the hottie you were talking to when you came off the stage by the way?"

I grinned. "You mean Ryan?"

Kat rolled her eyes as she adjusted her bag on her shoulder. "No, before he got there."

"Oh, that's Max. You know, the record producer who helped Liv with that guy a little while ago?"

Liv's eyes lit with recognition and Kat hummed thoughtfully, clearly already considering moving on from Leo. "What did he want?" Liv asked and I cleared my throat lightly.

"He asked me to do a test recording at his studio. He said he liked my voice," I winced as they both squealed, their reactions not that far off of Ryan's—though definitely more high pitched. "Relax, okay? I'm not doing it."

"What?" Liv shrieked and Kat squawked her outrage too. "Why not? It's a great opportunity. What do you have to lose?"

"Yeah," Kat linked her arm through mine. "I would kill for an opportunity like that and here you are, throwing it away."

"You want to sing?" I said, surprised, and she shook her head.

"No, I just mean an opportunity. *Any* opportunity." Kat's jaw was tight and I sighed. Maybe they were right, just because a music career was risky didn't mean I couldn't do the test recording while finishing out my degree. It didn't even mean the test recording would lead anywhere—the studio could easily pass.

"I'll think about it," I conceded as we neared the fork in the path of the trees and Liv smiled.

"We're going shopping at the mall, do you want to come?" Kat said, snapping a piece of gum enthusiastically.

I winced. "I wish. I have an essay due tomorrow morning about censorship: then and now." I gestured with my hands as if it were a movie title and Liv snickered. "I won't be home for dinner tonight either, Ryan and I are trying the whole dating thing."

"I love that you slept with him *before* you'd even consider a date." Kat snorted. "Try before you buy is an excellent philosophy."

I rolled my eyes. "It wasn't intentional."

Kat grabbed for Liv and pretended to kiss her. "Right, it was just your wild, animal lust—" I slapped her arm, laughing and Kat grinned.

"Have fun," I said, blowing them both kisses and turning away towards the apartment as they headed towards the upper part of town where the mall sat. "Don't do anything I wouldn't do."

"That leaves frighteningly little off the table," Kat called and I laughed.

Ryan was early. He'd texted to say he would pick me up at seven, *wear something nice* he'd said and my brain had gone into overdrive. Nice as in, fancy restaurant? Or nice as in, sensible, modest? I needed more information so in the end I had opted for black skinny jeans, my only pair that didn't have rips in the legs, and a high necked flirty red top. I'd kept my make-up light but was attempting to do something with my messy hair when there had been a knock on the door.

I cursed as I finished curling the short lengths and then made my way to the door, checking the time on my phone. I opened it with a scowl and then drew up short at the bouquet of flowers that were obscuring Ry's face. He leaned around the side and gave me a grin before holding them out. My hands automatically reached to take them, even as I knew my mouth was still hanging open. He'd bought me flowers. *Flowers.* Nobody had done that for me before. Ever.

"I didn't get you anything," I blurted in a panic and Ryan laughed.

"The pleasure of your company is more than enough."

We stood on the threshold for a second more before I stumbled back a step and then went in search of something to put the flowers into. They were beautiful, brightly colored and sweet smelling and I let the smile that had been building break across my face as I entered the kitchen. Liv looked up from peering inside the fridge and gaped.

"Help," I pleaded and she snorted, grabbing a pitcher from the cupboard that I was pretty sure she'd stolen from *The Box* and filling it with water.

"Go on," she said, offering me a quick pat on the shoulder. "Finish getting ready, I'll get these in the water for you."

"Thank you!" I pressed a quick kiss to her cheek and hurried back to the hall where Ryan still stood, looking bemused. "You're early," I grumbled and he shook his head.

"By two minutes?"

"I needed those two minutes!" I complained as I pulled on a set of sandals with chunky heels and then stood up to grab my jacket.

"You look gorgeous," Ry said, voice low and I looked up to find his eyes on me, heavy and hot. He cleaned up well too, it was a similar outfit to what he'd worn to the History mixer just sans the blazer.

"Thank you for the flowers," I said, realizing I'd been in too much shock earlier to do so. "Where are we going?" I pulled the door closed behind us but stopped at his brief touch on my arm. Ryan pressed two fingers under my chin and gently tilted my face up to meet his, his mouth was warm and he kissed me thoroughly, unhurriedly, sipping at my quiet, breathy moans as if they alone were all he needed as sustenance.

He pulled away slowly, lips lingering, before giving me one last peck and offering me his hand. I took it and he grinned. "I wasn't sure what you'd like so I figured Italian was a safe bet."

I smiled, looked like I might still be getting pizza for pizza-night then. Ry said the place he'd booked was up near the mall and I nodded, most of the restaurants were near that end of town—mostly I was reeling about the fact that he'd actually made us a reservation. I had always been the one taking charge in my relationship with Aaron and before him I'd mostly just had flings.

The early evening air was still warm as we made our way through the winding trail in the park. The green area ran through the center of town and one of my favorite things about living in Sun City was that everything was close enough to walk to. I could drive and stored my truck in the underground parking beneath my apartment complex but there was just no need to drive while I was living in the middle of town. Campus, the mall, *The Box,* all of them were under a thirty-minute walk away and on nights like these, with a warm hand in mine and the stars peeking out behind the canopy of leaves, it felt like paradise.

We made idle chatter about classes and the upcoming football game as we walked and by the time we got to the Italian place *Giorgio's* I was certain that this was the best date I'd ever been on. And we hadn't even made it to the food yet.

Things were comfortable with Ryan. The little brushes of his legs against mine and the small smiles he sent me whenever he thought I wasn't looking were making my heart race and I was glad that even though we'd already had sex it hadn't detracted from my desire or the tension at all.

"So about my upcoming game," Ry said and I glanced up at him from the carbonara I had been twirling around a fork. "Would you maybe want to come?" I could see from the way he bit his lip that he wanted me there and I covered his hand with mine as he tapped at the table waiting for my answer.

"I'd love to, though I have to warn you I know nothing about football."

"You literally dated my co-captain," he said disbelievingly and I shrugged.

"We didn't talk about sports much."

"Well, it would still be great to see you in the stands," he said and smiled. "It's a home game too so you wouldn't need to travel."

"It's a date," I said and then blushed because *hello* we hadn't even finished the first one yet. Ryan just grinned, pleased and maybe a little smug as he scooped up another slice of pizza.

"So this is your final year of study, right?" he asked and I nodded, if Davis didn't kick me out first then I would be graduating in a month or so. "Where are you going after you graduate?" I appreciated the fact that he'd said it like it was a given, like I didn't have a hearing this time next week that could make or break my academic probation. All thanks to fucking Taylor.

"I'll be staying here," I said with a shrug. "I bought my apartment outright and I like it here. I figured I'd see what colleges were hiring after graduation and try and get in as a TA maybe. At this point I'm just hoping they don't kick me out before I can graduate." Ryan nodded grimly and I winced, not wanting to kill the mood. "What about you?"

"I've got another year of study," he said with a wry smile, "training to be a therapist takes a little longer than other courses." He paused and looked at me slyly. "So I guess we'll both still be here in the Fall."

I tried and failed to hide my grin. "Looks that way."

"What about your family?" Ryan asked and my stomach dropped. "Won't you miss them staying here permanently? Or are they local?"

"I don't have any family," I said sharply and his eyes widened, instantly making me regret my tone and words. I tugged at the ends of my hair. "I mean, I have my mom but we're not close. I don't speak to her at all, really."

"Oh," he said carefully, looking around the restaurant awkwardly and I knew he wanted to know why, wanted to know *me* and I supposed if I wanted to have friends or... more, that knew the real me then I needed to let them in a little. Offer up a bit more of myself than I had in the past.

"She's an addict and the only time we talk is when she's hitting me up for money," I said emotionlessly, it was a simple and irritating fact. Didn't seem to matter how often I changed my number, she would show up at some point, trying to guilt trip me into letting her stay or borrowing cash. "I moved out as soon as I was legally able, headed to Arizona with the money I'd saved up and got a job at a club in Phoenix. Then my Gran died. I combined the small inheritance she'd left me with everything I'd been able to save and applied for a bunch of scholarships. I got in at Radclyffe, bought the apartment and the rest is history." It was odd really, how your life could be summarized in a few short sentences that minimized the pain, the loneliness. The days that had turned into weeks that I'd lived off of cheap noodles and tap water, how thin I'd been when I'd moved to Sun City and how my life had begun to change when I'd rented out the room to Taylor for relatively cheap.

"I'm sorry you had to go through that," Ryan said quietly,

squeezing my hand. He seemed to sense that I was done talking about it and turned back to his pizza, swallowing a bite with a huge square of pineapple on top before speaking again. "We grew up very differently," he said it off-handedly, like it didn't matter to him, like he didn't see me differently. "My family wasn't well-off but we were comfortable. We lived in Detroit for most of my life before my folks decided they hated it here and filed to move to Canada."

"Oh wow, really? That must be hard having them so far away." I couldn't empathize at all but I could imagine that if you actually liked the people you were related to then it must have been difficult for him.

"Yeah it was a big change, they moved to Toronto with my sister, Tate, and I came here." He smiled and reached for his phone, flicking it open to show me the photo on his home screen. Ryan's smile in the photo took over his whole face as he peered down at the chubby blonde toddler sitting in his lap.

"Big age gap," I said and then smiled. "She looks adorable."

"She is," he said and the proud big-brother look on his face made me feel both sad and happy. I'd never had a sibling and it was something I'd both wished for and been happy about—I wouldn't have wanted another kid in the same position I'd grown up in, but the idea of having someone who would love you and shelter you the way that siblings often did...

"You're lucky to have each other," I said softly and Ryan leaned across the short space between us and pressed a sweet kiss to my mouth.

CHAPTER TWENTY

HEAVEN - FINNEAS

I stood staring at the solid wood door to Professor Dick's office. Whatever happened inside was going to change things, I could only hope that whatever transpired allowed me to still graduate and didn't affect my permanent record too badly.

It had been an odd week in the run-up to Friday. Ryan had ended our date with a chaste kiss to my cheek at the door while Liv stood watching like a chaperone from the living room, but he had met me for coffee as usual on Tuesday and we'd made out as he walked me home. Kat had been at the apartment more than usual and Liv had been conspicuously absent. I'd finally thrown out my flowers from Ryan yesterday and only because they'd become so bare that I'd had to face that it was time for them to go. Class was still the new norm, Davis acting like I didn't exist—even going so far as to leave me off class emails, though thankfully Nick kept me in the loop. At this point, I just felt tired. Tired of Davis being a dick for no good reason other than his personal vendetta against women in academia, tired of having to fight so damn hard for dreams that just seemed to be slipping further and further away.

Several texts popped in one after another from Liv, Ryan and Nick, all wishing me good luck in the meeting, and it felt like my breaths came a little easier knowing that somebody had my back at least.

The door swung open and Davis peered down his nose at me, the first eye contact we'd had since the disaster at the mixer.

"Get in," he said curtly and I rolled my eyes discreetly as I followed his instructions, tugging at the white collar of my shirt so that it fell flat.

There were two other people waiting inside the office behind Davis' large wooden desk. A stool sat in front of it that was so low down I knew that Davis had likely done it on purpose so I would have to look up at them while I spoke. Assuming they even gave me the chance.

"Do you have a representative from the student union accompanying you?" the first of the newcomers asked, a petite woman with her hair in a bun so tight it tugged at the edges of her face. Glasses perched precariously on her nose as she stared at me while I sat down.

"I wasn't aware that I was allowed a rep," I said carefully and the woman frowned, throwing an irritated glance in Davis' direction that had hope flaring in my chest.

"Your department head should have informed you of this prior to your meeting," she tried again and I shook my head. The other unfamiliar figure in the room looked disinterested in the exchange, watery blue eyes instead roving the office space.

"He didn't," I said again and Davis said nothing, made no denials and the woman jotted a note on her clipboard.

"Very well, a note has been made. Just so you are aware, we are recording these proceedings to help with our later verdict."

She raised an eyebrow at me and I nodded. "Please verbalize all responses."

"Er, right. Yes, of course. Whatever you need," I said, dread curling into a lead ball in my stomach and making me feel lightheaded.

"We're here to address a formal complaint made by Taylor Walcross. Are you familiar with the student in question?" The woman appeared to be in charge and I glanced at Davis to find a sour look on his face.

"Yes."

"What was your relationship with the student?"

"She was my best friend up until recently and she also rented the spare room in my apartment." I fought to clear any tension from my voice as the woman nodded stiffly and the man scribbled several notes of his own.

"Taylor has claimed that you have harassed her multiple times in public as well as forcibly removed her from your premises." The woman said it as if it were a statement of fact and I frowned. "As you are aware, we have a no-tolerance policy when it comes to bullying and physical violence at Radclyffe and we are taking this matter very seriously."

"I dispute those claims," I said formally and tried to remember what Bryn and Leo had advised me to say when I'd sat down with them for coffee during the week.

"Honestly, they don't have a leg to stand on," Bryn had assured me, fluffing her blonde hair confidently as she spoke. "I mean, what evidence could they have? You didn't touch her and you've gone out of your way to avoid her, right?" I'd nodded and Leo had frowned, not seeming as optimistic as Kit's sister.

"I don't know," he said slowly, face pulled into a characteristic frown, "they take claims like these really seriously because of safeguarding–"

"He means they don't want to get sued if someone gets

hurt," Bryn cut in with a wolfish smile. "But they can't just kick you out on Taylor's word alone."

We'd hashed out what statement I would give and my palms had been sweaty the whole time as Bryn and Leo went back and forth, theorizing whether or not my future was wrecked.

"I would like to see the evidence of the alleged harassment as, by my recall, none occurred," I took a breath that shook and clenched my fists as I pulled my head back into the room, trying to ignore the weight of the eyes on me. I was used to performing, this shouldn't be any different. *Though normally everything you've worked for doesn't hang in the balance while you sing.* "Taylor left my apartment under her own free will after I requested she leave. No force was used. To be frank, I'm not sure why we're here when there's zero evidence against me and my apartment is private property." I'd done it, had delivered my small rehearsed speech and now I would be relatively spit-balling.

"Do you really believe we would have pursued this complaint if there wasn't significant evidence, young lady?" the mousy-haired man tutted as he ran his watery eyes over me in disapproval. "We have several witnesses who were able to confirm your presence at the sorority house where the student took refuge *and* confirmed that the student had sustained bruising to her arms and face caused by you. That places this into University territory."

"That's simply not true," I insisted. "I didn't lay a finger on her. Do you have any photographic evidence of this? Or proof that any injuries she sustained weren't self-inflicted?" Fuck. They were going to side with Taylor. That sneaky bitch had convinced her new housemates to testify on her behalf and I was going to lose *everything*. I held my breath, willing my panic to subside. I hadn't lost yet.

"We have a duty of care to our students regardless of where

the incident occurred," the woman explained patiently, adjusting her glasses and sniffing down at me, "and your disregard for your studies and other students has been well documented on your record by the head of your department." She gave a small nod in Davis' direction and I clenched my jaw.

So they had no evidence except the word of a bunch of sorority girls and the bullshit Davis had been creating to get me off the course. It was like Leo had said to me during our coffee meeting, they wanted to make this potential mess go away in whatever way was easiest. Unfortunately for me, that didn't bode well. *Fuck this.* I shook my head. "I'm so glad you're recording this session Ms...?" I blinked. Had they even introduced themselves before interrogating me? I didn't think so, unless I had missed it during my nervous fretting.

"Sunderland," the woman answered coolly but her eyes flicked to her colleague and I smirked. So they had bungled this right from the start, then.

"Ms. Sunderland," I said with a harsh smile. "Thanks so much for clarifying on the record Radclyffe's stance on alleged crimes that happen off campus involving its students. I suppose this means that the next time anyone from the school is attacked or assaulted you'll be able to step in to ensure the perpetrator is appropriately punished."

Her colleague threw her an irritated glance and Sunderland's mouth gaped for a second before she closed it and shook her head. "I don't think we have any other questions for you," she said quickly. "Do you have anything else you'd like to add in your defense?"

"Yes," I said, standing and scooping my bag from the floor. "I'd like the record to show that I requested evidence, more than just 'she-said-he-said', and none was presented. I'd also like to ensure that the panel is aware that the student in question slept with my boyfriend and has gone out of her way to harass *me*, thus ending our friendship and her casual tenancy. This complaint makes a cruel mockery of the school system and I'm sorry that Taylor wasted both your time and mine."

There was something suspiciously close to a smile on Davis' face as I swept from the room and I knew that he would be using this to push even harder for my suspension. But *fuck me*, if this is what the world of academia really looked like then why was I fighting so hard to get into it? *What do I have without it?*

I let the door close quietly behind me and pulled out my phone as I made my way down the stairs. That... couldn't have gone worse really.

Jamie: Where are you right now?

Ryan: Home. Y? How was the meeting?

Jamie: Have you ever seen a train wreck?

Ryan: ...want to come over?

Jamie: I'll be there in ten

The walk from the campus to Ryan's felt like a blur, I couldn't remember if it had been sunny or if the pathways had been busy. Had just been lost in a whirlwind of my own thoughts with no escape. Had I made a mistake in there? Was there some way I could have salvaged that before I'd decided to do what I did best—dig in deep and go for the jugular?

My future, all of my hopes to actually make something of myself, everything I'd done to get here... The long hours at the club in Phoenix, spending all of my free time working and saving while I was still in High School, nearly starving myself for a year so that I could move here and become something *more*. Were all those sacrifices now just wasted?

Ryan opened the door, took one look at my face, and pulled me into his arms. He cradled my head against his chest as he stroked my hair.

"What happened?" he said quietly and I shook my head, pulling back and finding his lips in a hard kiss that left us both breathless. There would be time for talking later but for now...

"Just help me forget it," I whispered and Ryan hesitated before nodding, kissing me again but it was too soft, too tender, and I nipped at his lip savagely, wringing a groan from him. His hands slid past my waist and over my ass in a smooth circle that had fire singing in my blood and then he slapped one cheek before soothing away the sting with the palm of his hand.

"Upstairs?" I asked and Ryan nodded, spinning around and moving up the steps with athletic grace while I panted. He led me along the corridor to his room and I paused in the doorway before walking in. This was the first time I'd seen his room. Ry seemed to have the same thought and he blushed a little as he swept a t-shirt off the floor and into a small hamper under his desk. The rooms were all fairly similar in the house, gray carpets and beige walls, though Ryan's easily had the best view overlooking the park, I thought as I stood by the window.

Ryan stood behind me, gathering my hair in one hand with gentle fingers as he pressed kisses to my neck. My head lolled against his shoulders and he pressed in close to my back. I arched my spine, letting my ass rub against the growing hardness in his sweatpants until he bit my ear lobe in admonishment.

"What?" I murmured, voice husky as he licked and sucked at my neck and his hand came around to brush across my breast through my shirt.

"You asked me to help you forget," he said in a voice just as low, full of just as much want, "so stop distracting me."

Ry's hands traced down the buttons of my shirt, undoing them one by one until the white lace bra I had on was exposed and he turned me around and bent his head to mouth one nipple through the sheer material.

"You are so beautiful." He traced the other nipple with his tongue, humming in pleasure when it tightened for him. "You deserve to be worshiped." He bit down lightly and I gave a quiet gasp. His hand moved to the clasp on the front of my pants and he glanced up at me for approval before undoing it and sliding the zipper down. Ryan palmed my pussy through the white lace of my panties, holding my hips still with his other hand as I tried to relieve the tension myself. "Can I taste you?" he asked, kneeling down so his lips were a hairsbreadth from the white lace, his warm breath leaving me throbbing. "Let me fuck you the way you should be fucked, the way you need it, Jamie."

I whimpered as one finger traced the outline of me through the material. "Yes," I gasped and he dipped his hand inside my panties, stroking softly, going deliberately slow as if he couldn't see how ready for him I was.

"Has anyone ever fucked you as good as I do?" he murmured, pressing down hard on my clit until I saw stars before easing up and tugging my trousers down my legs, nudging me to step out of them. He stood and backed me up against his desk, nudging my legs apart from where I'd squeezed them together in an attempt to give myself a fraction of the relief I needed.

Ryan tugged his sweatpants down and fisted his hard length and my mouth watered as I watched him, wanting to drag my tongue along the underside and make him scream. He smirked as he got on his knees again, looking up at me, but didn't let up as he worked himself, leaning in to press a long, hot kiss to my pussy.

"I asked you a question, Jamie," he let the words brush against my clit with his tongue and I couldn't breathe as he sucked it into his mouth with a groan of pleasure. My eyes darted down to his lap where his hand slowly pumped his cock and a drop of moisture began to leak down his head. I watched it, mesmerized, until his tongue slid inside me and I called his name. "Still waiting..."

"No," I panted as my thighs shook, "nobody fucks me as good as you do, Ry."

He gave an *Mmm* of satisfaction and then his mouth was on me again, tongue lathing against my clit and a finger slowly sliding through my wetness to find purchase deep inside me. I reached for the back of his head, stomach muscles contracting as he suctioned with his mouth and destroyed me with his tongue while I moaned his name.

Ryan pulled away for a moment, eyes glazed with lust as his hand moved faster on himself and suddenly I knew what I wanted. He read it on my face and nodded. "Whatever you want, you're in control."

The last vestiges of panic from the meeting faded away with his words and I pressed him back so I could move away from the desk. "Lay back," I said softly and he obeyed, watching me from the floor as I walked over to him and straddled his lap. He watched me, blue eyes burning and mouth still wet from between my legs.

"Are you going to ride me?" he asked, voice throaty and I felt his cock twitch against my leg. I considered him, the way he looked beneath me, taut muscles of his chest rippling as he held himself still. I shrugged off my shirt but left on the bra as I stood back up and moved over him, settling down so that my legs were spread over his face instead. He smirked and anticipation had the cool air feeling sensual against my dampness.

I sat on his face slowly and Ryan enthusiastically licked me, pressing his tongue into me deeply until I writhed over him, unable to stop myself from grinding down as he brought me to the edge of an orgasm. His moans of enjoyment had me panting as they tickled the sensitized skin and I pushed away before I could come, the slickness of my pussy as it rubbed against itself sending little vibrations of pleasure through me as I moved back and slid down onto his cock in one motion. Ryan moaned my name as I rode him, slamming myself down over and over until all I could do was rock my hips frantically against him.

He pulled me forward so I could rest against his chest as he took over, driving into me until my orgasm crashed over me unexpectedly, leaving me gasping as I tightened around him and felt climax take him too.

I couldn't move, my muscles felt like jelly and my breathing was slow as we lay there on the floor, our bodies slick with sweat.

"Thank you," I whispered, my mind was finally quiet. Ryan ran a hand up and down my spine and pressed a kiss to my head.

"Are you ready to talk about it now?" he asked and I felt like maybe I was.

CHAPTER TWENTY-ONE

AS THE WORLD CAVES IN - SARAH COTHRAN, WUKI

THERE WAS SOMETHING ABOUT THE ENERGY AT A football game that reminded me of being on stage. The lights, the sounds, the electricity in the air as the players charged around. I had no idea what the rules were, mostly I just cheered whenever I saw Ryan—much to the irritation of Aaron in his number thirteen jersey. He'd never invited me to a game and I'd never asked to come to one, I'd never really cared much about sports but Kat sat on my left with her face painted in deep purple stripes reflecting the school colors as she yelled and pumped her fists.

I'd leaned over and asked her what was happening and she'd shrugged with a broad grin on her face, thrust a fist into the air and declared, "I have no idea! I'm just happy to be here!" It turned out Kat had never been to a game before either. Liv had stayed home to study and I missed her, it felt like she'd been pulling away from me over the past week and I couldn't work out why.

"Kat, do you think Liv's okay? Like, have you noticed anything weird?" I winced as a large cheer went out and almost obscured the words. Kat threw me a quick look before darting her eyes back to the game.

"Weird like how?" Kat bit her lip and I watched her intently. She was the worst secret keeper and if I hadn't known better, I'd have thought that maybe she knew something I didn't.

"I don't know, she just hasn't wanted to hang out with me much recently and every time I get home she's in her room... we used to have dinner together at least once a week but now I'm lucky if I even see her that often. I mean, it's a Saturday night and she decided to study."

"Oh." Kat wrung her hands and then immediately dropped them when she saw me notice. "Well, maybe she's PMSing."

I eyed her doubtfully. "Is there something you want to tell me?"

"Nope, can't think of anything at all," she said cheerfully and then gave another loud cheer, cutting off any other protests I might have made. She was definitely hiding something and I felt hurt settle onto me like a familiar second skin. I had finally found some friends who weren't massive d-bags and they were being... I wasn't sure if *shady* was the right word, but it definitely didn't feel good.

Kat's shoulders sagged and her bright green eyes swam with tears as she spun around to face me abruptly. "Okay, fine, you got it out of me."

I blinked, the weight in my chest easing slightly. Maybe they didn't all hate me if she was willing to dish?

"She's into you."

I stared at her. "What? Who is?"

"Liv," Kat said, fingers squeezing tightly together as she watched me.

I burst out laughing. "You're ridiculous, you know that?"

Kat didn't laugh and my smile faded quickly. "No. Tell me you're fucking with me."

Kat shook her head slowly from side to side and I groaned. "Oh man, I can't believe you told me! No wait, I can't believe she kept this a secret from me!"

Kat winced. "You're clearly into Ryan and she's upset, okay? Just give her some space."

It felt like there was too much spit in my mouth and I swallowed, looking away and back to the match as Ryan got possession of the ball and I gave a half-hearted cheer.

"You're wrong," I said. "There's no way."

Kat shrugged. "Suit yourself."

I cursed, Kat was a gossip but she wasn't usually a liar. *Fuck.* How had this happened? I liked Liv a lot, she was gorgeous and funny and sweet but I was—

My eyes found Ryan's back, standing in position as I looked on from the bleachers. I liked Ryan. I had for a long time if I was being at all honest with myself. Liv was amazing and she deserved the world, but what I really needed from her was a friend. I'd made that decision right after I'd kissed her at the bar and hadn't regretted it since.

I pushed my hand through my wind-blown hair and tugged out the tangles impatiently. "This is a fucking mess," I said and Kat nodded her agreement. "How long have you known?"

"I don't know," she said, avoiding my eyes. "A week? Maybe two?"

Fuck. Liv had liked me for a while then and there I was, waxing on about Ry and having him over to the apartment...

"Hey," Kat said, placing a cool hand on mine, "don't beat yourself up. You didn't know and she didn't want to tell you. So just pretend I never said anything okay? Liv will get over you."

Clearly I was predictable. I sighed, trying to ease the chaos of my thoughts by focusing on the match. We were up by two points. Or tries. Or whatever the fuck this sport used. But it looked like we were winning and if nothing else, this was a great time to simply sit back and enjoy watching Ry's muscles work.

"How are things between the two of you?" Kat said, nodding to where Ryan stood and clearly trying to keep my mind off of the bomb she'd just dropped about Liv.

"Good I think." I smiled slightly as Ryan looked up and spotted us in the crowd, shielding his eyes against the bright lights highlighting the game and waving. "He's different to anyone else I've ever been with."

"I'm glad," Kat said and then smirked. "Aaron was an ass. About time you dated someone half-way decent."

I laughed and smacked her arm lightly. The truth was that if Taylor's complaint came back in her favor and I was suspended, I still would have had possibly the best few months at college since I'd arrived because I'd got to spend them with Ry, Kat and Liv. I hadn't realized I was lonely until suddenly I was no longer alone. I wasn't sure how long it would take them to reach a decision and let me know, bureaucracy tended to take a while, but given how desperate Davis was for me to be gone...

A whistle blew and Kat and I shared oblivious looks as the people surrounding us cheered and clapped. "I guess it's over?" I said hesitantly as people began to gather their stuff and make their way down the steps to leave. The campus didn't have its own stadium but regularly used the one across town for practices and matches. It had been a little bit of a trek to get there but if it made Ry happy I would go to every single game.

They stood too and headed for the exit. The small parking lot was packed with people and cars attempting to leave and they stood off to one side nearer the changing rooms, waiting for Ry, Kit, Xander and Leo. I hadn't really paid the other guys much attention as they'd played but it still boggled my mind that such different guys were all on a team together, it definitely challenged my own jock bias. Just then Cody and Brad stepped out of the small building and sent me half-smiles and I nodded. When I thought about jocks, those two were definitely more what I pictured. Not the ever-cheerful Kit with his bright blue hair and multitude of piercings.

He came out of the changing room with Leo, ruffling his hair before he spotted me and Kat and then charged over.

"Hey guys, you did great!" Well, at least I'd thought they had.

"Thanks," Leo said slightly stiffly while Kit slid his lip piercing back in.

"Can't believe you guys came and watched," Kit said with a grin once his arrow was secure in his lip again.

"It was fun," Kat said with a shy smile at Leo and I tried not to smirk.

"Yeah, especially because we had no clue what was going on," I said enthusiastically and Kat glowered at me. "So we made up our own rules like, when Ry gets the ball he had to pass to the person with the second cutest butt. Though Kat and I disagreed a little on that front, right?" Kat took half a step back from Leo and I laughed with Kit at the expression on her face.

"It definitely sounds like a more interesting way to play the game." Kit winked and Leo frowned.

"It's a bit inconsistent though," he said and Kit clapped a hand over Leo's mouth with a laugh as his eyes widened.

I shot Kat a look that said *I told you so* and she sighed.

Strong arms swept around my middle and I shrieked in delight as I was turned around, the smile on my face dying when I found Aaron and not Ryan behind me.

"See boys," he said with a sneer as he dropped me, "I told you I could still make her squeal."

I felt rather than saw Kit and Leo step up on either side of me but I kept my eyes on Aaron as I rolled my eyes. "Oh honey, your brother made me squeal louder than that. Just ask Cody."

A snarl formed on Aaron's face and I turned away flicking my hair back at him as I flipped him off over my shoulder. A small scuffle sounded and my mouth dropped open as I spun back to see Aaron held on his knees by some sort of pressure point, his hand twisted in the air as Max grasped it.

"Max?" I said in a voice slightly higher than usual. "Um, what are you doing?"

He gave me a nod, eyes hard on Aaron as he squeezed his hand before letting him up. Aaron scrambled away, eyes large in his face before walking over to his second-rate sports car. "Asshole tried to grab you," Max said in a hard voice, brushing back a piece of his usually-gelled hair from his face and I blinked stupidly at him. That was the second time he'd stepped in to help me in a situation with a guy, maybe he had a white knight complex but right now I couldn't complain.

"Well, thanks," I said, still confused. "What are you doing at the match?"

"I'm an alumni," he said with a small grin that showed off his white teeth and I realized that was why he was dressed so much more casually. "I leave town tonight and thought it would be fun to catch a game before I go."

A warm arm slung around my shoulders and I breathed in the warm, familiar smell of Ry's aftershave before pressing a quick kiss to his cheek. "Hey," I smiled and his eyes lit up.

"Hey," he said softly, gazing down at me and then clearing his throat as he noticed his friends staring. "What's going on?"

"Just Aaron being an ass," I said nonchalantly. "This is Max, from *The Box*, you remember?"

"Right," Ry said with an easy grin, holding his hand out for the other man to shake. "Nice seeing you again."

"Yeah you too, good game." Max nodded to Kit and Leo who had been joined by Xander before turning back to us. "Hey, do me a favor? Talk to your girl for me about the studio?" He sent me a wink and I smiled tightly, knowing Ry was never going to drop this now.

"Of course," Ryan said easily. "Did I hear you say you're leaving town?"

"Tonight was my last night," he confirmed and I held in a sigh, knowing Ry was only going to double down now that he had that knowledge. "Good seeing you all," he said with a smile that grew a little bigger when his eyes fell on Kat. "Don't forget to call," he said to me, handing over another business card and I nodded casually as I took it.

"Thanks again," I said as he walked to a sleek looking sedan and waved behind him. As soon as he was far enough away, Ry opened his mouth and I shot him a warning look. "Don't even start."

"Are you really not going to consider it?" he pleaded, blue eyes blinking at me adorably as if he could flirt me into driving to Arizona and singing at Max's studio.

"I already considered it."

"*Thoroughly* considered it," Ryan amended and I saw our friends drift away to give us privacy as the parking lot continued to clear out.

"I didn't half-ass it," I snapped and Ryan rubbed a hand across his jaw. "Academia, *history*, that's where my future is. Music is *risky*. My History degree is where stability and security, all those things that I never fucking had, will be. This is how I get there, how I can make something more of myself than my mother ever did." I hadn't realized I was yelling until he gently placed his hands on my shoulders.

"There's more than one path to get there," he said and I shook my head vehemently.

"I can't just quit," I said after taking a deep breath, "not when I'm so close to everything I ever wanted."

"And if they suspend you? It'll be on your permanent record, Jamie. There's not many schools who will take a chance on hiring staff with a record of harassment."

"But I *didn't* harass anyone!"

"They won't know that," Ryan sighed and pressed a long kiss to my forehead as my eyes filled with tears that I swiped away angrily.

"Just... consider it. Okay? I know you're scared—"

"I'm *not* scared," I hissed and he raised his hand placatingly.

"Okay, then what do you have to lose by just exploring your options? You love to sing. You can't even deny it because it radiates out of you when you're up on stage. So just go, do the recording, see how you feel about it. Going to the studio doesn't mean you're giving up on your History degree. You're not your mother, not even close."

I clenched my jaw as I took two steps back. "Thanks for psychoanalyzing me, asshole." I marched off towards Kat as Ryan called my name behind me. "I'm leaving. Are you coming with?"

Kat glanced behind me to where Ryan likely still stood and gave me a hesitant nod. I set off at a punishing pace, needing to get his voice out of my head. Not calling Max was the right thing to do. I needed to put all my focus and energy in one place—history. It was what I needed to do to have a better life. *But is it what you love?* An annoying voice that sounded irritatingly similar to Ryan's whispered and I shoved the thought away. Love had nothing to do with it. I liked history, had been good at it in high school, though a lot of the fun had drained out of it the longer I'd had Davis as a professor.

I had a plan. Go to college, rent out my spare room, study hard, graduate top of my class and then move into a TA position or research fellowship until I could get a full-time role doing something similar. It paid well, was relatively easy on my brain and was interesting enough that I wouldn't get bored. But more than anything it was *prestigious,* I wouldn't be Poor Jamie Silver whose mom was an addict, I'd be Jamie Silver—professor, or TA or whatever I could manage. But I wouldn't be the girl of my past any more.

My phone dinged with a notification and I huffed angrily as I pulled it out, expecting it to be Ryan. I stopped mid-stride and Kat asked if I was okay. I stared down at the email on my phone in disbelief.

Dear Ms. Silver,

Thank you for attending the hearing on Friday, we greatly appreciated your cooperation. However, due to the severity of the incident, coupled with your aggressive and disruptive behavior in class this year, we see no other option but to suspend your studies until further notice. Should you wish to appeal—

No. This couldn't be happening. It was a bullshit complaint and the probation had been sketchy as fuck to begin with too. Nick had been right, I should have contested it then and there and Davis wouldn't have been able to screw me over, but I hadn't imagined that I could actually end up *suspended.*

My record was ruined.

I showed Kat my phone numbly and she mouthed the words as she read them, eyes flying wide as she began to rant about the unfairness of it and how could they do this to me? All the fight went out of me, drained away like I'd been punctured by Taylor's stab in the back and Professor Davis' stab to the heart. *Now what?* It was the only thought that swirled around in my head. What was I supposed to do now that my carefully laid plans, the hopes I'd had for the future I'd worked so hard for, were now just nothing but pipe dreams? Well, I knew what my mom would do, obviously, but I wasn't her, was I?

"We can appeal the decision," Kat said brightly, as if that would fix everything. It wouldn't erase the way I felt right now, knowing that this institution that I had poured everything into was willing to give up on me. *They didn't care.* Were happy to take the word of a fucking backstabber and misogynistic prick over me—who'd only ever had straight As, didn't cause trouble despite my excess partying, I'd never been so much as reprimanded before Professor Dick started teaching me. He had hated me since the beginning of term and I was sick of it. Fuck him. Fuck Radclyffe for their shitty procedures that never helped anyone anyway, and fuck Taylor.

"Yeah," I said blankly, taking my phone back and sending a screenshot of the email to the group chat we'd created a couple of weeks ago. A few messages popped in immediately and Ryan tried to call. I didn't want to talk. Right now, the only thing I wanted was to get blazed out of my brain and never think about this shit again. *Like Mother, like daughter I guess.* I walked back to the apartment quietly with Kat and waved her off when she offered to see me inside. Then I headed down the stairs to the underground parking garage, climbed in my truck and started the engine.

CHAPTER TWENTY-TWO

THE JEWELLER'S HANDS - ARCTIC MONKEYS

I SAT IN THE TRUCK FOR A WHILE WITH THE ENGINE running. Not sure where I was going or what the plan was, just feeling like I needed to get away. Sun City had felt like a refuge of sorts for a long time, a place where I could rewrite who I was and choose who I wanted to be. But the past always comes back to haunt us and while I could choose a new path it couldn't change the one that had brought me here.

I put the car in reverse and pulled out of the lot, it was almost empty in there and I felt absurdly grateful. My truck was steady and reliable but it was also huge and a little difficult to maneuver so I was relieved to have the empty space either side of me. I stopped at the exit and shot a quick text to Liv, telling her not to worry and that I would be out late, before heading smoothly up and out of the underground parking space. I drove aimlessly for a while, just content to let my hands guide me.

I found driving soothing, not as soothing as singing but 'working it all out on the stage' was the last part of the process for me. I couldn't sing about it until I knew what was bothering me, sometimes I didn't even realize that anything was until I had my guitar in hand and tears running down my face. Emotions were a bitch, hard to understand and even harder to control.

I drove past Ry's house, the windows all dark, and glanced out at the park that the rest of the town campus seemed centered around. The trees had become full again, leaves swaying restlessly in the breeze, and I knew how they felt. It felt like I'd blinked and somehow my life had changed again. First when I'd found Liv and then when I'd found Ryan. Then when I'd got that email earlier, the one that had the power to change my future in a hundred words or less. Strange how something so small and intangible could leave such large ripples.

I drove on, heading past the mall and then the mini stadium where I'd watched my first football game earlier that day. I'd experienced a lot of firsts here, some of them good and some of them bad. I didn't want to let Radcliffe University affect how much I loved this place, these people, but it had. I'd felt on the outside before, but now I was even further away from everything I'd wanted, it all came to a screeching head with that email. With fucking Taylor and what it all boiled down to—I wasn't good enough. I'd tried and scraped and struggled to become something more than the girl whose mom was an addict and whose dad had skipped town. I didn't want people to look at me and think *oh yeah you can see she's had it bad*. Yet even after all I'd done to get here, the promise of more, the promise of the life I fucking deserved had been snatched as quickly as snuffing a flame.

Of course, pretty blonde girls like Taylor whose rich momma would take care of them would never have to worry about their place in the world. Neither would Aaron. Perfect plastic people ready for cookie cutter lives, filling themselves with drugs just to feel something. I tapped the steering wheel angrily with two fingers, hating the direction my thoughts were spinning, knowing I needed to shut them down before I became truly self-destructive but I was spiralling deeper and deeper and hating them more and more for having this fucking effect on me. For being able to tear me down in ways their words and actions never could. They had it better, even in their fragile empty lives, they would always have it better.

They don't have what you do, I reminded myself. *Love, more love than you know what to do with. Friendship and people who care in ways you'd never dared hope for.* I shrugged off the thoughts. Love could only get you so far.

A bright sign up ahead had me turning off the main road and into a tiny parking lot outside of a bar. It wasn't on the main strip, which explained why I'd never been here before, but it seemed fairly busy and I could only hope that the too-loud music might drown out my thoughts.

I sank into an empty stool at the bar, swinging my jean-clad legs around as I ordered a vodka. *Fucking Devil's juice,* Kat had called it and she had been right. It was a nasty drink for a nasty person, cheap and sour and I could practically feel how it would numb my throat before the drink was even set down in front of me. Hoped it would numb more than that. It was almost dark in there, like they didn't want you to look too closely at the drinks or the person next to you, all low-hanging lights and the drinks came in heavy glasses that made me wonder how much I'd actually paid for my drink. I'd never had a problem with drugs or alcohol, had always known the difference between drinking for fun and drinking because you *had to*—before the sadness or the anger could swallow you up and spit out only the worst parts of you. Sometimes it didn't matter how hard you tried, we all turned into our parents in the end.

I nodded my thanks to the baby-faced bartender and picked up the cool glass, swirling the clear liquid from side to side as I contemplated it. For some people depression felt heavy, for me it felt light. The lightness of not giving a single fuck and I supposed that was in itself, fairly heavy. Like your body was empty and you could feel every inch of your soul shriveling in the sunlight. Trying to work out how much to let it consume you before the cracks started showing, needing to know how much of a fuck you wanted people to give and only showing *just enough*. It hadn't been a problem for me in a long while and yet here I was, slumped down and falling faster, dizzy at the bottom of a spiral with nothing to hold on to.

You're not your mother, not even close. But wasn't I though? Ready to bury myself in whatever could make the pain, the failure, the hopelessness go away? Who wouldn't want to turn that part off? To just take one little sip and never have to break through the haze? I raised the glass to my mouth, let the scent of the alcohol fill my nostrils, let the liquid brush my lips and felt that *tug*. The same one I'd been feeling for weeks now whenever worry about Taylor or Aaron or the upcoming hearing had left me breathless and each time I'd found myself at Ryan's door.

The glass hit the red napkin with a thud as I placed it back down, untasted. *Me*, I realized slowly. *I* wasn't someone who wanted to run away from the pain, I never had been, and for one stupid letter to shake me so thoroughly... I clenched my hand and then released a deep breath. I would rather stand out in the deluge and let the rain fucking lash me than take a step closer to being like *her*. To letting one more set-back drag me down, drag me back to who I could have been. Who I almost was.

I stood and slid the expensive drink to the guy sitting next to me. "Enjoy, I don't want it."

He sniffed it and winced but I was already gone, the stool top still spinning as I walked unhurriedly to my truck. I still burned with anger, betrayal, but at least that soul-crushing blankness had eased a little. Just enough for me to get in the car and take a steadying breath as I pulled away and back on to the road.

I switched on the radio, my truck was too old to have an aux or bluetooth for my phone, and hummed mindlessly to whatever song was playing as I drove on, not sure where to go but knowing I wasn't ready to go home yet. A sign for Phoenix flashed on my right in the light from my headlights and my mood sank a little again as I wavered, caught between the future it seemed like fate wanted me to have and the one I wanted for myself.

I squared my jaw and made the turn. It seemed only right, only fitting, to come back here to the place I'd run to as soon as I could get away from my mother. She loved me, but her love was a brand of poison that had been killing me slowly—it wasn't even just the drugs, though that had been bad enough, it was the constant parade of other addicts she'd had in and out of the house, like they were in some club only the lowest of the low knew about.

The drive to Phoenix took about forty-five minutes on a good day and at this time of the night the roads were quiet. Nothing but me, my thoughts and the sound from the radio breaching the night. The time on the dash told me it was just after one and I blinked at it blearily, I must have been driving around Sun City for longer than I'd realized while I'd been wallowing.

I clenched my jaw, ignoring the pain that spiked up to my temple. I'd made the choice once before, in this exact place, that I wouldn't be held back. Not by my mom, society—nobody. That included the snooty-ass academics at Radclyffe. So why was I letting it shake me this badly? Who gave a crap what they thought of me? *Party girl. Slut. Not cut-out for academia.*

Those were just things people said, not who I was fundamentally. If I walked away now, if I refused to give myself a second chance to be something—anything—then didn't that make me just as bad as them? I felt oddly adrift, like tonight could be another rebirth of sorts and the night was malleable, waiting for me to decide what to make of it. Like anything could happen.

Decision made, I drifted into a quiet parking lot outside of a mall and pulled out my phone. I could vaguely remember the name of Max's studio and quickly typed it in, hitting the button for directions. It actually wasn't too far from here. Funnily enough, it was only a stone's throw from the old club that I had sung and waitressed at years ago. It was a 24-hour kind of affair with more seedy clients than there were tips, but if I had to I could wait Max out there til morning.

I deserved to take a chance on myself, the same way I had before. I owed it to that girl who had scrimped and saved and worked her ass off to get where I was now. Sometimes it took more than one try to get something right, what mattered most was that I kept on going.

I pulled up outside the studio, unsurprised to find the lot empty and the only lights on were in what looked like a security box. The building was painted a shade of mint that made it look closer to a bakery than a recording studio and I felt my stomach rumble as I thought about pastries for a second. I parked and sat in the darkness, blowing out a long breath as I tried to decide what to do. Whether this was a step I actually wanted to take or just one I felt like I *had* to take. I had options. I didn't need to do this. And sure, music wasn't the career I'd picked for myself but what sane person who loved it like I did would turn down this opportunity? Maybe Ryan had been right, I didn't want fear to take this from me. So *what* if they rejected me or decided I wasn't good enough? I. Had. Options.

I let out another deep breath, unbuckled my belt and leaned forward to rifle through my dashboard compartment for the emergency stash I usually kept in there.

My hand closed around the cold metallic tin and I grinned a little, finally feeling something inside of me settle. This wasn't like the vodka. This was for me, for fun, for lightness—not because of someone or something else, but I still sat there for a second longer, making sure I felt secure in that before I lifted the joint to my lips.

I lit the zoot inside the cab with a lighter that I'd stashed in my pocket and then let my head fall back against the headrest of my seat. I sat and smoked and reminded myself to just breathe for the duration of the joint and then flicked the ends out of the window. The time on the dashboard now read three-thirty and I blinked at it slowly before glancing at the web page I'd used to find the studio's location on my phone. Was it too early to leave Max a voicemail? Surely not, he was a working guy, he'd likely have his phone on *do not disturb*. I had nothing to lose. Probably. Plus, I was getting bored, there was nothing good on the radio and munchies were starting to hit me until all I could think about was that little Chinese place around the corner that I'd used to love. I needed a distraction.

I pulled another pre-rolled joint out of the tin and then put the box back in the dash, hitting call on my phone before I could second guess myself. Or order Chinese food. I stuck the zoot in my mouth and inhaled as I lit it, sparking it up, and then almost choked when Max said a cautious, "Hello?"

Fuck, I hadn't thought he'd be awake. What was I supposed to say? I settled on, "Hi," and silence flooded the other end of the line.

I took another drag and thankfully didn't cough as Max said, "Um, who is this?"

"Oh, sorry, it's Jamie. From The Box?" I tapped my fingers

on my thigh and waved at the security guard when I noticed him watching me out of his window.

"Are you... okay?" Max sounded confused and concerned and I smothered a laugh.

"Yeah, sorry for the late... early... call. I'm at the studio. I was going to leave you a message."

"You're at the studio now?" Max's voice rose and I nodded, hastily following it up with a quick, "Yeah."

"Okay, I'll be there in ten."

"Oh no that's okay, I can wait til morning. I was going to head across the street—"

"Stay where you are," he said sternly and it was clear that he knew exactly which club was across the street. "I can't sleep anyway so I'll meet you there." He hung up before I could say anything else and I winced at the sharp beeping noise as the call cut-off.

It didn't feel like much time had passed at all before Max's sedan pulled into the lot. I rolled down my window and airily tipped some ash.

"That was fast."

He didn't look like he'd just come out of bed, though he seemed a little tired. Max sniffed the air and shot me a look of sheer exasperation. "What are you doing here? You weren't driving about stoned, were you?"

"I've come to sing!" I laughed and Max's lips twitched. "And no, of course not. I didn't think you were going to be awake so I thought I'd kill time." I opened the door to my truck and hopped out, wincing as the fresh air hit me all at once and I momentarily felt everything spin.

"You look a little pale," Max pointed out unhelpfully and I frowned at him. "What made you change your mind about the test recording?"

· · ·

"I got suspended," I said, like it was no big deal and Max stopped short of unlocking the doors to the studio.

"From Radclyffe? Why?" He sounded genuinely shocked and I grimaced. Better I told him now to save myself any disappointment if this was going to be a deal breaker.

"Because my best friend slept with my boyfriend, so I slept with his brother and best friend and sent him a photo and then he leaked that picture everywhere."

Max's jaw was slack and he fumbled his keys before he cleared his throat lightly and concentrated on the door. "Why would that get you kicked out?"

"My professor hates that I like girls and guys. And my ex-bestie complained that I'd harassed her after I kicked her out of my apartment." I stubbed out the last of the joint and followed Max inside with a quick nod to the security guard who simply turned back to his tiny TV.

"That... got you suspended?" he said in disbelief and I shrugged. "Did you complain about the professor? I mean at worse that's discrimination—"

I sighed. "I'm here to sing Max, so let's get on with it if this isn't a deal breaker."

"It's not," he said decisively.

"Do you need to like, check with someone higher up? Or like, with your PR department?" I said as he led me up some stairs and to a room marked '1'.

He let out a quick laugh and I eyed him warily. "Figures." He held out his hand for me to shake. "I'm Max, owner of AZ Records, parent company of what's soon going to be our Sun City label."

I shook his hand limply. So Max wasn't just a record producer—he was the *owner* of the fucking label? And I'd told him I'd had a revenge threesome. *And* I'd smoked a lot of weed, partially in front of him. Had I already blown this to hell? I didn't know what to say so I settled on, "You're expanding?" and he snorted as if my answer pleased him.

"Yes. So if we sign you there'll only be a short commute time." He'd said *if* but he hadn't already shown me the door so that had to be a good sign. Right?

"Why are you even here at," I checked the time on my phone, "almost four in the morning? I mean it was weird before but now that I know you own all this shit..."

His jaw clenched for a second before he relaxed, holding open the door that led to the microphone booth behind the mixing decks. "I have insomnia."

"Oh," I said and walked into the room, letting him follow behind me and decided to let that slip by. "So what do you want me to sing?"

CHAPTER TWENTY-THREE

NO. 1 PARTY ANTHEM - ARCTIC MONKEYS

MY THROAT HURT, I'D SOBERED UP AROUND THE fifth song Max got me to record but everything still felt warm and fuzzy. I was having... fun.

Despite the fact that Max was the big boss and therefore should have been intimidating, it was hard to feel like that when he was pretending to rock out to an air guitar. Plus, I'd guessed correctly before, he was only four years older than me at twenty-five. He'd bought the studio with family money and surprisingly, that hadn't rankled me. He was clearly doing this because he loved it and he was good at it too, he knew way more about music theory than I did.

"Are you on any socials?" Max asked as I span in the office chair next to the mixers.

"What? Oh, no. Had to delete them when the nude was leaked."

Max gave me a sympathetic look but nodded. "Well, we're definitely going to want to get you back on them at some point, especially that one that's so hyped right now—TakTic?"

I snorted. "Right, yeah sure."

"So if you're down with it, I'm happy with everything that I've seen. You'd be the first new artist signed to our Sun City label."

I blinked. Just like that? "Really?"

Max smiled and it transformed his face, lighting his eyes and making a dimple pop in his right cheek. "Do you know how many people I could sit and jam with for, say, five hours?" He raised an eyebrow. "You're talented, Jamie. But more than that, you're down-to-Earth and genuinely nice. Which is always a plus. Take some time, get a lawyer to look over the contract, but we can sign a prelim agreement now to show that an offer has been made if you want it or need it for an employer or something."

This was really happening. I pinched my arm. "What exactly are you offering me?"

"A contract to sing for us, it'll be a mixture of your own stuff —some of your covers will be fab for TakTic—and we have songwriters on the team. Unless that's something you're also into?"

I shrugged slightly. "Only when the mood takes me but I don't think they're very good."

"You never know," he said, standing and stretching. "You could always work with one of our writers and turn what you already have into something better."

I nodded thoughtfully, that did sound like something I'd enjoy, similar to when I'd sit and play around meshing songs for covers.

"What changed your mind in the end?" Max asked as he rifled through papers in a drawer next to him. "About coming to do the test recording I mean."

"My mom, actually," I smiled wryly and he raised one honey-coloured eyebrow at me.

"You guys are close?"

"Not at all," I said and a small smile curled his mouth and he nodded like he could relate. "It's funny really, sitting in here with you singing, getting offered a contract—did you know I used to sing at the strip club across the street?"

Max handed me the prelim paper to sign and a pen and smiled. "Small world, I guess. You're a local then?"

"Not really, I moved here from Tempe originally to get away from... everything. Wound up in a dingy apartment I could barely pay for and working at Marco's." I tapped the pen against the paper after I signed my name and then handed it back.

"You talk to her much?" Max said, looking away and somehow that made it easier to open up a little.

I shrugged. "Not if I can help it. Sometimes she just texts, other times she just turns up like everything is normal, like *we're* normal." I sighed and rubbed my temples. "She knows a lot of people who also know a lot of people, you know? Hard to stay on the down low when they're all connected at the proverbial hip."

"That's rough," he said, but it didn't feel dismissive, more like he was commiserating. "My folks and I don't talk much either. They thought that opening the business was a dumb idea." Max smirked. "Of course, that was until I earned my first mil, then of course they acted like they'd practically had the idea for me to open a record label."

I snorted. "Don't say that in earshot of my mom, otherwise she'll be hitting you up for money as well as me."

He winced. "Drugs?"

"Sure, or booze, depends on the day."

Max handed me a copy of the actual contract they wanted me to sign and stretched his long body out, bones popping as he slumped back down.

"You know, I think I might be able to sleep now," he mused and I laughed.

"Worst bedtime story ever." I stood and he dragged himself up too.

"You've got my number," he said wryly and I grinned, "so call if you have any questions, or you know, if you want to chat some more." I nodded and he cleared his throat lightly. I bit back a smile, glad that he was almost as awkward with his emotions as me. "Let me know as soon as you can if you're going to sign. I'll be back down in Sun City in a week or so anyway to check out the new premises. You can come too if you like?"

I got the impression that Max was lonely. He was nice, funny, and clearly knew what he was talking about and maybe I wanted to be his friend or maybe I just felt bad, but I found myself nodding. They said it was lonely at the top, I guess Max would know.

He showed me back out the front entrance and the sunlight had me shielding my eyes. I was sober enough to drive, thankfully, but I was in desperate need of food and a coffee. I waved to Max as I unlocked and stepped into my truck.

Yesterday felt a million miles away. Yesterday, I'd been kicked out of college. Today, I'd essentially been offered a record deal. A broad smile swept over my face and faded only when I checked my rearview mirror before I reversed. I swore as I stomped on the breaks and glared at the familiar figure standing behind my truck.

I didn't dare get out. Instead, I rolled down my window and called, "Hello, mother." I poured as much sarcasm and disdain into my voice as possible and didn't know whether to feel relieved or bad when she didn't notice. "How the fuck did you know I was here?" I glanced over at Marco's suspiciously. I hadn't ever told her I worked there but the place was seedy enough that it didn't surprise me that she had contacts there.

"Is that any way to greet your mom?" she said, gesturing to the rolled down window and holding out her arms as she moved around to the front of the car. We shared the same dark hair, though hers was thin and graying, and the same mole above our lips. The years, or, more accurately, the drugs, hadn't been kind to her. I didn't get out of the car. "Karly told me you were here," she said when I remained silent, "if you'd answered my texts you'd know that I live here now. Isn't it great? I'm so close-by, we could visit—"

"What do you want?" I kept my tone curt, disinterested. "Money? I don't have any."

"Now, why would you assume that? You know I love you baby—"

"Let's skip the bullshit routine," I said, hands flexing on the wheel. "I don't have any money on me and even if I did I wouldn't give it to you to snort away. What part of me moving out and not answering your calls don't you get?" She stared at me, a hand pressed to her chest like I'd wounded her and my gut churned, making me feel queasy. "I don't want you in my life. Ever. Not if you're going to be like this."

"Benji, baby," she tried and I clenched my jaw so hard I feared my teeth would break as my eyes burned. God, she had to ruin even this. Not a single moment of fucking peace in my life.

"I'm done. Have been for years now. Get clean or don't fucking contact me again," I was trembling but I meant the words. I didn't want anything to do with her, not until she sorted her life out, if that day ever came would be up to her to decide.

She said nothing, eyes watering as I rolled up the window and reversed out of the space. I tried to control my shaky breaths, tried to ignore the guilt that gnawed at me the way she relied upon. *What if she really needed me this time? What if I could help her? What if I'm all she has left?*

I turned on the radio and let the sound drown out my thoughts. The truth was that I'd tried to help her. Had given her money, had put her in rehab, I had *tried*. The same couldn't be said for her. Just the fact that she was associating with people like *Karly* told me everything I needed to know about whether or not she was clean. It was... awful, and I wasn't sure if I'd ever think of her and not feel grief at what we might have had, but I needed to move on. I needed to put that shit behind me once and for all. I'd been so caught up in my hang-ups of the past, I'd almost missed out on something amazing. *Ryan's never going to shut up about this. Smug bastard.*

A sign for a pancake house caught my attention and I immediately banked a right to go through the drive thru and then sat in the parking lot while I scoffed the thick, fluffy goods down. I grimaced at the leftover stickiness of the syrup on my hands afterwards but ran a hand over my stomach in satisfaction. Worth it.

I took a sip of the black coffee before placing it carefully into one of the many cup holders this truck offered. I'd have preferred a latte but I'd only had twenty dollars on me, so black would have to do.

The caffeine perked me up and as I drove back towards home I felt the anxiety that seeing my mom had dredged up begin to fade away. It was always like that when I saw her—she'd try and convince me she was there for me, to see me, that she'd missed me. Maybe in her own twisted way she really believed that. But it always ended the same, her crying, me slamming the door, and usually finding myself a couple hundred bucks lighter too. I'd said last time would be the last, and I'd meant it. Maybe now she'd take me seriously. I sighed and reached for my coffee, unfortunately it didn't seem likely.

My phone chimed with an incoming message and I glanced at it quickly while I was at a red light. Just Liv, calling me a hoe. She clearly thought that I had spent the night with Ry, which I supposed was fine. Though she'd only have to check-in with Kat or one of the boys to know that wasn't the case.

Truth be told, I wasn't sure what to do about Liv. We were still getting to know each other in a lot of ways, but in the ones that counted she was the closest thing I had to a best friend and I didn't want to lose her just because I was dating Ry. I didn't know whether I should confront her and clear the air or just continue on and let the chips fall where they may.

I sighed, deciding to go with option two until I had any indication that Liv wanted to talk about it. Right now, I had more pressing matters—like finding a lawyer to look over this contract before I signed anything. Max seemed nice enough but I didn't want to accidentally hand over my soul.

It was still early so the traffic was light and as I drove back past the mall I felt nothing but relief. Sun City was home, regardless of some stupid University that apparently hated threesomes. Ironically, I knew personally of a couple of good ways they could let loose...

I snorted as I pulled into the underground parking, back where I'd started and yet infinitely different. The sun was bright outside and it hit me for the first time how exhausted I was—I sniffed delicately as I grabbed my phone and empty coffee cup —and how badly I needed to shower off the weed sweats.

I called out to Liv as I made my way into the apartment, exhaustion dragging my steps and making me more confused than usual when I bumped into a familiar, svelte blonde trying to leave as I walked in. Well, normally svelte anyway, Bryn was looking naughtily rumpled and I grinned at her as we did an awkward side shuffle.

"Bryn." I grinned wider. "Nice to see you."

She gave up on all pretenses of sneaking out, instead sliding her heels back on and gaining at least a head and a half of height on me. Bryn smacked a kiss to my cheek and waved goodbye without replying as she made her way down the hall and I snickered.

"I thought *I* was supposed to be the hoe?" I said as I walked through the lounge to the kitchen and dumped the to-go cup and Liv came out of the bathroom in a cloud of steam, long hair wrapped up in a towel and face a little pink.

"What?" she asked and then her eyes ran over my likely tired eyes and rumpled hair. "Are you okay?"

"I saw Bryn leaving," I said with an eyebrow waggle and Liv paled. "Hey, it's okay. Invite over whoever you want. And I'm fine, I went on a long drive."

Liv looked like she didn't know what to address first, she chose to ignore the comment about Bryn. "A long drive where?"

"Phoenix," I said as I strode past her to the hall and kicked off my shoes before heading to the bathroom. "Now, I need to shower off this funk and get some sleep, I'm dead on my feet."

Liv bit her lip. "I have questions."

I waved her off. "I'll fill you in later. After I've showered and slept preferably."

'Okay," she nodded and swung the towel off her hair, rumpling it to make sure it didn't drip, and then handed me the wet towel to hang back up. "I think there's something going on later at *The Box?* Nick and Ryan asked me to tell you to come."

"Sounds good," I said, though I was a little worried that Ry hadn't texted me himself. I closed the bathroom door and shucked my stinky clothes. "I'll fill you in then."

I'd made the mistake of falling straight into bed with my hair still wet, something I was now sorely regretting as half my hair had dried in mangled clumps and the other half was sticking up like I'd been electrocuted. Liv had taken one look at me after I'd stumbled out of my room with puffy eyes and fallen about laughing. I'd flipped her off and gone in search of cereal.

"It's 6:30PM," she said and I shrugged.

"I just woke up. It's breakfast time."

Liv rolled her eyes but the smile stayed on her face so I thought perhaps now was the best time to gently enquire about last night. This morning. Whatever.

"So. You and Bryn?"

Color immediately stained her cheeks and she looked away, fussing with a mug on the counter and swiping away invisible crumbs. "What about Bryn?"

So she was going to play it like that? "Oh, I suppose I imagined her attempting the walk of shame yesterday." I paused, "Earlier." *Fuck.* I felt like I had jet lag but I'd only gone on an hour's drive. Admittedly the joints I'd smoked had been fat—*mental note: keep smaller zoots in the car.* I didn't even want to think about what sort of stupid shit I might have said to Max yesterday.

I spooned another scoop of lucky charms into my mouth and crunched loudly while I waited for her answer.

Liv sighed. "Yes she came over. Then she left. Okay?"

"Was it good?" I drank the milk out of the bowl and widened my eyes when she grimaced. "It was *bad?*" Who'd have figured? Bryn had the confidence of someone who was good in bed. I wiped a trickle of milk off my chin and Liv blinked at me as I licked it off my hand.

"It was fine," she said, turning away and placing the mug in the sink. "It's just that I sort of like someone else."

Oh shit. Maybe I shouldn't have pushed this. Was she about to confess?

"Wow," I said after the silence stretched on for a couple seconds too long. "That... sucks. Do you think they like you back?" I asked carefully and Liv shook her head.

"No, but it's okay. I'll get over it." Her eyes met mine in the window above the sink and I wondered if she knew that I understood. I moved closer to her and she pulled away, moving to the door as I placed the bowl in the sink. I made to turn away until I saw Liv's raised eyebrows and turned back to wash the bowl with a quiet laugh.

"Anyway," Liv said, "we're supposed to be meeting everyone at *The Box* in like twenty minutes for some surprise or whatever. So hurry up and sort all of that out." She gestured to my hair and face and laughed when I made a face.

"Thanks for giving me *so* much notice. What am I supposed to do with this mess?" I gestured to my hair and Liv looped her arm through mine.

"Come on," she tutted, "I'll fix it."

Liv was a miracle worker. Or a witch. I wasn't sure yet. She owned more beauty and hair products than me and Kat combined if I had to guess, but somehow she'd wrangled both my hair and face into looking somewhat presentable.

"Wow," I said, I looked... *glossy*. Liv beamed, pleased as I surveyed my face in her mirror. "You should totally do something with this."

"What do you mean?" Her nose wrinkled adorably and I bit my lip on a grin.

"Take my photo." Liv stepped back, angling her phone and I shook my head. "I mean of my hair and make-up. For your portfolio."

"I don't have a portfolio," she mumbled but took the picture anyway.

"Well you do now," I grinned. "You said you weren't sure what you wanted to do and I think you'd make a great personal stylist, or maybe a make-up artist! To the stars!" Liv laughed and I joined in before letting my smile fall away. "I mean it though, you're good at this and clearly enjoy it—why not?"

Liv didn't answer, just looked lost in thought as she sat on the edge of her pink bed spread. I patted her on her head as I stood. "Okay, well thank you—I'm going to go and get dressed."

She nodded absently and I hurried to my room after quickly freshening up my body in the shared bathroom. I pulled on a cute cropped ringer tee, tartan mini skirt complete with jingly chains, fishnets and my big boots. Liv had done my make-up to perfection but I added on a bold red lip to match my grungy look. I grabbed a jacket off the back of my door and my phone from the nightstand and came out of my bedroom to find Liv waiting for me.

She tapped her foot impatiently. "We're going to be late."

I rolled my eyes. "We live like five minutes away."

It was slightly crisp outside as we walked to *The Box* and I smirked when we walked in at exactly seven. Liv huffed at me but I smiled as I turned to the booth at the back and found Ry, Kat, Nick and the boys all waiting for us.

"Hey," I called as we approached, "did somebody save us a seat?" They scooted down the benches and Liv and I perched on the ends opposite each other. I was gasping for a drink but Ryan looked ready to burst so I thought it might be best to listen to what he had to say first. "What's up? Liv said you had a surprise or something?"

Nick pulled out a piece of paper from his bag underneath his seat and passed it across the booth to Ry. He grinned broadly as he handed it to me. "Surprise!"

I quirked an eyebrow as I took it and pulled open what I could now see was an envelope. "What is this?"

"Just read it," Nick said with a slow smile.

I tugged it open, trying not to rip it too badly, and pulled out the letter inside. I unfolded it and felt my mouth drop open in a small gasp.

Eyes watering, I looked up at Ryan and Nick who looked smug as fuck. "You guys did this for me?"

"Of course," Ryan said, pressing a kiss to my temple and Nick smirked.

"I've been telling you to complain for months now," Nick reminded me and I sucked in a shaky breath and I nodded, clutching the letter to my chest.

Reinstated and a letter of *apology*.

"What is it?" Liv asked and I beamed, clearing my throat lightly before I read the most important section.

"*Please accept my most sincere apologies for the actions of the staff in question and for the school safeguarding policies that, ultimately, failed you. We hope that you will return to complete your final classes with us next week in good faith and spirit and should you wish to press charges Radclyffe will support you as best we can.*" I looked up and Liv was grinning. "It's signed by the Dean."

Kit gave a low whistle and I looked between Nick and Ry. "How did you get the Dean involved?"

Ryan looked me straight in the eye, lips twitching. "I booked an appointment."

Nick snorted. "He did not. He stormed into the Dean's office reception area ranting about discrimination and injustice and we were ushered in fairly quickly." Nick waggled his eyebrows. "She offered us *tea*."

"How refined," Kat said and I laughed. My heart felt light, like being suspended was a bad dream.

"I can go back to class," I whispered and Ryan's eyes were soft as he brushed a stray hair from my face and nodded.

"And," Nick said, "the best part is that Davis has been placed on administrative leave until a proper investigation can be held."

"Oh my god, really?" Fuck, had Christmas come early? "This is... thank you both."

Nick waved a hand. "It was easy, I had so much evidence that he would have been caught soon either way. I just expedited the process."

I smacked a kiss to Ryan's mouth and blew one to Nick. "Still, you guys are the best."

Ryan blushed and my heart squeezed. Too. Fucking. Cute.

"So are you going to tell us about *your* night now?" Liv said and I bit my lip to hide my smile. Thanks to Nick and Ryan I could finish out the last few weeks of my degree, graduate and *still* have the contract with Max's Sun City label.

"Wait, wait," Kit interrupted, "Leo and I *also* had a task."

"You did?" I hesitantly accepted Kit's phone from across the table and he grinned.

"It was a group effort. We collaborated," Kit winked and I felt a tinge of nerves run through me.

"This isn't evidence of an orgy, is it? Because I can't believe you would do that without me—"

"Just look at it!" Kit crowed and I laughed and then gasped as I took in the truly awful photo on his phone. The flash had gone off and highlighted the red veins in Aaron's eyes, his usually carefully arranged blonde hair was unkempt and sweaty, but the real kicker was the line of coke racked up on top of—

"Is that a pool table?" I asked and Leo smiled for once, leaving me staring because *fuck* he was actually pretty when he wasn't frowning.

"Yep," Kat said smugly. "Xander showed it to the Coach this morning."

"You did?" I breathed, the phone hanging forgotten in my hands.

Xander grinned. "I was just so concerned about Aaron's severe coke problem."

I started laughing and couldn't stop, tears ran down my face and Liv tutted as she wiped away any smudged make-up from under my eyes as I wheezed. "Oh my god, is it my birthday? Did I forget or something?"

Kit smiled, revealing a flash of the piercing in his tongue. "We couldn't prove he leaked that photo of you, so we figured why not get him back in a Jamie-approved manner? Anyway, he got kicked off the team, apparently his dad was *furious.*"

"I'll bet," I murmured, feeling oddly empty after my laughter had run out—but it was in a good way. I was smug as all hell that Aaron had gotten what he deserved, but I wasn't invested in him anymore. The revenge barely tasted sweet, though I definitely appreciated their gesture. "Thank you guys, you're all... well, I don't know what I'd do without you." A chorus of *aw* sounded and I waved them off irritably.

"What was this Liv was saying about you doing something last night?" Ryan had a tight edge to his voice that made me stare at him for a moment before answering. Was he jealous? His jaw clenched slightly and I restrained a grin.

"So last night..." I explained how I'd driven to Phoenix and done the test recording for Max and Ryan's eyes warmed, pride smoothing his face as he beamed.

"So?" Kit demanded. "Did he offer to sign you?"

I grinned. "He did!" I practically squealed the words and Ryan wrapped his arms around me in a fierce hug, brushing his lips against my cheek and then my ear.

"I'm so proud of you," he whispered and tears rushed to my

eyes and heat pooled between my legs. Who knew validation did it for me?

I smiled up at him as Xander stood and pushed his way down the bench, declaring he was buying us all drinks to celebrate. I could barely breathe through the joy that flooded my system as I looked around at everyone chatting, could barely believe how crazy things had become in just twenty-four hours.

I glanced back over to Ryan and he immediately smiled at me but there was something in his expression—

"Drinks!" Xander announced and I accepted mine gratefully. "To new beginnings," he said a little more quietly, with half a glance at Liv, "and friends."

I cringed half-heartedly at the cheesiness but joined in on the toast as we clanked our cups together.

"Will you come back to mine?" Ryan asked as he leaned into me.

I smiled. "I was about to ask you the same thing."

He laughed and kissed me deeply, tongue briefly twining with mine before he pulled away with a smirk. I grinned, kissing his cheek. It was crazy how your luck could change so fast.

CHAPTER TWENTY-FOUR

SLOW - RUMER

WE'D LEFT THE BAR AFTER A FEW MORE ROUNDS OF drinks, both of us enjoying the time with our friends but also ready to be alone. Neither of us were particularly buzzed and I felt content as we strolled through the park back to Ryan's. I'd thanked Nick again before we left and reminded him that if he ever wanted to pursue a complaint against Taylor that I'd have his back, the same way he always had mine. He'd pressed a quick kiss to my cheek and smiled but said nothing else, which worried me a little. We'd become fast friends after being paired up on a group project but I hoped he knew that we were more than just course-buddies.

"Are you okay?" I asked Ryan as we turned the corner just outside of the park entrance and he looked down at me with a smile.

"Of course," he said and raised our hands between us so he could kiss my fingers. "I'm so happy for you."

"I can't believe you went to the Dean for me," I murmured, heart pounding as I still tried to process it. Nobody had ever put themselves on the line like that for me before. Nobody had cared enough to.

"There's very little I wouldn't do for you," Ry said softly and I swallowed hard as I met his eyes for a moment before looking away.

"Oh my god," I breathed as I looked up and saw a familiar blonde head in the distance accompanied by a stern looking skinny woman.

"Is that—"

"Oh my *god*," I repeated, a grin breaking out across my face as we drew a little closer. I hadn't even thought about what it meant for Taylor that her complaint had been found to be false. She had her big suitcase thumping along behind her as she followed her mom to the sleek car parked a little way down from Ryan's house. "They kicked her out! I can't believe it. Pinch me. Today has been too good to be true."

Ryan chuckled and pinched my ass and I shot him a look as we continued on past Taylor who looked like she was crying as her mom shoved a box into the backseat. Other than a small bit of smugness, I mostly felt relief—who knows, maybe she would clean herself up and find a better life for herself. I hoped so, anyway.

My hands shook but I didn't know why as we got to the door and Ryan put his key into the lock and let us inside. It was blessedly quiet and I'd never been more grateful for the party-boy lifestyle of his other roommates than right then, when electricity seemed to spark between me and Ryan. What was different? We always had this level of heat, attraction, but this somehow felt like more. The way that Ryan's eyes moved over me, like he wanted to devour me, felt like more.

My tongue tied as he took a step toward me and slid his fingers over my cheeks and into my hair, tilting my head up towards his with a gentle tug that had me clenching for him.

The kiss swept over me and left me breathless, his tongue moving in gentle movements as if coaxing me to fall further into him, to relax, to trust him. But I already did. I couldn't pinpoint when it had happened, but somewhere along the line, Ryan had become the person I turned to when I needed someone. The first person I called after a shitty day, the one I immediately thought of when I got good news or saw a cute cat. He was... oh fuck, I was in *love* with him.

The realization made me gasp into his mouth and Ryan pulled me closer, inviting me to taste more, to take *more* and I wanted it. Wanted him.

I pressed closer, letting my hands fall to his chest and stroke along the toned muscles I could feel beneath his sweater. Ry nipped at my lip and I laughed darkly, knowing I was getting to him. I twisted my hands into his thick, dark hair and kissed him harder, wanting everything he could give me.

His breathing was heavy as he pulled away, eyes hooded and mouth red from our kisses. He took my hand in his and led me through the hallway and up the stairs to his room. My heart resumed its unsteady beat as the door closed softly and Ryan turned, his eyes hungry but his touch gentle, almost reverent as his lips found mine again.

He sipped slowly from my mouth, wringing little whimpers from me as he pulled my jacket off one shoulder and then the other. His hands were so warm against my skin and I shivered, wanting his heat everywhere—against me, on me, in me.

He smiled as if he knew how eager I was but continued to torture me with soft, slow kisses and barely there touches until I was desperate for him.

Ry's hand finally pressed solidly against one breast through my shirt and I moaned when he stroked my nipple. "You know..." he said slowly as he lowered his mouth to my chest, sliding the material of my top up and out of the way and

225

pulling the cup of my bra down. "One of the things I love most about you..." My breath left me in a hiss as his tongue slid around the nipple, tightening it with pleasure, and then became shallow as his words registered, specifically the L word. "...is how responsive you are." He took the nipple firmly into his mouth and sucked while his fingers stroked and teased my other breast. "You love to be touched." He smirked. "And I love to touch you."

Three times. He'd said the L word three times, was he trying to tell me something? Ryan chuckled like he could see my brain working and I let him distract me as he pulled off my top and moved down my body. His hands ran down my back, sliding the zipper on my mini skirt down and he moved to the floor as stroked down my calves, encouraging me to step out of it.

His eyes roved over my skin, smiling at the stiff peaks of my breasts as I stood there in my boots, fishnets and panties. His hands stroked the back of my knees and it felt so sensitive that I gasped and he grinned when I lifted a leg and he was able to slip off one boot. I offered him the other foot and he kissed from my knee to my ankle as he slid off the other.

"Beautiful," he murmured and a flush stole my skin as I looked down at him.

Ryan reached for the waistband of my fishnets, shimmying them down slowly, stroking at the small red marks the band left on my lower waist and pressing his mouth to my inner thigh as he left lingering kisses all the way up... and then back down.

"Why," I panted, "are you teasing me?"

"I told you that one day I'd take it slow with you," he replied with a smile that was pure desire and maybe a little something more. "So here I am, taking it slow."

I wriggled uncomfortably in just my panties, sure that they

were soaked and as Ryan pressed a kiss to the front of the lace he gave a moan of satisfaction. "I love how wet you are for me."

There it was again, that L word. He looked up at me as he hooked his fingers under the string of my panties, waiting for me to nod, to tell him I wanted this.

I took his hand in mine and helped slide them down my thighs and it looked like he hardly breathed as he watched me become bare for him.

Ry leaned in as if helpless, glancing up at me once to see my nod before pressing his tongue to my folds and making me shudder. A finger brushed over the sensitive bud that had grown hard for him, pulsing with need as he smoothed over it, feeling my wetness on his fingertips.

"You are perfection," he groaned as he sank his finger into me and slid his tongue over my clit. His other arm came around me, settling on my ass and pulling me firmer against his mouth as my hips rocked against him. My hands fell to his shoulders as I steadied myself against him, a jolt running through me as I looked down to find those blue eyes watching me as he feasted.

My breaths rattled as I watched his eyes close and felt his tongue smoothly slide through my center. A second finger joined his first, curling against my sensitive inner walls as he pressed down and my eyes flew wide. Just that fast I was coming on his tongue, my hips completely out of my control.

I could feel the heat in my cheeks and the slickness between my thighs as Ryan pressed one final kiss between my legs before standing up. I felt unsteady on my feet and Ry's hands slid under my elbows, supporting me like always. He pulled me closer and I bit my lip at the sensation of his clothes against my skin.

I rested my head against his shoulder and pushed my fingers into his hair, smiling when I felt him relax.

"That was..." I wasn't sure how best to describe it. Hot and yet infinitely tender.

"Mind blowing? The best you've ever had?" Ryan suggested and I felt his mouth curve up against my hair.

I laughed as I pressed against him, feeling the hardness of his erection through his jeans. "I was going to say it was a good start." I placed a hot kiss to his neck and felt a shiver work its way through him.

"You're insatiable." Ryan grinned and I laughed.

"Me?" I pulled out of his arms, skin pebbling in the cool air as I sank to my knees. "I'm pretty sure you're the one that's been left wanting."

"Never," he said softly. "I've never been more satisfied." Strangely, I believed him.

My hand stilled on his zipper as I raised an eyebrow. "So you don't want me to...?"

A deep chuckle vibrated through him and I grinned. "Only if you want to. This isn't tit for tat."

I slid the zipper down slowly, loving the way he sprang out at me as I wrapped my hand around his thick, hot length. I dropped a kiss to his head and he gasped, I smirked as I began to pump him slowly.

He jumped against my hand, eager for my touch and I tightened my grip around him as I licked and kissed my way up the underside of his cock until his face was tilted back, his throat working and bottom lip between his teeth as I teased him.

Moisture began to gather the longer I stroked him, both at his tip and between my legs, heat stirring again. I licked his away, my tongue luxuriating at the soft feel of him in my mouth before I took him in fully and Ryan groaned.

His hand tugged at my hair gently, a shout falling out of his mouth as I took him in as deeply as I could, suctioning as I hollowed out my cheeks.

I twirled my tongue around his head as his hips began to push his cock in and out of my mouth. I could feel his muscles tensing and hear his soft grunts as his movements sped up before he paused entirely.

"I don't want to come in your mouth," he said roughly. "Right now I need to be inside you."

I stood and helped him pull off his sweater, smiling at the way it rumpled his dark hair. He pulled his jeans down, dick bobbing in the air, and my mouth dried as I watched his muscles tighten and release. Ry prowled forward and slid his arms around me, holding me close to his chest and I reached up to kiss him. Everything was just pure sensation, the heat of him against my stomach, the rasp of his stubble against my cheek and my neck, it was a slow torture and I needed release.

Ryan walked me backwards to his bed and I wanted to stretch out as I felt his soft sheets against my back.

He kissed up my stomach towards the underside of my breasts and I moaned as he tasted the sensitive skin there. I grabbed his chin and raised his head up. "Enough playing," I said huskily and he kissed me, cutting off the words with a desperation that surprised me as he lowered himself to his forearms, body sealed against mine.

I wriggled against him, wanting our bodies to be touching everywhere and Ryan murmured my name. I rolled us over gracelessly and laughed breathlessly, stopping only when his cock nudged against my entrance and instead moaned.

Ryan propped himself up against his pillows and I braced my hands against his headboard as I tauntingly rolled my hips across his, luxuriating in the feel of him hot and ready beneath me.

"Do you want me to ride you?" I breathed as I bent lower

towards his ear, pressing us even closer together. His hips rose as he thrust against me, the top of his head barely filling me before he pulled away.

"Yes," Ryan said hoarsely and I obliged him, sinking back onto my thighs and taking him deep inside me until my body shook with restraint and pleasure. I wanted to give myself a second to adjust but I couldn't help the rocking motion of my hips, couldn't stop after my name slipped out of Ryan's mouth like a prayer and a curse rolled into one.

I pressed myself down and onto him over and over until Ryan sat up, wrapping his arms around me as our bodies moved frantically, chasing the pleasure we knew we would find waiting. I started to come again, whining his name, begging him for more, to *please please fuck me harder* and Ryan didn't hold back. Not until I was a shaking mess, orgasming around his cock. He pumped into me one more time, hands twisted in my thick black hair, and called my name as he came. His kiss was salty with sweat but I didn't mind as he laid us back down with me sprawled against his chest, head tucked under his chin.

We both panted lightly as we tried to get our breath back and I kissed his cheek casually as we stayed there, curled up in one another. Once my legs were no longer like jelly I stood and grabbed his jumper, tugging it on so I could go to the bathroom. It hit around mid-thigh and something in Ryan's eyes grew hot again as he looked at me in it while I walked out of the room.

I quickly peed and hurried back to the room, missing his warmth, quickly curling back into Ry's side.

"All good?" he said quietly and I nodded, waiting patiently as he went to the bathroom too, pressing a kiss to my forehead when he got back. "So you're going to continue taking classes?"

I huffed a small laugh, he wanted pillow talk? Not that I

minded at all really, it just felt like an odd segue from *Hey please screw my brains out* to talking about my plans for the future.

"Yeah, I might as well finish the degree seeing as I actually can now." I smiled at Ryan but his answering smile seemed a little... dim. He looked up at the ceiling when he spoke next, as if looking at me was painful.

"Have you got a place in Phoenix or do you need to look for somewhere?" he asked nonchalantly and I stared at him for a second, his slight unease making more sense now.

"I already have a place," I said and he frowned, confirming my suspicions, "here in Sun City."

He whipped his head towards me so fast that I knew that it would hurt later. "What?"

"Max is opening up another studio here in Sun City, there's no commute and I'm not going anywhere." I watched his face like a hawk for even the smallest of clues and was rewarded when the tension vanished, a relaxed smile taking over his face.

"Oh, good. Cool," he said and I bit back a laugh even as something inside my chest melted. He had thought I was leaving him, running off to Phoenix to record music and yet he'd *still* put me first. Was still prepared to support me and my dreams no matter what.

"Why?" I said, running a finger up his chest. "Would you miss me?"

"Considering I'm pretty sure I'm in love with you," Ryan said and I could hear him swallow in the quiet of the room, "yeah, that's a safe bet."

My heart thudded almost painfully in my chest. "You love me?"

He looked at me head on. "Yeah."

"Well, that's a relief."

"It is?" He sounded shocked and disbelieving and I let a grin sneak across my face as I nodded.

"Yep, because I'm pretty sure I'm in love with you too."

Ryan grinned and for a second we just smiled at each other like fools before Ryan broke away and pressed a kiss to my throat. "Well, that works out well don't you think?"

"Mmm," was all I could say as my lips found his once more.

Continue the Sun City
series in 2023 with...

ACKNOWLEDGMENTS

Big love and thanks to the whole booktok and bookstagram community for sticking with me on my author journey and squealing about this book with me—your support means everything. Special mention to Callie, Ciara, and Helena, you guys are the best.

Thank you to Hannah, my talented Alpha reader who helped me shape this book into what it now is, I'm forever grateful for your insight. Big love to my ARC team, you guys are the loveliest bunch and I'm beyond thrilled that you're with me on this journey.

Lastly but not leastl-y... I'm sending all my love and gratitude to my partner, Connor, who is only too happy to let me ramble aloud while I figure out the plot or the characters and watches all my silly Tiktoks with me. You are everything.

Finally, thank you to you, the reader—I couldn't do this without you. **Continue reading for an excerpt of the next book in the Sun City series *Fall Hard*.**

CHAPTER ONE

Love sucks. I wasn't much of an expert, I'd only really fallen once—but there was only one thing worse than loving someone who didn't love you, and that was watching them fall in love with someone else. So there I was, about to do something that was probably a terrible idea—but lately all my ideas seemed terrible, so what could one more hurt?

I'd gotten to the club earlier than I cared to admit and immediately headed to the bar for a drink—I'd made a mistake not having anything before I came out, that was for sure. Luckily, the neon rainbow stripes that encased the front of the bar had made it easy to spot and I'd claimed a seat there on the tall black bar stools with ease.

I had been to a club only once in my life, when I'd just turned eighteen and managed to sneak out of the house, and I'd forgotten how loud and... sticky, they were. Dark too, only the rainbow lights tracing the edges of the walls, DJ booth, and the small smattering of tables tucked into a few alcoves adding a soft multi-coloured glow to the room.

The girl I'd been watching for the past half-hour pushed

away from the bar and made her way to a packed corner of the club. Her blonde hair was an unnatural white that seemed to change color with the disco lights and was almost the same color as her skin. I kept my eyes on her retreating figure as she paused by a skinny white guy wearing a ripped tee emblazoned with Britney Spears' face. Her hand dipped into the pocket of her high waisted jeans as she leaned in close to the guy, then she moved back to the bar. Done. Easy. I could do this. Probably.

I sighed, barely even feeling the buzz of the last three drinks I'd had against the strange tingling numbness that moved through my chest recently. It had been happening for a while, ever since I'd moved to Sun City and accidentally fallen in love with my best friend.

She was out with everyone else right now, gone to some football match her boyfriend, Ryan, was playing in and I'd told them I had to study. I snorted into my cocktail at the thought. I couldn't even remember the last time I'd gone to class.

I waited til she reclaimed her seat a little further down from mine and then I ordered another drink, the steady pulse of Christina Aguilera's *Dirty* making my heart feel like it thudded too hard. Her top was red and off the shoulders, not unlike something Jamie might have worn—

I gulped the drink the bartender handed me as I shook off the thought.

"Whoa. Steady there. You know they put alcohol in those things, right?" The girl grinned at me and I swallowed before offering her a smile. If you didn't know better, then what I was about to ask her might seem perfectly natural coming from my lips—tonight, I looked the epitome of a party girl. I'd loosely curled my hair and let it run free over my shoulders, put on my highest pink velvet chunky heels and let my sparkly eye make-up be the only accessory needed to match the pink sequin mini dress.

"Well, there's a little mixer too. Got to stay hydrated." I laughed breathlessly and bit my lip as the girl's eyes moved over my bronze legs, made longer by my heels, and back up to my face. "Listen..." I leaned in close and a flirty smile tugged up the corners of her mouth. "I, um, was wondering if you have any pills?"

She leaned back, a look that might have been disappointment flashing across her face as a cheer went out in the crowd at the next song, before she nodded. "Sure. What are you looking for?"

"Ah, you know."

An eyebrow raised at my answer and I wanted to curse. "Sure, but do you?" I didn't answer and she rolled her eyes. "Look, are you sure you want to—"

"I'm sure," I said firmly. "I've just never done this before. My friend usually buys," I lied, clearing my throat a little and her eyes narrowed slightly before she nodded.

"Fine. How many do you want?"

"Just one."

Another eyebrow raise. Crap. I was so clearly out of my depth. I'd thought this would be good for me, to get out of my own head for a while, but maybe it was just another mistake.

"Thirty," the girl said and I barely held in my surprise. That seemed like a lot for one pill, but I couldn't say for sure if she was ripping me off or if I was just hopelessly naive. Either way, it didn't matter. Thirty dollars was nothing in the face of the inheritance my parents had given me to essentially stay out of their lives, another form of hush money—their signature move.

I slipped the cash out of my clutch and she rolled her eyes as I tried to be surreptitious about it and failed.

"Have a good night," she said dryly, handing me a clear baggie and then shoving away from the bar.

"You too," I murmured, the words lost in an old Taylor

Swift song as I shook the pill free and examined it closely. Was I supposed to take the whole thing? I glanced around to see if I could maybe ask the white-haired drug dealer but she'd disappeared into the crowd on the dancefloor. I didn't even know what this thing was or how it would make me feel—what if I had an allergic reaction? I tried to shake the thought off. *What would Jamie do?*

Jamie would have already taken the pill by now and not given it a second thought. Yet here I was, having second, third, and fourth thoughts. I didn't need to do this—not to have a good time, and not to prove anything. But I just felt like I needed... *something*. Change, or maybe just an end to the aching hollowness that seemed to follow me around lately. It had been a rough year.

My palms were getting sweaty and I tossed the pill back and forth between my hands, not wanting it to melt or something. *Just do it.* I let out a slow breath as I brought my hand to my mouth and then paused. Was I supposed to swallow it whole? Chew it? Crap, I should have just asked Jamie—

I reined my thoughts in before I could get lost in my own head again, wondering what she was doing right now, whether the match had ended and they'd all gone to *The Box* for drinks after. *She's with Ryan. Her boyfriend. Having a great time without you.*

I swiveled the seat so I faced outwards and could watch the dancers, the ache in my chest reverberating around the bass of the music.

She was the reason I'd come here. Jamie. Or one of them, at least.

There were people like Jamie, so comfortable in their skin it seemed almost inhuman to me. She'd had her nudes leaked by her ex and was barely phased. She didn't break. How could you not envy someone like that? Who knows exactly who they are?

"For you," the green-haired bartender said from behind me and I looked up in surprise as a shot of tequila was placed next to me on the purple counter, alongside a cocktail.

"Oh, sorry! I didn't order this."

"No, doll. *She* did." He smiled at me and nodded his head off to the left where a familiar, blonde head smirked at me. Bryn.

"Right," I murmured, opting not to pick it up. "Thanks."

I hadn't exactly come here looking for company, not the familiar kind anyway. I came here to get lost, to be someone new. While I knew from the way she flirted every time she saw me that Bryn would happily take me home and help me forget, I didn't look Bryn's way again.

For one night, I wanted to be someone else—someone unafraid to take risks, who doesn't pause to think or rationalize all the different ways a situation could go wrong, someone *scary*. That was one of the things I loved about Jamie. With her, you never knew what might happen next.

And so I found myself in a gay nightclub, buying drugs for the first time, getting ready to dance with strangers, just so I could pretend for a little while. To escape my own skin, like I wasn't the girl in love with her best friend, the girl that got kicked out of school, or the girl disowned by her parents. I put the pill on my tongue and swallowed it with the last of my drink before the shaking of my hands could persuade me to rethink my decision. Tonight, I was free.

How long would it take to kick in? I swung my legs idly to the beat and returned the smiles of a few people dancing in the middle of the floor. It wasn't a big club and the bar took up a lot of room, spanning the whole of the back wall, but the layout twisted and turned into small nooks where people were laughing or making out. Posters had lined the walls in the tiny corridor that had led to this larger dance floor, advertising the events coming up, so I knew that on Fridays they did karaoke and there was a drag show one Monday a month. Karaoke made me think of her though, not that what Jamie did with her voice should be cheapened down that way, and I fanned myself with my hand lightly as the heat from the club made my cheeks flush. Or maybe that was just the alcohol—it was wild to think about how far I'd come since leaving St Agatha's, the religious college I'd been kicked out of after being caught in a kiss with my female teacher. I had a fake ID, because I wasn't going to be twenty-one for another ten months, I was fully independent, and my dress just about covered my ass.

I sighed as I reached absently for the drink Bryn had sent over, dumping the tequila into the tall glass of orange liquid. This wasn't working. Sitting in a club and waxing poetic about my best friend was the exact opposite of what I was trying to do there.

The drink was fruity and sweet and I wrinkled my nose as I sipped it. I was pretty picky about the cocktails I drank, and this one was a little too syrupy to really be my thing, but the guy behind the bar was busy and I was thirsty. So overly sweet, flirty cocktail it would have to be.

The rhythm of the music changed to something bassier, the thud of it echoing through my chest as I let my shoulders relax. I glanced to my right and smiled at the pretty redhead collecting her drink. She had freckles similar to mine, coasting along her nose daintily, and her dress was a green silk that looked so weightless on her it could have floated away.

"Wanna dance?" I half-shouted over the music and then swallowed the rest of my drink quickly when she nodded with a big grin, grabbing my hand and tugging me out into the middle of the floor. Now, not everyone at gay clubs was actually gay, she could just be there with friends, but when she stepped closer and slipped a pale arm around my waist to tug me closer,

I melted. She smelled like summer flowers, sweet and heady, and her gold eyeliner sparkled in the lights of the dance floor as her eyes dropped to my lips.

I didn't even know her name. But that was exactly what I'd wanted, right?

We laughed and swayed our hips to the music, a song I vaguely recognized but wasn't paying much attention to as the room swirled into a haze of rainbow lights and glitter.

"I love your eyeliner," I said into the redhead's ear, letting my lips brush the shell, and she grinned at me. "Pretty," I breathed as I pulled away and stroked a thumb idly underneath her eye.

The song changed, something heavy and angsty that made us throw our hands in the air and jump as high as we could manage without breaking an ankle in our towering heels. A group of people waved to her off to my right and she kissed my cheek before dancing over to them. I waved her off airily, not even feeling the disappointment as I swayed and bounced to the music, barely feeling the hands on my skin as I twirled between dancers. I don't know when I closed my eyes, couldn't remember deciding to do so, but the room felt like it was overwhelming my senses in a riot of color and sparkles when they flickered open. The cheesy disco lights were going strong and the girl I was dancing with had glitter in her hair that I stroked fondly, twining it around my finger as her brunette strands shone red under the lights.

This was what I'd been looking for, to just get lost for a little while. The emptiness in my chest that had threatened to overwhelm me the longer I stayed in the apartment had faded, replaced with laughter and the scent of honey shampoo.

Someone bought me a drink. Then two, then three, and the next set of hands that settled lightly on my waist steadied me when I hadn't even realized I'd been swaying.

They smelled nice, like jasmine or clementine, something flowery that danced on the edge of fruity. I inhaled deeply as I rested my head on their shoulder, slow dancing despite the Carly Rae Jepson song that blasted out around us.

I didn't want to move, tiredness settling into my arms and legs as I relaxed in this stranger's arms, but my throat was parched. I pulled away slightly too fast and bit the inside of my cheek as the pleasant haze I'd been drifting in threatened to send me down a swirling ravine that I knew would leave me puking.

"Sorry," I slurred. "Need another drink."

"I think what you need is to go home."

I wrinkled my nose. That voice sounded familiar.

I forced my eyes open and squinted in the flashing lights—when had they turned on a smoke machine? I clutched the woman's arm as I fought to assess myself for a second. It wasn't often that a smoke machine could trigger my asthma but for some reason my lungs felt sluggish anyway, like I was breathing in syrup.

"Hey, you're okay." The voice was so strong that my body relaxed, like it had just been waiting for orders. "Come on, I'll take you home."

A slither of coherency cracked through my senses and I frowned as I focused on familiar blue eyes that were, annoyingly, pinched with concern.

"I'm not going home with you."

Bryn rolled her eyes, thick dark lashes casting fascinating shadows across the high points of her cheeks and I struggled to focus on her words for a moment. "I'm not propositioning you, Olivia. You're absolutely fucked right now. You need to go home."

A giggle burst out of my mouth and I clamped a hand over my lips before letting it drop. "You said fuck."

Bryn wound an arm through mine and tried to guide me to the exit. "Come on."

"No."

We ground to a halt and a breath that even I could recognize as sheer exasperation escaped her.

"No?"

"No, I'm not going to sleep with you."

"Oh, sweetheart. I doubt you could even locate a boob right now—I'm taking you to *your* home, not mine."

Without thinking, I reached out and placed a hand on her chest. She was wearing a gauzy silver mesh top that sparkled prettily and I instantly coveted it, especially because it managed to feel silky rather than scratchy. We both looked down at the hand that cupped her left breast. It was full, bigger than my palm could comfortably cover, and Bryn looked bemused as she reached out and gently tugged my hand away.

"Come on."

I didn't argue. I would probably feel a thousand shades of embarrassed about this tomorrow, but right now I couldn't deny that the thought of my bed waiting for me sounded like bliss. Well, that and maybe some fries. Salty, greasy, goodness.

"Yes, yes, fine, we can stop for fries if somewhere is open."

I blinked, not realizing I'd said the last part aloud. Whatever. As long as I got my fries, I didn't care that I'd touched Bryn's boob. Plus, Sun City was a student town—of course someone would be selling fries at... I checked my phone and hissed as the brightness seared my eyes. Wow. Three AM. Not bad. Not bad at all.

I didn't think I'd gone out partying by myself in, well, ever and tonight I'd actually had a good time. There weren't many times in my life that I'd been able to just feel... good. Carefree.

"I'm sorry to hear that," Bryn said as she steered me around a bush that had appeared out of nowhere and I blinked at her in confusion.

"Am I still saying all this to you out loud? I thought I was just thinking stuff."

Bryn snorted. "Jesus you're wasted. What did you even take?"

"A pill."

"Of?"

I shrugged and the pinched look on Bryn's face reappeared again but I tuned out before she could try and lecture me some more.

Fingers snapped in front of my face and I waved my hand in protest. "What?" I glanced around us, confused. "Where are we?"

Bryn's hand cupped my jaw, tilting my face up to look into her eyes and for the first time I realized she was slightly taller than me. I tugged my face free from her grip.

"You mean you don't remember the part of this very, *very* long walk home where you whined and complained until I agreed to go to *Paulies* with you to get fries?" She shook her head, somehow still managing to look good even under the gross fluorescent lights in the diner.

"I think these lights are giving me a hangover." I grimaced as I tried to shield my eyes with my hand but a second later the pain was forgotten as a carton of hot fries was pressed into my palm. "You are beautiful," I moaned, shoveling two in my mouth and wincing slightly at the burn. There was only one thing ruining this.

I thrust the fries into Bryn's arms and she fumbled slightly as she caught them.

"What are you—"

I reached down and unclasped my shoes, sighing in relief as my toes touched the cold tiled floor.

"Liv, no—"

I grabbed my fries back out of Bryn's hands and spun for the door, the world whirling around me as I moved too quickly.

The night air was cool and still smelled like heat from earlier in the day. It was late—or early, depending on how you looked at it—but plenty of people still milled around. Bryn caught up to me a second later, my shoes dangling from their straps in her hands as she muttered under her breath.

"Your feet are going to get cold."

"They're fine," I said absently, munching on a fry as I started away from the town and down the path that led through the park. Despite it being paved, the twigs and errant rocks immediately stabbed into the soles of my feet and I hopped a little as I walked, trying not to drop my food. "Ow."

The trees were bushy and full, though it was too dark to see the lush green they'd turned a little while back, and the moon just peaked out from between branches. For a second I just stood there, staring up at the sky as I continued to eat my fries, the stars swirling around my head and the night air barely touching my skin. My hand scraped the bottom of the box and I frowned as I stared down into it.

A sigh startled me and I turned wobbily to see Bryn watching me. "You want to stare at the stars some more or can we get you home? You must be cold."

"It's the summer."

"It's also almost four in the morning."

"Huh."

I hobbled forward a few more steps and Bryn watched me, shadows partially obscuring whatever expression was on her face—not that I particularly cared what she thought anyway.

"Come on." She turned so her back was to me and I waited for her to walk away, confused when she crouched a little. "Well? Are you coming?"

I stepped carefully across the small distance separating us and hopped onto her back, her arms coming up under my legs as I hooked mine around her neck.

"Do *not* throw up on me."

I giggled as we walked, a little confused about what we were doing and how we'd got there—didn't Bryn live up by the mall? *So why was she walking with me through the park?* The odd swaying motion soothed me until my cheek was pressed against her hair and I jumped when she nudged me before sliding me off her back. I stumbled and her arms caught me under my elbows, our faces close enough in the dark that we could have kissed.

Her eyes were so blue that they stood out against the darkness, and I stepped closer as my eyes dropped to her mouth. I'd noticed that Bryn was beautiful before, you would have to be blind not to, but she seemed practically luminescent in the dark.

"Liv—"

My mouth brushed across hers, featherlight, reminding me of another kiss, another girl as I fought the haze descending on me, sighing as our mouths parted. "Jamie..."

Bryn slid away and I hadn't realized how cold I was until her warmth left. She fumbled around in the dark, reaching under the matt for the spare key Jamie and I left there and unlocking the door.

"Come on," she said quietly, guiding me inside and helping me into bed when I pointed to my room across the hall.

I shimmied my dress up and over my head and heard Bryn leave as I climbed into bed naked, not bothering to wash off my make-up.

"Here," she said a second later, setting a glass of water down on my immaculately tidy bedside table and then straightening again to leave.

248

I caught her hand before she could go. "Stay."

"Liv, I really don't—"

"Please," I mumbled as I snuggled down into my comforter and lifted the edge for her to join me. I relaxed once she slid off her shoes and settled next to me. "Stay."

"Go to sleep, Olivia."

"Bryn?"

"What?"

"I'm sorry I touched your boob."

She chuckled quietly and the sound followed me into a dreamless sleep.